"I'm going back, Whitney."

"Well, of course, Gabe. I know that."

Gabe looked up at the ceiling as he spoke. "Not just to Seattle. I mean I'm going back to the law firm. To the fast track, the glitz and glamour, the big bucks."

"Well, if that's what you want, then that's what you should do." Whitney's voice was flat. "Don't let *me* stop you," she added sarcastically.

"Look, I know you don't approve!" Gabe exploded. "You think I should stick around here, looking for my *roots* or something. Well, you know what? I don't *care* about my roots. My being born half-Indian was an accident of birth, nothing more."

Dear Reader,

February is the month for hearts and flowers, and this month's Superromance selections definitely call for a few hearts to be lost—and found.

In Patricia Chandler's *Mooncaller,* Dr. Whitney Baldridge-Barrows knows she should hate Gabriel Blade. He's planning to turn the Havasuapai village where she works into a tourist resort. Instead, she finds she's losing her heart at the bottom of the Grand Canyon....

Texas journalist Lacy Kilpatrick comes home to a family feud. Though her family calls sexy Austin Fraser "the enemy," and forbids her to see him, Lacy discovers she has other ideas. Lynda Trent weaves lighthearted romantic magic in *If I Must Choose.*

And sparks really fly between Tatum McGillus and Jonathan Wright. In Tara Taylor Quinn's *McGillus V. Wright,* hero and heroine stand on opposite sides of the law. Besides that, the timing is wrong, and the two agree on absolutely nothing. This is one relationship that will need a miracle in order to survive.

Louisiana author Anne Logan sets *Dial "D" for Destiny* in her home state, where Lisa Le Blanc is hot on the trail of her missing sister, Dixie. And the trail leads straight to Gabriel Jordan. But the man denies ever speaking to Dixie. Still, she's sure he knows more than he's telling, and sticking close to him is the only way to discover the truth. Strangely, her heart seems to be in danger, too....

And speaking of hearts and flowers, this year's edition of Harlequin's popular Valentine anthology, *My Valentine,* features short stories by four favorite Superromance authors—Margot Dalton, Karen Young, Marisa Carroll and Muriel Jensen. Be sure to look for it wherever Harlequin books are sold!

Happy Valentine's Day!

Marsha Zinberg,
Senior Editor, Superromance

Patricia Chandler

MOONCALLER

Harlequin Books

TORONTO • NEW YORK • LONDON
AMSTERDAM • PARIS • SYDNEY • HAMBURG
STOCKHOLM • ATHENS • TOKYO • MILAN
MADRID • WARSAW • BUDAPEST • AUCKLAND

ISBN 0-373-70582-4

MOONCALLER

ABOUT THE AUTHOR

The idea for this book came to Patricia Chandler after she herself spent a week in an Indian village at the bottom of the Grand Canyon. "It was beautiful and fascinating down there—but also boring, since every day was *exactly* the same."

In her writing, Patricia draws upon both her experience living in twelve states and her academic background. "My degree in sociology helps me understand my characters from a social as well as an individual perspective," she says.

Patricia lives with her husband in Chandler, Arizona. Between the two of them, they have six grown children.

Books by Patricia Chandler

HARLEQUIN SUPERROMANCE
489—DECEPTION BAY

HARLEQUIN AMERICAN ROMANCE
497—AT HER CAPTAIN'S COMMAND

With love, to Stu and Fe, and thanks for
introducing me to Shangri-la

PROLOGUE

COYOTE WALKED ALONE upon the earth. The land smelled rich and fertile, but the People had not yet come to cultivate it. Coyote was so hungry that his bowels were chewing at his stomach, and he howled with pain. Then, near the Edge of the World where the sumac grows, he spied great clusters of plump, red berries. Quickly he reached out his hands to gather them and fill his howling stomach, but then he saw Wise Old Man, father of the People, sitting among the sumac.

"Whose land is this?" Coyote asked Wise Old Man.

"It is the land of the People," Wise Old Man replied.

"Where did they get it?" Coyote asked craftily, hoping to lay claim to the land himself. "Was it given to them by their ancestors?"

Wise Old Man replied, "Of course not. They borrow this land from their great-great-great-great-grandchildren. They must take good care of it because it belongs to the children of the future. So that the People will not forget this, the children of the future have placed stalks of red berries where the sumac grows. These berries are theirs, and no matter how hungry we get, we must never eat them. They are only there to remind us that the land belongs to the children yet to come."

"What will happen, Father, if we eat the berries?" asked Coyote as he slyly circled behind Wise Old Man, where Wise Old Man could not see him.

"*I do not know,*" Wise Old Man replied. "*No one has ever eaten them.*"

To himself Coyote said, "*The Old Man thinks I am a fool. He just wants to keep the berries for himself. Besides, how could I owe anything to people not yet even born?*"

So behind Wise Old Man's back Coyote ate the berries. He ate great handfuls, until his stomach was so swollen he could not even move, laughing all the while at the trick he had played on Wise Old Man.

Very soon the palms of his hands began to itch, and then the soles of his feet; and by the time the moon had risen to her place in the sky, he was covered from head to foot with an itchy, blistering, bright red rash. Now he howled louder than he ever had with hunger. He scratched his hide until it bled. But he could not scratch himself everywhere at once, so he hid himself deep in the woods where he could scrape his raw, itching hide against the bark of the cottonwood trees, and where no one would know of his shame, that he had forgotten the children of the future. . . .

CHAPTER ONE

WHITNEY BALDRIDGE-BARROWS, M.D, mesmerized by the guttural voice narrating events that had taken place before the time of man, was jolted back to reality when that voice was abruptly silenced by the click of her tape recorder. The tape had run out.

With the air of having just returned from a long journey, a journey of time as well as of distance, Whitney brought herself back to the reality of the small, dingy café where she occupied a booth at the rear. On the table in front of her were her tape recorder, a dented tin ashtray and a glass that had held iced tea, now containing only a bent straw and an inch of melted ice upon which floated a tired lemon wedge.

Slouched on the rump-sprung vinyl bench opposite Whitney, Jesse Sinyella pursed his lips, Indian-style, and nodded his approval.

"You've got a real rarity there, Dr. B," he stated in his precise, formal voice. "That's one of the most ancient Coyote myths. Goes back seven hundred years, maybe more. I haven't heard Billy tell that story since I was a kid."

"I recorded it the last time he was in the infirmary," Whitney replied, pleased. "It's the only time I can get him off the firewater long enough for him to string two coherent sentences together."

Pursed-lipped, Jesse nodded again. "It's a good thing," he stated, "this that you're doing with Billy." The uninflected way he pronounced every syllable gave his speech a monotonous, singsong quality. Although he'd been born and raised in Northern Arizona and educated at the Phoenix Indian School and Arizona State University, it was obvious that English was not Jesse Sinyella's first language. "After him, there will be no one to tell the old stories. Your tapes will allow our children to hear their past."

Whitney smiled. "It pleases me to do it." She also spoke with a slightly formal tone, which she unconsciously adopted whenever she conversed with Jesse.

He was, after all, Tribal Chairman, the most powerful and respected man of the Havasupai tribe. Never mind that he was also, at Whitney's own age of thirty, the youngest man ever elected to that position. Never mind that he was soft-spoken and unassuming almost to a fault. The authority was there, and he carried it with innate dignity on his solid shoulders.

"Children *need* to know their past," Whitney continued. "They need to know who they *are*." She sighed. "I only wish someone had gotten to Billy before the whiskey addled his brain. What a storyteller he must have been!"

"He was good," Jesse agreed. "I remember winter nights when I was a boy, all of us kids sitting around the woodstove in the trading post and Billy talking to us about the old days."

He took a drag on the cigarette he held between thumb and forefinger, then raised his head to blow slow, deliberate smoke rings into the air. "He was so old even *then* that we thought he must have known Coyote personally."

"It's too bad you didn't think to write down his stories," Whitney remarked, a note of regret in her voice.

Jesse shrugged. "I was only a child," he said, sending another series of smoke rings into the air. "A child does not know his world is passing into time. By the time I *did* know it, I was already far down my own path." Reflectively, his gaze followed the smoke rings upward until they dissipated in the down-draft from the ceiling fans.

In the summer sun, the café was like an oven, and the fans rotating sluggishly overhead did little to circulate the stale air. A fly buzzed angrily against the hot plate-glass window. Beyond the window, not the slightest breeze ruffled the hard-packed red dirt outside Gwe Watahomigie's Red Rock Café.

Gwe Watahomigie, proprietor, waiter, cook and absolute autocrat of the Red Rock Café, was wiping the counter with a dry corner of his grimy apron.

Behind Jesse's left shoulder, at the far end of the lunch counter, Whitney could see Baaq'baaq and his grandson Benny'wi, head to head over a checkerboard. While her tape rewound and Jesse Sinyella pondered his smoke rings, Whitney propped one elbow on the table, rested her chin in the palm of her hand, and contemplated the faces of grandfather and grandson.

Only eleven years old, Benny was the spitting image of his grandfather. Both faces were blank, as if no one lived behind their eyes. Like hollow men, with no past to give them pride and no future to give them hope.

In earlier times the old man would have had wisdom and knowledge to pass down to Benny. But there was nothing to pass down now, for the wisdom was outdated and the knowledge unnecessary. The People no longer followed the old gods who had ensured their survival since the Beginning Time in this canyon, Supai Billy Hamadreeq had told her. They no longer ran toward the rising sun.

Now they were like this man and boy, who sat together in the pungent confines of the Red Rock Café.

Each had a greasy red bandanna tied around his long, even greasier hair. Each had a cud of tobacco bulging in his cheek, and each showed the same indifference toward the spittoon in the corner that made Gwe Watahomigie curse earnestly and viciously under his breath whenever one of them aimed a jet of tobacco juice at the floor.

And yet Benny'wi was one of the better students at the Indian school. In a few years he could go away to the Indian Boarding School in Phoenix; after that, college was not beyond the realm of possibility. Yet in reality, Whitney knew, the boy would probably end his education at the fifth grade. That's what most of them did.

Then he would join his father, driving pack mules up and down the tortuous eight-mile trail between the canyon floor and the mesa called Hilltop, that indistinguishable spot in the arid northern Arizona desert where this hidden canyon opened up into the outside world. A mule-skinner, Whitney thought sadly, when he might have been anything.

The spirit is gone, she lamented silently, not for the first time. *Now there is nothing left except the old stories.*

And even those were almost gone, embodied as they were in a single, frail old man who spent half his time in her infirmary and the other half in the lockup, sleeping off his latest lost battle with firewater.

Whitney wasn't sure when or how it happened that *she* had become the keeper of the old stories. She wasn't even Native American. She was only an Indian Health Service doctor, serving a year on this isolated reservation, the most remote and inaccessible outpost in the entire Indian Health Service.

Possibly it was just because the stories needed to be told, and she was willing to listen. But most probably, she had already admitted ironically to herself, it was simply because she had the tape recorder.

Reversing the cassette in her recorder, Whitney snapped the lid shut and held it close to her lips.

"Recorded June, 1993," she began, her clear soprano a dramatic contrast to the guttural raspings of the ancient storyteller whose taped voice had just recounted the Coyote myth. "On the Havasupai Indian Reservation, located at the bottom of the Grand Canyon, Supai, Arizona. My informant is Supai Billy Hamadreeq, who claims without documentation to be one hundred years old, the oldest man alive in the Havasupai tribe. Supai Billy was once a powerful song shaman—that is, he dreamed songs that foretold the future. But now he dreams no more songs, nor has he trained any younger man to replace him when he joins Those Whose Names May Not Be Spoken. He is old, he says, and all his gods are old with him. The People are at the Ending Time, and there is no future to sing."

Suddenly Benny looked up from the checkerboard. "The helicopter!" he announced, as Whitney became aware of the faraway whir of rotors growing progressively louder overhead.

Beyond the window, the top layer of dust on the hard-packed earth swirled upward. Particles of red dirt sprayed against the thick plate glass. Benny leapt to his feet, jerked open the café's screen door and raced outside, for the moment not a hollow man but an eager, excited little boy.

A flurry of red dust gusted in behind him, which caused Gwe Watahomigie to curse even more fervently under his breath.

"Kids!" he muttered bitterly, taking another swipe at the counter with his apron. "Like he's expecting something from the Sears and Roebuck, maybe!"

Jesse Sinyella took another drag on his cigarette, then ground it out in the battered tin ashtray. He slapped the flat of his hand on the table and pushed himself up and out of the booth.

Whitney looked up from the tape recorder, automatically switching it off with her thumb. "Expecting something?"

"Yep." Jesse's heavy face was as devoid of expression as his voice. It was only his choice of words that indicated to Whitney he wasn't exactly thrilled about whatever was arriving on the afternoon flight. "That land shark, Hobie Stoner, is flying in with his sleazeball lawyer to address the Tribal Council."

"Stoner?" Whitney couldn't place the name.

"Hobart Stoner. As in Stoner Fantasy Resorts International." Jesse fixed his black eyes on her and waited for her gasp of recognition.

It came; and then she slumped backward against the cracked vinyl. "Oh, Jesse!" she wailed. "What are you going to do?"

"Do?" he repeated. He broke into the slow, phlegmatic smile that never quite reached his eyes. "What else can I do? I'm going to meet the helicopter."

Whitney dropped her tape recorder into the black fanny pack belted around her waist, right beside the walkie-talkie that was as much a part of her as her arms and legs. Then she slid out of the booth. The vinyl clung like fingers to her perspiring skin.

"I'll walk over with you," she offered. "I've never seen a land shark up close."

A rising column of red dust swathed both the helicopter and the spectators who had gathered to witness one of the high points of life in their isolated village. The wash from the propeller flung bits of dirt that stung their skin like needles.

By the time Whitney and Jesse arrived at the clearing that served as a helipad, the helicopter had descended to hover just above the tops of the cottonwood trees. Then Smilin' Jack Hannigan, veteran pilot of the Grand Canyon Helicopter Service, touched down on the cleared patch of red dirt. The rotors slowed and then stopped.

Smilin' Jack clambered out of his aircraft and bellowed cheerful greetings at the circle of spectators, mostly children, who regarded him solemnly. Undeterred, he ambled jovially around the circle, feinting like a shadowboxer at one boy, clapping the shoulder of another.

"Did'ja get your grandpa to quit cheating at checkers yet?" he demanded of Benny'wi. He patted a tiny girl on the check. "How's that pretty mama of yours?"

The children's faces remained expressionless; it was only the shy shuffling of their bare feet in the dust that told Whitney they were enjoying Smilin' Jack's banter enormously.

Behind Smilin' Jack, the belly of the helicopter swung open. A trio of passengers exited the aircraft and stood waiting for Smilin' Jack to offload their bags. They were the usual intrepid types who made the harrowing helicopter ride half a mile into the bowels of the earth—hikers and campers, all dressed alike in shorts and hik-

ing boots, with baseball caps or flapping Australian
outback hats like those worn by Crocodile Dundee.

Then another trio emerged. This group was nothing
like the first, and Whitney knew immediately that these
had to be the land shark and his entourage.

Only the first of the three, a statuesque young woman
with an artfully tousled mane of sun-streaked hair, was
appropriately dressed for a trip to the bottom of the
Grand Canyon. And even her safari outfit, complete
with high-heeled, goldtone-and-snakeskin boots, looked
more Rodeo Drive than Eddie Bauer.

The second member of the trio wore green plaid pants
and a green polo shirt with an initialed gold crest on the
pocket. *H* and *S* were the initials, all intertwined with
intricate whorls of gold braid.

The man was in his early sixties, Whitney estimated
with an automatic professional eye, but his trim, toned
physique looked much younger. *His pampered, pum-
meled, massaged physique,* she amended mentally, noting the smooth, tanning-salon bronze of his skin and the
lack of muscle development beneath it.

She also noted the gleaming white of his teeth, relent-
lessly displayed by a smile as practiced as a politician's.

"So that's what a land shark looks like," she murmured to Jesse. But the land shark was not the one who
caught her attention and held it.

The dark figure of a second man appeared in the
doorway of the helicopter. It was the quick flash of a
sunbeam reflecting off his metal-rimmed glasses that
drew Whitney's eyes to his face, but it was the face itself that riveted her.

There was something raw about it, as if it had been
begun and then for some reason left unfinished. His
forehead sloped back too far, and the bridge of his nose

was almost a right angle; his cheekbones were too prominent and his jaw too blunt. His hair was as black as Jesse's, only cropped in a more cosmopolitan style. And his skin, although darker than Jesse's, had a coppery cast.

Dressed in black, like every villain in every cowboy movie Whitney had ever seen, he wore a splash of red knotted around his neck that was in fact a quite civilized silk tie but might well have been a bandanna.

Crouching in the doorway of the helicopter, he looked like a big black cat—*a panther,* Whitney thought irrationally—ready to spring. Almost . . . dangerous.

He raised one hand to shield his eyes, gave the surrounding landscape a fastidious once-over and then stepped down from the helicopter to join the others.

Whitney had to smile at her own over-active imagination. What could possibly be dangerous about an attorney—for she assumed the man was, to use Jesse's words, "Hobart Stoner's sleazeball lawyer"—wearing a perfectly proper business suit and squinting like a displaced city slicker into the hot Arizona sun?

It took Whitney Baldridge-Barrows, M.D., trained observer of the human condition, a full sixty seconds to put all the pieces together and realize that the person she was looking at was a half-breed.

GABRIEL BLADE PAUSED in the dazzling glare of the sun as it reflected in waves off the sheer sandstone cliffs, and cursed. The heat enveloped him like a sauna.

He dropped awkwardly from the helicopter to the ground, trying to avoid stirring up any more dust than was absolutely necessary. Then, seeing the fine red particles waft upward anyway and settle on the hems of his black summer-wool trousers, he cursed again.

He scanned the circle of children who were inching closer to the helicopter. Every child appeared to be accompanied by a dog, and every dog by half a dozen of its closest friends.

Gabe thought that he'd never seen so many dogs in all his life! And they were all panting in concert, their tongues lolling in the dirt and their ears alert, as if waiting for him to commit some social gaffe so that they could bite into him.

He felt unpleasantly conspicuous, not because of the dogs, which no doubt viewed *all* newly arrived passengers as fresh meat, but because of the children. Every one of their round, red-brown faces were aimed in his direction, their black eyes pointed directly at him.

It's the damned suit, Gabriel Blade thought, irritated with the children for noticing and with himself for caring. Exactly right for the cool, rainy Seattle day he had left behind. Exactly right, in fact almost obligatory for the law offices of Parkhurst and Brandenberg.

But to these kids, most of whom had probably never even seen a man in a suit before, he must look ridiculous, wrapped in a layer of black wool on what must undoubtedly be the hottest day of the year! *I must look like an undertaker,* he thought, then reconsidered. These kids probably wouldn't even know what an undertaker was!

"Well, Gabe, my man, what'd I tell you?" Hobie Stoner slapped Gabriel Blade on his hot, itchy, wool-clad shoulder. "Does ol' Hobie know a gold mine when he sees one, or what!"

With his other arm he made a grand, sweeping gesture that laid claim to all he surveyed: the dusty clearing, the towering, red canyon walls, the cluster of wide-eyed children and their mangy mongrels, the stocky Indian man striding purposefully across the helipad toward them with a half-grown little Indian girl at his side.

The Indian wore jeans and a blue chambray shirt, unbuttoned down the front to reveal a red-brown, hairless chest and a thick midsection that suggested a sedentary lifestyle.

The man's face looked heavy and dull, but his black eyes studied Hobie Stoner with a shrewdness that made Gabe suspect it would be a mistake to underestimate him.

"Mr. Sinyella?" Hobie boomed, transferring his hand from Gabe's shoulder to that of the Indian. His other hand shot out and grasped the man's right hand before he had even offered it. *"Jesse!"* he amended engagingly as he pumped the man's hand with enthusiasm. "Businessmen like ourselves don't need to stand on ceremony, now do we? Hobart Stoner here, and I'd be honored if you'd just call me Hobie. Good of you to meet me!"

With a hand at the small of her back, he propelled the statuesque Rodeo Drive blonde slouching gracefully at his side toward Jesse.

"I'd like to introduce you to my assistant, Mimi Samples."

The woman's long red acrylic nails dipped graciously into Jesse's rough brown paw and lingered there. *"Mimi,"* she murmured.

"And Gabriel Blade," Hobie finished. "Gabe. My attorney."

The instant their eyes met, Gabe sensed the Indian's almost palpable hostility. For a tense moment he wondered if the other man would refuse to shake his hand. Then Jesse Sinyella extended his arm as if it were made of wood, and gave Gabe's hand a single, downward jerk.

"Mr. Blade," he acknowledged curtly. From bitter experience Gabe recognized the source of the man's hostility: Gabe's mixed blood. On the Seattle waterfront, where he had grown up, mixed blood meant divided loyalties; it offered an easy excuse to hate. Obviously it was the same down here. Resentment rose like hackles along the back of Gabe's own neck. *I have an enemy here,* he acknowledged, his every combative instinct rising to the occasion. *So be it.*

Still flashing his teeth, Hobie reclaimed Jesse Sinyella with a chummy arm around his shoulder and reverted his attention to Mimi Samples, having long ago discovered that her lush blond beauty was as conducive to discussing business as old whiskey, which he also used on occasion to great advantage.

Hobie never misses a trick, Gabe thought wryly. He even felt a certain contemptuous pity for the unsuspecting Indian, who was already outgunned, outmanned, and outmaneuvered, and didn't even know it.

A gold mine? Gabriel Blade looked around the great red bowl in which he found himself. He conducted a quick and informal feasibility study.

The sheer, perpendicular walls were at least a thousand feet high, he estimated, and surrounded in turn by the dazzling limestone walls of an even higher outer canyon. The lofty red walls and the towering white cliffs behind them shut out all but a narrow strip of blue sky.

But greenness and lushness and life spread itself across the broad canyon floor. It was a stunning contrast to the several hundred miles of parched desolation they'd driven across to get to Hilltop, the middle-of-nowhere mesa where the helicopter had picked them up and dropped them like Alice in Wonderland down this rabbit hole.

Possibly a gold mine, he concluded. If it was handled right. And for sure there was no one who could handle it better than Hobie Stoner.

Smilin' Jack unloaded the last of the bags from the hold and boarded passengers for the return trip to the surface of the world. Then, like departing royalty, he gave a final salute to his assembled subjects and clambered back into the cockpit of his aircraft.

"Clear!" he shouted out the window. The children and their assorted dogs scrambled off the helipad.

The rotors started up, grew louder until they echoed like thunder off the sheer canyon walls, and the aircraft lumbered into the air. It hovered aloft for a moment just above the cottonwood trees, then shot straight up. By the time the red dust had settled in its wake, it had become nothing more than an blurry sunspot in the brilliant blue strip of sky.

In the silence left behind on the ground, Gabe became aware of voices in the background, rising and falling in heated discussion. It was the trio of newly arrived hikers, dickering with some of the Indian boys over the price of packing their supplies into the campground.

The voices were mortifyingly familiar. But they weren't taking place on this hot summer day at the bottom of the Grand Canyon. Muffled by the drone of the interminable Seattle rain, it was his own voice that Gabe heard, bargaining with strangers over the small change in their pockets.

Burning with shame that was as real now as it had been twenty-five years ago, he turned on the three young hikers. "Why don't you give them what they want?" he barked. "It's no skin off your—"

Belatedly he remembered the crowd of smaller children, their inquisitive black eyes growing rounder as they watched the black-robed stranger turn almost as red-faced as the scrap of cloth that encircled his neck. Hobie Stoner, hearing Gabe's angry voice, shot an astonished, raised-eyebrow glance over his shoulder.

"—nose," Gabe finished lamely. He was furious with himself for what he had revealed by his unthinking gut reaction. Luckily, no one appeared to have noticed.

"Sure, man," shrugged the hiker wearing the Crocodile Dundee hat. He looked askance at Gabe, as if Gabe were some as yet unknown form of insect life. "No problem. We just figured it's, like, *expected*."

"He's right, you know." The voice came from among the crowd of children. "They *do* expect to dicker. It's all part of the game."

It was an intriguing voice, high and musical, trilling as sweetly as the birdsong that filled the dusty air.

Especially intriguing, Gabe noted with a bewildered frown, as it possessed a definite and most incongruous eastern-prep-school drawl.

Turning in the direction of the voice, he looked down to discover among the children the half-grown Indian girl who had accompanied Jesse Sinyella. "I doubt very much that it's a game to those kids," he began in the pompous tone of adults who have never talked to children.

Then he stopped short.

For the possessor of the musical voice with the pronounced Yuppie drawl was most definitely not a half-grown Indian girl. She was a woman. Not much taller than many of the children who surrounded her—the barely five feet of her didn't reach even as far as his shoulder—but undeniably a perfectly formed little woman.

Startled, Gabe reached up with thumb and forefinger to straighten his glasses.

Her white cotton camp shirt outlined her figure enchantingly, revealing modest but womanly curves, and a waist that Gabe suspected he could encircle with his two hands. The shirt was open at the throat, where he glimpsed a bead of perspiration trickle downward and disappear into the shadowed cleavage between her small breasts.

She was so damned . . . *cute!*

It was the first word that popped into Gabe's head, and even after casting around for a more eloquent adjective, it seemed the most accurate. All sorts of cute-isms ran through his mind. *Cute as a button. Cute as the dickens.* The oversize sunglasses that hid half her face made her look like a tiny, Disneyesque mosquito. *Cute as a bug.*

No, she was definitely not a half-grown Indian child. In fact, except for the straight black hair that curled under slightly at her shoulders, she hardly looked Indian at all. Her skin was golden rather than red-brown, her body fine-boned instead of thick and sturdy.

But neither did she look like a tourist. As rugged as this terrain appeared to be, this delicate little woman wore nothing more substantial on her feet than a pair of woven leather huaraches. Indeed, she looked as if a heavy hiking boot might easily snap one of those fragile-but-shapely little legs that extended from the wide-legged khaki shorts she wore.

The woman reached up and pushed the huge sunglasses up into her hair. "Whitney Baldridge-Barrows, from Boston," she said in a brisk, assertive tone that nevertheless managed to sound like the tinkling of glass wind chimes. "I'm the Indian Health Service doctor at Supai Village."

The city and the name certainly explained the eastern-prep-school drawl, Gabe thought, as he dutifully told her his name and mentioned Seattle. But neither the name nor the accent fit the exquisite, doll-like woman who stood before him.

For the woman was not Indian.

She was Asian.

SEEING THE LAND shark's sleazeball lawyer at closer range, Whitney realized that, except possibly to her, he was not tall. He wasn't actually much more than medium height, but carried himself with a posture so erect that he appeared a good deal taller.

"Shall we go?" she asked, gesturing toward the Indian children who were already filing off the helipad with the luggage in tow. The older boys had taken the heavier pieces, while parceling out the lighter ones to each of the younger children.

Even the smallest shared in the work and would share in the reward, Whitney knew, watching two tiny toddlers grapple manfully with a small leather case she sincerely hoped was not a camera. It was one of the things she admired most about the Indian way—the spirit of cooperation rather than competition. It was what had ensured their survival for the thousands of years they had lived in this inhospitable land; it was also what was threatening their survival today.

She wondered if the frowning VIP at her side even noticed the kids' behavior. Probably not, she decided. People like these kids, along with waitresses, hotel maids, taxi drivers, and the like, were just part of the nameless and faceless masses, no more than the grease that made the wheels of his life run smoothly.

Looking up at him, however, Whitney was surprised to see that his eyes were indeed following the children. "We're going to *walk?*" he sputtered incredulously.

"Yes," she replied.

"In *this* heat?" he persisted. "You mean there aren't any courtesy cars?"

Whitney shrugged, shaking her head as if to emphasize her helplessness in the matter.

"Shuttles? Cabs? *Anything?*"

Whitney continued to shake her head, her small mouth tilting at the corners. If she were not so well-bred, Gabe suspected with increasing irritation, the tiny smile that tugged at her lips would probably be a smirk.

"Well, as a matter of fact, there are no motorized vehicles at all in the canyon," Whitney told him. "But I suppose we might be able to find you a horse—"

A note of amusement crept into her voice as she indicated the several unkempt specimens who were grazing, ground-tied, at the edges of the helipad. Beneath each horse lay at least one panting, scratching dog, seeking shelter from the blazing sun in the shadow cast by its broad belly.

"—or maybe a mule?"

Now Gabe heard the suppressed laughter in her voice break through. It sounded even more than before like glass chimes tinkling gaily in the wind, but it did nothing to improve his rapidly deteriorating mood.

"Fine," he assented grimly. "I'll walk."

By the time they reached Gwe Watahomigie's Red Rock Café, Gabe had loosened the double Windsor knot in his tie and unfastened the collar button. A little farther along, he shed his jacket and folded it over one arm.

From his breast pocket he retrieved a square of white linen and mopped his brow.

Finally he undid the buttons of his monogrammed silk shirt and rolled up the cuffs. His black suitcoat, no longer folded, was slung carelessly over one shoulder.

At this rate, Whitney concluded while pretending not to notice the impromptu striptease, by the time they reached the Lodge he could very well be buck naked.

The thought was not altogether unpleasant.

CHAPTER TWO

THE NAME ON HER PASSPORT was Quan Jwa Gee. But that wasn't her real name. That was the name given her in the orphanage where she was taken after being found, abandoned, in a police station in Seoul.

The fifteenth of August, the Republic of Korea's Liberation Day, was the date chosen for her birthday. It was a common birthday in the orphanage. Seven was the age assigned to her, although of course there were no medical facilities available in the orphanage to make that determination. She could just as well have been six, or eight.

By seven—or six, or eight—she would have known her world; its customs, its sights and sounds and tastes and textures. And she would have known her place in it. There must have been people she knew, a place that was home. She must have had a mother, or someone who cared for her, or else she would not have survived at all. By the age of seven, or six or eight, her roots would have already been firmly established, and her taproot already gone deep.

But those years were a total blank to her.

Oh, occasionally, there was something she almost recognized, a fragment of a memory—a snatch of color glimpsed from the corner of her eye, a smell, a sound that was foreign and yet not—but the instant she tried to grasp it, it was gone.

She remembered nothing. Or if she did, it was lost in the trauma of her departure, when she left the country where she had spent the first seven or so years of her life, to live in one as alien to it as night is to day.

Sometimes it seemed to her that she was really born at the age of seven when, having been legally declared abandoned, she was adopted by an American doctor and his wife who lived in Boston. When she ceased to be Quan Jwa Gee and became Whitney Baldridge-Barrows.

During the time she lived in the orphanage, it was believed that she was mute. She never uttered a sound—not a word, not a laugh, not a cry—from the night she was found in the police station in Seoul until she had been living with her new American family for nearly a year. Then one day, out of the clear blue sky, she suddenly began speaking complete sentences in perfect English, with no trace of any accent except the broad *A*s and dropped *R*s of her parents' nasal New England dialect.

Her upbringing had been typically and unremarkably American. She had been a Brownie and then a Girl Scout, played the clarinet in the junior high school marching band and become captain of the debate team at Concord Academy, just outside Boston.

She had partied for a while at Radcliffe and then settled down to the disciplined course of study that culminated in her graduation with honors from Harvard Medical School.

There were months, even years on end, when Whitney Baldridge-Barrows completely forgot Quan Jwa Gee. But then, without warning, she would catch sight of herself in a mirror, or turn a street corner and come unexpectedly upon a reflection of herself in a shop window, and for an instant she wouldn't recognize the face staring back at her.

It didn't look at all like the other faces that inhabited her world. It was flat and heart-shaped, with slanted black eyes that rested on top of prominent cheekbones—narrow slits of eyes that practically disappeared when she smiled. The face had golden skin, delicately arched brows that swept upward as if in perpetual surprise, and small, bowed lips.

It was a face so classically Korean that it appeared in ancient scroll paintings and historic temple carvings from Pusan in the south to Ch'ongjin City in the north.

It was the face of a stranger.

WHEN WHITNEY FIRST CAME down to the canyon, she had wondered how the Indians would perceive her—as a member of the dominant white culture of the "uptop world," as they called the world outside their canyon, or as part of an ethnic minority like themselves.

Neither, she had concluded wryly after a few months. They seemed to see her as no more than a purveyor of pills, a dispenser of advice that they largely ignored, indistinguishable from the long line of Indian Health Service docs who had preceded and would follow her.

Despite the beauty of the canyon, which attracted tourists from all over the world, it was hard for the Indian Health Service to get doctors to work on this reservation and almost impossible to get them to stay.

The workload was crushing. The doctor was on call twenty-four hours a day, seven days a week, never able to get out of the canyon, nor even to get out of range of the walkie-talkie. And there was no help in the clinic, so the doctor had to do everything: mix drugs, start IV's, run the lab work, take X rays, repair injuries and do the paperwork. All this in addition to the routine daily care, and often everything except for the paperwork at the same time.

Under normal circumstances, the round-the-clock availability was more an inconvenience than a problem; in an emergency, it could make the difference between life and death. And sometimes did.

THE DAY AFTER the arrival of the real-estate developer and his entourage, Whitney paced back and forth in her empty clinic, feeling decidedly out of sorts.

Usually at this time of morning, every cheap plastic chair in the waiting room would be occupied. Old men who couldn't urinate and old women crippled by arthritis would sit in stoic silence, staring at the red dust on the floor that no amount of sweeping could keep clean. Babies would be crawling through it, coating their red-brown skin with a darker crust of red, while mothers engaged in terse, monosyllabic gossip in their native tongue over the children's heads.

But on this particular day the clinic was empty, although there appeared to be more people milling about the village square than Whitney had treated during her entire six months in the clinic.

Apparently they had all come to get acquainted with Hobie Stoner. From the open door of the clinic Whitney could see the predatory gleam of his perfect white teeth as he flashed his indiscriminate smile at one and all. The moral equivalent of a politician's baby-kissing, Whitney grumbled to herself.

Like every white man who'd ever exploited a tribe of Native Americans, Hobie had brought his own contemporary version of wampum. Instead of glass beads and blankets, he had chartered a helicopter to fly in enough ice cream to make the whole tribe sick for a week.

The ice cream was packed in dry ice in coolers, and he and Mimi Samples were handing out half-gallon containers as if they were prizes at the bottom of a Cracker Jack box. Children and adults alike tore open the containers and devoured the ice cream right on the spot, using the plastic spoons that Hobie had thoughtfully provided.

The man was a wheeler-dealer all right, Whitney thought sourly. To the Havasupai, who had to pack in all their supplies by horseback over a trail that required an entire day to descend, ice cream was a commodity more priceless than glass beads and blankets had ever been.

The third member of Hobie Stoner's party, Gabriel Blade, was nowhere in sight.

Maybe the hotshot lawyer considered it beneath his dignity to participate in barefaced bribery, Whitney said to herself. Well that, at least, would be a point in his favor! But more likely he was sitting over his second cup of coffee in the Red Rock Café at this very moment, watching the impromptu ice-cream social through the smudged plate-glass window and planning the next step in the conquest of the unsuspecting Havasupai.

In disgust, Whitney turned away from the door. So far this morning Chili had logged in only two patients, one of them being Jesse Sinyella, waiting in the examining room for his daily injection of insulin.

"You know you should be doing this yourself," Whitney reminded him as she joined him in the examining room.

"I know, Dr. B, but..." Jesse began.

As Whitney rolled the tiny vial of insulin between her hands to mix it, he pushed up his sleeve. Quickly and efficiently she inserted a needle through the vial's rubber stopper and drew out Jesse's dosage. Then she swabbed a spot on his upper arm, jabbed the needle just under the skin and injected the milky fluid.

"... but it doesn't hurt as much when you do it," he finished, wincing just a little.

"It wouldn't hurt when you do it, either," she retorted with mock severity, "Once you learn how. As a matter of fact, I have kids as young as five injecting themselves!"

"I know," Jesse repeated. He arranged his round face into a sheepish expression. "I guess I'm just chicken."

Jesse wasn't chicken. Whitney knew that. Cowardice simply wasn't the Indian way. Over half the Havasupai Indians were diabetic, many dependent on insulin, and most administered their own injections with equanimity.

Except when they forgot. Or when they were too busy. Or when they ran out of insulin and didn't get around to coming into the clinic to pick up another vial. Or when they just didn't feel like it.

Whitney found the Havasupai to be the most frustrating patients she had ever dealt with.

It was hard to get them to think in terms of preventive medicine, impossible to interest them in good nutrition. It was a challenge just getting them to complete a course of antibiotics instead of discontinuing the medication as soon as they felt better. Then, of course, when the infection flared up again, as it always did, they'd return to the clinic with their nearly full bottle of pills and complain that the medicine hadn't worked.

If it hadn't been for Jesse Sinyella, Whitney wasn't sure she would have lasted these six months in the canyon. Because the village was so small, she ran into him everywhere—at the trading post, at the post office, at the Red Rock Café.

When she needed to arrange an air evacuation—"evac," as the locals called it—for a sick patient, he was always available to place her call to the uptop world via the shortwave radio in his office. When she needed supplies, when she needed an interpreter, when she needed someone to listen to her problems and be counted on to forget them later, he was there.

Things would have been much more difficult, maybe even impossible, she often reflected, if he hadn't been there to explain Indian ways to her, and her ways to them.

No, Whitney had concluded a long time ago, Jesse was no coward. She had formed her own opinion as to why he came to the clinic every morning for the injection he just as easily could have administered to himself at home, which was why she let him get away with it.

Seeing the chief, the Tribal Chairman himself, who except for his diabetes was healthy as a horse, routinely visit the clinic was a good example for the rest of the tribe. It made them view health care as maintenance, rather than something to be considered only as a last resort. Patient cooperation, while not at the level Whitney would have liked, had increased appreciably since Jesse started coming in every morning.

Whitney withdrew the needle and Jesse stood, rolling down his sleeve and buttoning the cuff.

"By the way, Dr. B," he said, draping a companionable arm across her shoulder as they walked down the corridor toward the waiting room. "How'd you like to have dinner tomorrow night with me and Stoner and his flunkies?"

"Oh, I don't know, Jesse," she began. "I'm afraid Mr. Stoner isn't my first choice for a dinner companion...."

Then, unbidden, an image of one of Hobie Stoner's flunkies flashed into her mind. It made her hesitate. "Why me?" she asked, playing for time.

"You'd really be helping me out," Jesse said. "I don't like that bunch. That Stoner never gives it a rest—I think trying to eat with him batting at my ear all night will probably end up giving me an ulcer. And that stuck-up, snooty half-breed lawyer of his..."

"Why do you dislike Mr. Blade so much?" Whitney interrupted. "Or is it just lawyers in general?"

"I'm not big on lawyers, that's true. But this one, especially... well, he's an apple, Dr. B. And I don't trust apples."

"*Apple?*" Whitney repeated, mystified.

"Red on the outside, white on the inside," Jesse recited in his somber, singsong voice as if quoting a religious axiom.

"Oh, Jesse! How can you say something like that? I've never known you to be a bigot!"

"It's not bigotry, Dr. B. It's just a fact. *Your* people—the whites, I mean—don't trust the Indian in him; why should we trust the white?"

Whitney bit back a cutting remark with a vengeance that left bloodless white imprints on her small, bowed underlip. Her self-control surprised her.

Usually she spoke her mind with little regard for the consequences, and that trait hadn't endeared her to some of her colleagues. Many called her pushy. A few even said, privately *and* in public, that she had a Napoleon complex. But this remark of Jesse's, coming as it did from a man she knew to be intelligent and educated, and one she considered a good friend as well, left her speechless.

It also repelled her. She didn't like knowing this aspect of his personality. And it created in her a sneaking empathy with the man Jesse had called an apple, who was stuck, through no fault of his own, with a foot in each of two worlds without really belonging to either one.

She knew how that felt.

She often felt that way, herself.

"Besides," Jesse continued in a conciliatory tone, trying to reestablish their earlier, bantering mood, "Stoner keeps pushing that gorgeous, blond assistant at me all the time. If I'm not careful, he's going to have us in bed together before either one of us knows what's happening!"

Whitney tacitly agreed to the cease-fire. "Poor baby," she forced herself to respond lightly. "So you want me there to protect your virtue?"

"Let's say that I like to make those kinds of decisions for myself," Jesse temporized, looking down at her with a rare twinkle in his eye. "And I like them to have *nothing* to do with business."

Whitney gave in, laughing. "All right, Jesse, sure. I'd be happy to meet you for dinner. What time?"

"Come on over after you close up the clinic," Jesse replied. There was no need to discuss where, since the Red Rock Café was the only place in the village where residents and campers alike could get food without having to cook it themselves. "And thanks, Dr. B. I really appreciate it."

He gave Whitney's shoulder a companionable squeeze, then clamped his straw sombrero on his head and ambled out the door.

Chili, the clinic's on-again, off-again Havasupai receptionist, looked up from the yellowed tabloid she held in front of her face.

"Um, um, um," she volunteered in the flat, singsong voice that gave away the fact that, like all of the Indians in the canyon, English was not her first language. She pursed her lips, Indian-fashion, and gestured with her double chins in the direction of Jesse's retreating back. "He can leave his moccasins outside my teepee anytime."

Interpreting the monosyllabic grunts as one of Chili's infrequent attempts at witty repartee, Whitney turned toward her. "Teepee?" she queried with a grin. "You live in a duplex!"

"I know," Chili deadpanned. Her stolid moon-face almost flickered into a smile. "I heard that in a old John Wayne movie once." Then she snapped the yellowed pages between her pudgy fingers to dispel any wrinkles, and was once again engrossed in her reading.

Whitney noticed the date on the front page. It was right above the colored photograph of an eighty-year old grandmother who had given birth to twelve alien babies. The tabloid was nearly a year old.

Those little aliens should be walking by now, she said to herself.

Whitney wondered many things about Chili. She wondered how the woman managed to balance her ponderous body on that cheap plastic chair hour after hour, signing patients in and signing them out. She wondered if her huge breasts ever got in her way, resting as they did on top of her desk all day long.

She wondered about Chili's real name, her *Indian* name. Whitney had never heard it, because Chili was known throughout the reservation simply as "Chili

Pepper." The name had been given to her in her youth by some Mexican miners who had come to the upper mesa to mine uranium.

Looking at the straight black hair that flowed past Chili's undefinable waistline, her plain, round face and somber black eyes, Whitney sometimes wondered what there had been about this woman, now forever buried beneath layers and layers of flesh, that had once caused a group of lusty young migrant workers to nickname her "Chili Pepper."

"Chili," Whitney said abruptly. "Do we have anyone else scheduled for today?"

Chili peered over the top of her newspaper and scanned the waiting room. Then she turned her impassive gaze toward Whitney. "Don't look like it," she stated flatly.

Whitney pointedly ignored any sarcasm that might have been intended. "Well," she said, "I'm going down to pay a call on Billy Hamadreeq. It's been a couple of days since he's been in, and you know how forgetful he gets about his meds."

She walked back to her office, belted her fanny pack around her waist, then unplugged the walkie-talkie on her desk and dropped it into the fanny pack. "I'll be on the hand-held," she told Chili, "if anything comes up."

Chili, her lips moving with laborious concentration as she sounded out the story about the twelve alien babies, grunted noncommittally.

BILLY HAMADREEQ LIVED deep in Havasu Canyon, below the magnificent travertine waterfalls that had, centuries before, given his tribe their name: Havasupai—"The People of the Blue-Green Water."

Billy's wickiup, the traditional mud-and-brush shelter that he called home, rose like a gigantic bird's nest turned upside down in the middle of a garden patch slowly returning to nature. Whitney saw that the sleeping hammock tied between two ancient cottonwoods was empty. That told her Billy was probably inside his dilapidated shelter.

She coughed politely to let him know someone was coming.

Slowly the leather flap that covered the wickiup's low doorway was lifted aside, and an old man hobbled out of the dim interior.

He was as thin and brown as a stick. His body was stooped, and his skin hung on his old bones as if it had been handed down from a much larger man. Lank white hair fell to his shoulders, secured in place by a woven sweatband tied around his forehead.

Whitney noticed immediately that he was barefoot. She resolved to discuss it with him at the first opportunity.

"Hello, Uncle!" she called from a distance because Billy, whose hearing was as acute as ever, was nearly blind.

"Ah, *bqi'gthegee!*" Billy called, welcoming her with the Indian name he had given her.

In the beginning he had called her only *hay gu'u*, which meant "white tourist." After he came to trust her and respect her skill, he affectionately began calling her *bqi'gthegee*, Small-Female-Medicine-Shaman.

Sometimes, when he was adrift in that nebulous, soothing twilight world between sobriety and intoxication, he called her *vje'e*, daughter.

Whitney threaded her way through the parched brown garden. Only a few sickly tomatoes added color to the dead and dying vegetation. Billy's swaybacked old mule picked desultorily at the few roots and stems still surviving among the weeds, and she patted its bony rump as she walked by.

When she reached the clearing where old Billy waited, they clasped wrists warmly.

"Have you come for another story?" he asked.

"No, Uncle. I've just come to see how you're doing. We've missed you at the clinic."

"Too bad," the old man muttered. He kept his hand on Whitney's arm and leaned on her for support as together they made their way to a wooden bench beneath the shade of one of the cottonwood trees. "I remembered a story today. It was about . . . it was . . ."

Billy lowered his bony rump to the wooden bench, then leaned back against the rough twigs of the wickiup's outer shell. He closed his eyes, basking in the feel of the hot sun on his face, and furrowed his brow as he concentrated on the remembering.

Whitney settled herself on the edge of the hammock, slowly moving it back and forth with the heel of one leather huarache. "Never mind, Uncle," she said. "I don't have my tape recorder with me now, anyway. I just wanted to say hello. How're you feeling? Have you been eating?"

Billy shrugged. "The ladies at the church bring me food every day. I eat."

"And you've been taking your insulin?"

Again Billy shrugged. He raised his hands to his mouth and breathed into his cupped palms, then brushed them lightly down his body from shoulders to knees. It was an old Havasupai gesture, dismissing Whitney's question as one of no importance.

"You *must* take your insulin, Billy!" Against her best intentions, Whitney injected a shrewish stridency into her voice. "You're going to become much sicker if you don't!"

"I am not sick," Billy contradicted her gently, his eyes still closed. "I am only old."

"But you would *feel* better if you took better care of yourself! Living all alone out here the way you do, with only the Ladies' Aid Society coming by with food...! Who knows what might happen? Who knows?"

There she was, nagging again. Billy always did it to her. Sometimes she wondered why she even bothered—the old man never paid a damned bit of attention to what she had to say, anyway!

She swallowed the angry words that were rising like a lump in her throat and that tasted suspiciously like tears.

Leaning forward in the hammock, she fixed a critical, professional eye on the old man's feet. She ran a sharp fingernail along the bottom of one dusty foot and waited hopefully for a reaction—a sensitivity, a reflexive curl of the toes, an involuntary jerking away. There was nothing.

Then she reached down to palpate them. Her heart sank. With his eyes closed, Billy didn't even notice her touch.

The soles of his feet were as hard and cracked as old leather. That, combined with the poor blood circulation caused by his diabetes, made them as numb as stone. They were cold as stone, too, even in the one-hundred-and-ten-degree heat, and the bluish-white skin was swollen and mottled.

Whitney felt as cold as stone herself. "Billy," she implored, her hushed voice more compelling than her usual persistent prodding. "Billy, your feet. They really don't look very good. You need to wear something protective on them, like moccasins. Even sandals would help. An injury... if you step on a thorn, if you get an infection... it could be very bad for you, Billy."

But old Billy, eyes still closed against the sun, only patted her shoulder. "Tell me the news of the village," he suggested. "There are newcomers there?"

With the constant influx of tourists, there were always newcomers in the village; Whitney knew that Billy was not asking about those.

"How do you *know* these things?" she demanded, distracted in spite of herself, which she knew had been his intention. The frustration she felt with the old man reverted to respect and admiration, the other emotions she most commonly felt toward him. "They only arrived yesterday afternoon!"

"The wind tells me," Billy replied with perfect conviction, "and the birds, and the grass, and the rocks when they speak among themselves. I have lived in this place for so long that I know how everything is. When something is different, I know it. Tell me of these newcomers."

"Well," Whitney began after gathering her thoughts for a few moments of silence. "He's a lawyer, from Seattle. He isn't exactly good-looking, but there's something about him... It makes you want to look at him again." She fell silent for another moment while she pictured the lawyer from Seattle again in her mind.

"He's not too tall, not too short," she continued. "Dark. He's a half-breed, as a matter of fact."

"This is the only newcomer? For some reason I thought there were others...."

A most uncharacteristic flush crept up Whitney's face, deepening the honey of her skin to the shade of a summer peach. Embarrassed, she glanced up at Billy to see if he'd noticed.

He hadn't, of course. He could hardly tell a hawk from a hummingbird if both were perched side by side in one of the old cottonwood trees. But he did hear the mortified tone in her voice when she replied, "Yes, actually, there are two others."

And he understood even more than she what it signified.

CHAPTER THREE

MORNING ENTERED unobtrusively through the windows of the small frame house that Whitney called home for the time being. It draped itself in subdued shadows across the white walls and the brightly woven Indian rugs scattered around the floors. Though it was already past nine o'clock, the light was still as pale and gray as dawn.

It was the time of day the Indians called "little light." The sun was blocked by the towering red walls until well past ten o'clock, so that even in summer, most of the day was without sunshine.

As their ancestors had done before them for the more than fourteen thousand years they had inhabited this canyon, the Havasupai did the heavy work of the day at little light. When the sun appeared in their narrow strip of sky to heat the canyon like an oven, they rested in hammocks and old iron beds in the shade of the trees, or on the banks of the cold, clear creek that rushed through their canyon on its way to the Colorado River, and from there to the sea.

Whitney also took advantage of little light. Propping first one foot and then the other on the edge of a kitchen chair, she laced up her running shoes. Then she flattened the palms of her hands against the wall and began to do her hamstring stretches.

It was a good morning for a run. The clinic didn't open for another half hour, and she felt refreshed after a night of relatively uninterrupted sleep.

Often her sleep was not so uninterrupted. Because there were no telephones, the Indians used her house as an emergency room and came knocking on her door at all hours of the night. A fall from a horse. A kick from a horse.

Most injuries, in fact, had something to do with horses and a great deal more to do with alcohol. But there were other emergencies, too—a child who couldn't breathe, a slash from a knife fight, snake and scorpion bites.

Last night's single interruption had been less serious, although had it been much later, Whitney probably wouldn't have found it as humorous as she did.

About midnight, a young man had appeared at her door. His face was hidden by a shabby straw sombrero pulled low over his forehead.

"'Scuse me, Dr. B," he'd said in a voice barely above a whisper. He shifted his sheepish gaze everywhere except directly at her. "Could I get a...a...*ning hathb'ig*?" His voice faltered on the last words.

"A what?" Whitney repeated with a frown.

"...*ning hathb'ig*." The voice grew infinitesimally louder. "A *ning hathb'ig*. A—"

Whitney's mouth dropped open. "Oh. Oh, yes." She nodded quickly, sparing the boy the embarrassment of translating his request into English. Her Supai wasn't much more than passable, but she was able to piece the words together. *Ning*—make love; *hathb'ig*—literally, dam.

The boy actually had the gall to come to her door in what was practically the middle of the night to ask that she open the clinic in order to give him a condom!

Indignant words sprang to her lips, first among them an exasperated "No way!" But when he removed his floppy-brimmed hat to swat at the moths beating frenzied wings against the porch light, she got a better look at his face. She saw the abashed flush creeping up from his neck, making his red-brown skin look even darker.

She knew him, though only slightly. His name was Lone Arrow. He had recently returned to the reservation after dropping out of Phoenix Indian School, and now he worked as a mule-skinner with his father and brothers.

"I brought you my horse to ride," he offered as an added inducement. Looking past him, Whitney saw a nondescript nag, saddled and tied to the hitching post in front of her house.

Well, it was her own fault, she supposed. Given her constant admonitions to her patients to use condoms, both as protection against sexually transmitted diseases *and* to stem the rampant illegitimacy that had become a way of life on the reservation, she felt she could hardly refuse, even though the boy's timing was inconvenient, to say the least.

Sighing, she pulled the door shut behind her, not bothering to lock it—no one did, in Supai—and mounted the horse waiting apathetically at the hitching post. The animal took off at a lazy plod to cover the few hundred yards to the clinic.

I could have *walked* faster, Whitney had told herself wryly. Aloud she'd only said, "Next time, Lone Arrow, maybe you could manage to *plan ahead* a little?"

FINISHING HER warm-up exercises, Whitney opened the door and stepped out into the thin yellow-gray of the morning. She wore faded gray sweats. The color made her slight form almost blend into the gray shadows that hung like webs from the cliffs.

Her sweatshirt was emblazoned with a picture of an Indian mounted sloppily on a horse, a whiskey bottle clutched in one hand and a large red *X* across the bottle. The message below the picture read Don't Drink and Ride.

She filled her lungs with air thirty to forty degrees cooler than it would be by afternoon. As the morning breeze stroked her skin, an almost sensual chill prickled up her spine. She shivered. Gooseflesh rose on her arms, and her nipples puckered as though touched by an invisible lover.

Unexpectedly, in the distance, she heard the tramp-tramp-tramp of approaching footsteps.

The faint sounds would not have been audible at all were it not for the strange echo effect in the canyon. It was caused by the massive stone formations and the close, towering walls. Through the sandstone labyrinth, the distant footsteps echoed and re-echoed until they sounded like an entire platoon of foot soldiers.

As they came closer, Whitney could hear them striking the hard-packed earth with a steady, measured tread. She heard the hollow sound they made crossing the wooden bridge that spanned the creek, and realized the runner was coming from the direction of the Lodge.

Curious, she stepped back into the porch shadows. Except for herself, she had never encountered another runner in the canyon. The hikers hiked—that was why they came. And because there were no motor vehicles of any kind for transportation, everyone who lived on the reservation walked so much that they had neither the need nor the inclination to run simply for the sake of running.

The footsteps came closer, accompanied by their reverberating echo, and then Whitney saw a figure emerge from beneath a stand of cottonwood trees.

It was Gabriel Blade.

The half-breed, she was forced to remind herself, because at this particular moment there was nothing about him to suggest that his bloodline was anything other than pure, unadulterated Native American.

Given her years of medical education, it was impossible to turn off the trained observer inside her brain that automatically evaluated his physical condition. *Age approximately midthirties. Strong skeletal structure. Excellent musculature. Obviously in the prime of life. A healthy, vital, no doubt* virile...*male.*

His back was straight with shoulders thrown back, his upper body was red-brown like an Indian's and, like an Indian's, free of body hair. His smooth broad chest rose and fell with the same steady rhythm as his feet when they struck the ground.

He wore only blue Spandex shorts and a scant blue muscle shirt, high-topped running shoes and a plastic water bottle clipped to his belt. The supple Spandex fit exactly the way it was supposed to—like a second skin. It hugged his buttocks and the long muscles of his thighs, outlining and defining each contour with a gleam of taut, shiny fabric.

Funny, Whitney thought. Yesterday, in his sophisticated black suit and silk tie and buttoned-down shirt, it had taken her a while to recognize the Indian in him. This morning, his body half-naked in the pale, yellow-gray of little light, she was having a hard time seeing the Caucasian.

Except she recognized immediately that he ran like a white man. His heel came down first and hard, creating a divot in the earth with each step. *Hay gu*—white men—ran against the earth, old Billy Hamadreeq had told her once. They used the assault of their heels on the ground to hurtle themselves up and away from the source of their life and their strength.

But an Indian ran, or so Billy said, with his feet striking the ground nearly flat, so that there was no injury to the man or the earth, but rather a harmony, a oneness, an exchange of strength.

Sometimes old Billy's ramblings made a convoluted kind of sense to Whitney. Like now. Medically speaking, the white man's method of running jarred his joints, compressed his spinal column and contributed to all kinds of orthopedic problems later in life. The Indian's more natural gait was kinder to the joints and the entire skeletal structure, and allowed him to run almost indefinitely without tiring.

Gabriel Blade's long reaching strides looked deceptively slow, but quickly devoured the red ground beneath his feet. As Whitney watched, hardly moving, hardly even breathing, he came nearer and nearer to where she stood on her front porch. She could easily make out his sharp, hawklike profile and the arrogant lift of his head.

She shrank farther into the shadows of the porch, feeling uncharacteristically shy. Feeling that her frank and admittedly erotic scrutiny was somehow invading his privacy.

Without looking to the left or to the right, Gabriel Blade sped past her. Then he rounded the bend on the path that meandered past the tribal office, post office, trading post and finally Gwe Watahomigie's Red Rock Café, then disappeared from view.

Distracted by thoughts she only half recognized and would have vehemently denied *had* she recognized them, Whitney's eyes remained fixed on the curve where the half-naked body had vanished.

She wondered how far he was going. She wondered how soon he would be coming back. She wondered...

The walkie-talkie in her fanny pack crackled, bringing her back to reality with a jolt.

From the depths of the fanny pack, Chili's voice rasped through the still gray morning. "Supai Two to Supai One. Over." Whitney extricated her hand-held unit and raised the antenna.

"Supai Two, this is Supai One," she returned. "What have you got for me, Chili? Over."

Listening to the static-charged voice on the other end, Whitney refused to acknowledge the twinge of disappointment that tugged at her. There would be no time for a run this morning. Neither would there be time to wait for an encore performance from the... *virile*... and provocative Gabriel Blade.

She turned and headed back into the house to change from her sweats into something more befitting a practicing physician.

AT THE SOUND of footsteps echoing through the canyon, Jesse Sinyella looked up from his desk. He heard the footsteps from a long way off, their tempo as measured as the beating of a drum.

A runner in the canyon. Odd. Except for Dr. B's occasional early morning runs, Jesse hadn't heard a runner in the canyon for a long time...years. Not since Ric

Caldwell, the Indian Health Service doc with Olympic aspirations. Ric had spent two years working in the clinic, longer than anyone else had ever stayed, practicing medicine as well as his own special regimen of cross-country training.

Ric Caldwell. How long had it been now? Ten years? Twelve? Somehow time just got away from you, Jesse thought with a vague sense of dissatisfaction. He didn't even remember whether Ric had made it to the Olympics....

For some reason, the nameless runner irritated him, capturing his attention in spite of the work piled up on his desk. The thought of an unknown someone's winged feet flying through his canyon when his own could not made him feel restless and somehow resentful.

An image flashed into his mind. A raven. The spirit guide that had entered his soul to become the other half of himself at his manhood initiation, over twenty years ago.

Was it really twenty years ago?

The elders had taken the whole rite very seriously, of course. But the young boys, most of them coerced by their parents into participating, had clowned their way through it, laughing and shoving each other as if it was a big joke. They didn't believe the old traditions had anything to do with them.

But Jesse knew better.

The raven was glossy black, raucous and flamboyant. It had come to him after three days of fasting and then the traditional long, hot run up Wii'baaq'a—the red rock formation that looked like a man—to greet the rising sun.

The raven had stayed with Jesse all the way back to the men's sweat lodge, urging him to run faster, faster, so fast that sometimes Jesse felt he was actually flying.

Eventually it urged him to fly higher and farther than his limited experience in this womblike canyon home could ever have foreseen.

So high and so far that he had graduated high school, the only one out of his entire dormitory at Phoenix Indian School to do so. So high and far that he had gone on to Arizona State, graduating with a degree in business.

Then, inevitably, he had come back to this red womb, because the raven called him back, and because he could not stay away.

But now the raven in his soul felt very old. Now it dragged its tired wings through the red dust over which it once had soared. Sometimes Jesse felt as though someone had clipped those wings, and he, Jesse, had just stood by and let it happen.

He looked down at the papers in front of him. In the yellow-gray of little light, he was working on a proposal to be presented to the Tribal Council. Hobie Stoner's proposal, as a matter of fact.

He didn't like Hobie Stoner. And he didn't like Hobie Stoner's proposal, but he was required by the Tribal Constitution to present it to the Council anyway.

He thought briefly about the old days and the old ways, the days before the white man, the days he knew only from old Billy's stories.

The days of the legendary chiefs like Big Jim, Chief Manakaja, Billy Burro, Mark Hanna. When the tribe followed a chief because he was wise, not because he was elected. When the chief made decisions for his people, without having to consult a committee of duly elected council members, each with his own political ax to grind.

But that was long ago, over one hundred years ago. Before the treaties that trapped the Havasupai tribe in the less than six hundred acres contained in this canyon. Of necessity, the tribe had learned compromise. And for a time, when the tribal population had fallen below two hundred, it looked as though they would be compromised right out of existence.

Then the outside world discovered the hidden canyon, with its sheer red walls and magnificent blue-green waterfalls and fountains of travertine pools as symmetrical as if they'd been designed by an architect. They began to call the canyon "Shangri-La"—which indeed the Indians had done for thousands of years, although by a variety of other names—and now tourism had become the mainstay of the tribe.

And tourism had saved them.

But was the franchised and homogenized tourism now proposed by Hobie Stoner the sort of tourism that would benefit the tribe? Or only benefit Hobie Stoner?

The running footsteps came closer. They sounded as though they were passing right in front of the tribal office. Jesse resisted the impulse to go to the window.

Slouched at his desk, he became acutely aware of the paunch that settled comfortably over his belt. Self-consciously he sat up a little straighter and sucked in his belly. He could feel the softness, still there. He kept intending to do something about it, but...

Somehow time just got away from you, he thought again, with the same vague dissatisfaction.

He wasn't even married yet. Sometimes he teased his mother about that, and she teased him back, saying that it was no longer her responsibility, that today's young warrior must find his own woman.

And more and more often lately, when he thought of a woman of his own, the image of Dr. B came into his mind.

Whitney. Intelligent and caring in the bossy, take-charge way so much at odds with her diminutive stature and clear, childlike voice.

If the choice were his alone, with no one else's needs to consider... But there *were* other needs. There was the tribe, and the preservation of what was left of Havasupai blood, and the example he must set. But if the choice was his alone...

Listening to the footsteps of the unknown runner, Jesse was reminded again that Dr. B was a runner, too. His wandering mind became a jumble of the beautiful Korean doctor, the Olympic triathlon runner Ric Caldwell, Hobie Stoner with his sultry blond bait and half-breed lawyer, and a million other things he couldn't have sorted out if his life depended on it.

He was relieved when the echoes stopped and he could get back to work.

GABRIEL BLADE was a methodical man. Even the deliberate pace of his running demonstrated the self-discipline he imposed on himself in everything he did.

He moved as if he had never hurried in his life, never run from the shopkeepers of Seattle's Pike Street market with his pockets full of stolen food, never outdistanced the cops in the twisted back alleys between the Pike Street market and the Seattle waterfront.

But he hadn't always been that way. The kids with whom he had grown up on the streets of Seattle had called him "Switch" Blade, because he was so quick with a knife, and with his hands and feet in his own bastardized but effective version of karate. They called him other things, too. Like "Breed." But never to his face.

They also called his mother names—"drunk" or "whore" or "squaw," all of which she may have been at various times in her life, but none of which really described the sad and impoverished misfit who had been as much a mystery to Gabe as all the other unfathomables of his life.

GABE FOUND HIMSELF at the end of the red-dirt path. Directly in front of him stood a low building, built of slabs of red rock and weathered planks of wood. A hand-lettered sign painted on the plate-glass window said Red Rock Café. Another hand-lettered sign in the open doorway said Open, although Gabe could see no one moving around the dim interior.

He caught a glimpse of himself in the window. None of his old gang would have recognized the man reflected there, he thought.

The intervening years had eroded all traces of the unknown Anglo father who had unwittingly contributed half his genes. Now it was his Indian blood that showed plainly in the high nose, the prominent cheekbones, in the angles and planes of a face very much like the rugged land that was reflected around it.

Grown, Gabriel Blade no longer tried to pass for white. Grown, he no longer beat to a bloody pulp anyone who dared suggest he was not.

Past the café, the path became nothing more than an old, untended trail winding up the broken talus slopes that were the foothills of the monumental red walls. Not yet even breathing hard, Gabe found the beginnings of the trail that led east toward the rising sun, and began to climb.

CHAPTER FOUR

ON THE AFTERNOON Whitney was to meet Jesse for dinner, Little Mary Manakaja came into the clinic with a severe asthma attack.

Her mother, Big Mary Manakaja, had been trying various home remedies—Mentholatum rubbed on the child's chest, hourly doses of lobelia seeds and garlic pulverized in illicit rum—without success. Now Little Mary was hardly able to talk, using all her strength just to exhale. Her round moon face was nearly blue.

Whitney administered an injection of adrenaline, then started an IV. She put a pulmo-aid mask over the child's nose and mouth so that Little Mary could inhale the cool, moist, medicated air. For two hours she and Big Mary sat on either side of the exam table where Little Mary lay, telling her stories, making her laugh, doing everything they could to keep her from becoming bored and uncooperative.

When the crisis was over, Whitney turned an accusatory eye on Big Mary.

"This is your fault," she informed the distraught mother without an ounce of sympathy. "You *must* see that Mary uses her Ventolin inhaler every morning and every night, even when she's not sick. If you don't, one of these times it may be too late. She could die."

Big Mary hung her head, looking like nothing so much as an overgrown, chastened child. "The medicine spray was empty," she said by way of explanation.

"Well, you *must* come to the clinic to get a new inhaler *before* it runs out. You must not forget. You know that, Mary—I've certainly told you often enough!" Whitney knew she sounded harsh, but she had learned that often it was the only way to get the attention of the easygoing and imperturbable Havasupai.

Turning, she unlocked a glass cabinet behind her, took out an inhaler still packaged in its pharmaceutical tamper-proof shrink-wrap, and handed it to Big Mary. By the time the ruddy color had returned to Little Mary's face, tears were streaming down Big Mary's broad cheeks. She thanked Whitney over and over again in a pidgin mixture of English and Supai, then clutched her daughter to her breast and lumbered out the door.

Gritting her teeth, Whitney ran after them, handing Mary the new Ventolin inhaler she had left lying on the examination table.

By the time Whitney left for the café, darkening clouds hung ominously in the narrow strip of sky between the red walls. They trapped humidity in the box canyon like a lid on a boiling pot. No wonder Little Mary was having a hard time breathing, she thought. The closeness of the air affected even her, making the distance from the clinic to the Red Rock Café an uncomfortable trek.

In the evenings, Gwe Watahomigie made a few lukewarm attempts to create an air of festivity in the café. As she approached, Whitney could see candles in red glass containers shining through the plate-glass windows and red-checked oilcloths draped over the scarred tables and booths.

The effect was vaguely Italian. Gwe also added a few allegedly Italian dishes to his menu, but as far as Whitney was able to tell, it was just his same old fare with tomato sauce poured over everything.

Through the screen door, she recognized the scratchy wail of Gwe's most prized possession, an old-time jukebox. How he had gotten it down into the canyon was anybody's guess, because it was as big as a Las Vegas dollar slot machine, and just about as garish, twinkling with red and yellow lights that were mostly burned out.

She also recognized the song drifting dolefully out into the muggy evening air—"Sixteen Tons," by Tennessee Ernie Ford. It was a favorite among the old Indian men, many of whom had once earned good wages working in the uranium mines uptop.

As she drew nearer, Whitney saw that Baaq'baaq and Benny'wi were stationed in their usual spot at the end of the lunch counter, head-to-head over their interminable game of checkers. Other than those two regulars, only a single booth and the round table in the center of the room were occupied.

Seated in the booth were a collection of scruffy young hikers, obviously belonging to the several overstuffed backpacks stacked on the ground outside the café door. Gwe had a theory about backpacks. He figured that if he didn't allow them inside, the hikers and campers would be less tempted to use his rest room as a makeshift locker room.

At the round table sat Gwe's only other customers, Hobie Stoner and his dinner guests. They were arranged—"arranged" was the operative word here, Whitney thought wryly, for the seating struck her as too fortuitous to be accidental—with the hapless Jesse sandwiched between Hobie and Mimi.

Whitney stepped inside. Behind her, the screen door banged shut in a series of diminishing thumps.

Hobie and Gabe sprang to their feet. Jesse did the same a full twenty seconds later, after extricating himself from Mimi's clinging ministrations, but by that time it was too late. Gabe had already pulled out the chair beside him and escorted Whitney into it.

Sliding her chair forward at the same time that Gabe tucked it beneath her, Whitney unexpectedly found her ribs jammed hard against the edge of the table. With an impatient twist of her body, she wiggled the chair backward and felt it bump into Gabe, who was still standing behind her.

"Sorry," she muttered crossly. Six months away from Boston and she had already forgotten the ridiculous gallantries such as the opening of doors, the helping on of coats, the holding of chairs, that society required well-mannered men to perform and perfectly able-bodied women to tolerate!

But her flash of temper, she was forced to acknowledge, had less to do with feminism than with the very feminine Mimi Samples, an improbable combination of innocence and sensuality. She was seated across from Whitney, and had wrapped herself around Jesse like a snake. Gabriel Blade undoubtedly had his pick of golden girls like Mimi, Whitney guessed, angry that the thought made her feel small and dark and insignificant.

Whitney threw Jesse an apologetic look. She knew he had invited her specifically to deliver him from the advances of both Hobie Stoner and Mimi Samples. But unfortunately, Whitney could tell that she'd come too late to do much about either.

Hobie had already taken full possession of Jesse's right ear, while at his left, poor Jesse was launching a very half-hearted defense of his honor against the seductive Mimi.

In her gold-tone-and-snakeskin boots and gold-lamé sheath with a décolletage that plunged nearly to her abbreviated hemline, she was obviously knocking the socks off the normally unflappable Jesse. Her no-holds-barred, below-the-belt carnal blitz had superimposed a bemused smile on his usually dignified face.

It looked as though Jesse was going to have his hands full for the rest of the evening—no pun intended, Whitney thought wryly as her almond eyes threatened to disappear into a laugh.

"How nice to see you again, Whitney," Gabe said. His voice was low and intimate, with a show of teeth nearly as practiced as Hobie's.

He wasn't lying. She *was* good to look at, he had to admit, in her little denim skirt and baggy tank top. No bra, Gabe couldn't help but notice. He wondered if that was a concession to the heat or simply due to the fact that she hardly needed one.

He knew it was unprofessional to even notice, but something more basic than professionalism made it impossible for him to turn his eyes away.

The doctor wore no makeup, nor any jewelry except gold hoops in her tiny ears. As she turned to smile at Jesse and Mimi, then at Hobie, and finally at Gabe himself, Gabe could almost feel vicariously the heat in those golden hoops, warmed by their contact with her body, brushing against the delicate skin of her neck. He shifted uneasily on the hard wooden chair.

Cute, Gabe thought, just as he had the first time he'd seen her. But this time he found that he couldn't dismiss her as easily as before. She was cool and self-contained, especially compared to Mimi, whose scorching body heat seemed to raise the temperature of the very molecules of the air that surrounded her. Due to the same inevitable comparison, Gabe estimated the few square feet of shimmering lamé that barely preserved Mimi's modesty would probably have covered the diminutive Whitney from head to toe like a nun's cowl.

His first impression at the helipad, he realized now, had been much too superficial.

Beneath the fluorescent light overhead, her black hair shone with warm brown highlights, and the same warmth lay beneath her dusky, flawless skin. The tiny Asian physician was actually quite ·lovely, Gabe decided. He was disappointed that her small, symmetrical features were arranged into a bland smile that revealed nothing at all about what was going on behind them.

She was Korean, Jesse had told him when he'd asked about her. The only things Gabe knew about Korea were what he had been force-fed in school and what he had seen in movies. That, and an old war ended long before his time and largely forgotten.

Still, from those fragments his imagination could paint a picture of the woman Whitney might have been in ages past. Dressed in rich embroidered silks, waited on hand and foot by servants, her small, fine-boned hands idly occupying themselves with nothing more demanding than delicate stichery.

Obliquely he glanced again in Whitney's direction. He watched as she shook out her paper napkin and draped it across her lap.

No, he amended immediately. These hands, fine-boned and with a tracery of delicate blue veins along the backs, could never be the hands of a lady. They probably had never been idle a day in their lives. They were capable, competent hands, work-worn and dry, undoubtedly from the dozens of times each day that she scrubbed them between patients.

Gabe found himself inordinately glad that she had been born in this century. Still, she was so petite, so fragile, so like a little China doll that it made a man want to put her in his pocket and take her home for safekeeping.

Another man, of course. Not him. He wasn't a romantic. He preferred women like Mimi Samples, whom he had in fact sampled a few times himself, back in the days when Hobie was wooing him as he now wooed Jesse Sinyella. Big women, who gave as good as they got. Savvy women, who knew the score. Women who could turn a man inside out with their hands, and their lips, and their tongues, and make him forget everything, even his own name.

As he felt the involuntary reaction of his body to this train of thought, Gabe shook his head, angrily banishing the fantasy. He was disgusted with himself because he had no desire to remember the brief, intense and strictly physical relationship he'd had with Mimi.

He was more disgusted still when he realized it hadn't really been Mimi Samples he'd been thinking about.

Totally unprofessional, he reminded himself again with annoyance. Admiring beautiful female doctors was not even a side trip on the road to the partnership in Parkhurst and Brandenberg that was his ultimate goal.

Across the table, Hobie lifted a languid forefinger to summon Gwe. "My man, do you have anything in the way of a good Chablis?" he asked. "Or even a *bad* Chablis?" His droll wink circled the table, demanding audience participation. On cue, Mimi drew her attention from Jesse just long enough to titter dutifully. Gabe smiled thinly.

"No Chub-lee," Gwe grunted.

"Oh?" Hobie raised his eyebrows in mock-surprise. "Well then, whatever you have will be fine, I'm sure."

He spoke with a nonchalant gesture, implying that under the present primitive circumstances he was prepared to be magnanimous. Mimi tittered again. Gabe's smile was hardly more than a stretching of his lips across his teeth. It was obvious that the role of sycophant didn't sit well with him.

In a moment Gwe returned, plunking down in front of each customer a glass of tea with minimal ice and a tiny sliver of lemon.

Hobie looked at the glass as if he didn't know what it was.

"Alcohol is illegal on the reservation," Jesse explained diplomatically, trying to distract everyone from Gwe's unintelligible mutterings, which rose and fell with the opening and closing of the kitchen doors.

"Illegal?" Hobie sputtered in honest bewilderment. "But... but... how can it be illegal? Everyone knows how much drinking you people do!"

"Some tribes allow alcohol on their reservations," Jesse told him, each word carefully chosen to ignore the blanket indictment implicit in Hobie's use of "you people." "We do not. But those who want it always manage to get it, the same way they do in your world."

He lifted and lowered his shoulders in a fatalistic shrug. "We cannot inspect the pack animals when they return from Hilltop Mesa. And we have only two tribal policemen—it would be impossible to search the canyon for those who make moonshine for their own medicinal purposes."

"Well, that's one of the things we're gonna have to change around here, eh, Jesse, my man?" Hobie boomed, his joviality tempered by the suspicion with which he was eyeing his glass of tea.

Gwe returned to take their orders. Jesse and Whitney ordered Indian fry-bread pizza. Gabe, having been too distracted to read the menu scrawled on a blackboard over the lunch counter, was caught unawares. "I'll go with whatever the lady is having," he said.

"Ever'buddy doesn't take to fry-bread pizza like Dr. B does," Gwe warned Gabe, a sly insolence in his voice suggesting that his *hay gu* digestive tract might not be equal to the demands of Indian fry bread. "You maybe might oughta think about it."

He was disappointed when Gabe didn't heed his warning. It would have been a great joke to tell his cronies about the cowardice of the *hay gu*, too weak in the bowels to even *attempt* the staple of the Indian's diet.

"Okay, I got three fry-bread pizzas and three hamburgers," Gwe tallied after he had circled the table with his pencil and notepad, then shuffled back into the kitchen.

Whitney threw Gabe a challenging glance. "Do you like Indian fry bread?"

Gabe shook his head. "Never heard of it before," he admitted. "Am I going to be sorry?"

"Well, either you'll love it or you'll be up all night wishing you'd ordered a hamburger," she said. "It's pretty heavy and greasy because it's deep-fried, but it tastes good with all kinds of toppings—syrup or powdered sugar in the morning, melted cheese, ground beef, fried peppers and onions for lunch or dinner. Tomato sauce is the best, though—it sort of disguises the greasy taste."

Gabe began to wish he'd looked at the menu.

"So, Whitney," Hobie's voice boomed from across the table. "Jesse tells me you're a doctor. Quite an achievement, quite an achievement, especially for such a pretty little lady. 'Course I can't say I'm surprised. All you people go for things like that. Must be in the genes."

Whitney stiffened as though she had been slapped. Tilting her chin upward until her forehead was very nearly parallel with the ceiling, she looked down her lilliputian nose at Hobie Stoner.

"I wouldn't know about that," she retorted, each word exiting her lips like an ice cube. "I became a doctor because my father is a doctor. My *adoptive* father," she added with emphasis.

Temper, Gabe noted with admiration. It was an unexpected trait for a little China doll, but he liked it. And arrogant, too. Well, weren't physicians noted for that? It required a certain arrogance, he supposed, to take someone else's body in your hands and dare to presume that you could fix it.

Normally Gabe didn't like "arrogant" any more than he liked "cute," although he had to admit he was getting a kick out of both in this little doctor.

Not that it mattered.

He was here strictly to deliver the Havasupai tribe to Hobie Stoner and earn a full partnership in the prestigious Seattle law firm of Parkhurst and Brandenberg. And Dr. Whitney Baldridge-Barrows—what a moniker for a person no bigger than a minute!—cute or not, arrogant or not, had nothing at all to do with him.

His job wasn't to take her out. He didn't have to buy her dinner. He didn't have to invite her up to his apartment for drinks, and then seduce her. And he didn't have to wonder afterwards whether she had come into his bed *because* he was Indian, or *despite* the fact that he was Indian.

Most of the women he had known in his lifetime fell into one category or the other. Those he met in college, flush with their first taste of independence, were usually the former. Jill, whom he met during his law school days at the University of Washington, had been the latter.

Jill was cute, too, in the stereotypical, all-American way that should have led to student-body president, cheerleading squad and eventually a suitable marriage, 2.5 kids and a house in the suburbs.

But somewhere along the line, Jill's consciousness had been raised. She wore ragged jeans and torn sweatshirts and men's greatcoats that she bought several sizes too large for her at the Salvation Army.

She rented a drafty loft over a warehouse near the waterfront, although her parents lived in an exclusive northside town house. And at night the old brick building vibrated with the passing of unseen trains that sped along like great, mysterious night creatures toward a rendezvous at some station farther down the line.

Jill was an angry young woman, and had taken it for granted that Gabe was an angry young man. She'd never understood why his ambitions were strictly on his own behalf, not for what she earnestly regarded as "his people." And in the few brief years of their stormy marriage, she'd never understood that what he wanted was to be a man, not a cause.

WHEN GWE RETURNED with their dinners, Gabe eyed with thinly veiled apprehension the sodden lumps of fried dough smothered in tomato sauce, garlic and Parmesan. Then, following Whitney and Jesse's lead, and with the confidence born of living in a world where eating establishments were regularly inspected and duly graded by the United States government, he picked up his fork.

Conversation was stilted, consisting mainly of an animated monologue by Hobie Stoner. Even Whitney's tight smile was as artificial as Hobie's. Except for Mimi, who knew her job was to radiate sex appeal and did it with single-minded professionalism, no one else at the table seemed to understand the purpose of this pale imitation of a dinner party.

But Gabe did. Hobie liked to keep people off balance and guessing, and to that extent Gabe knew that the dinner was a huge success.

Hobie liked to toy with his opponents, in this case Jesse Sinyella, like a cat with a mouse. He lulled the mouse into believing, right up until the very last moment, that Hobie the Cat was just a big, lovable, cuddly stuffed animal; then Hobie crushed the mouse with a clawed forepaw that the poor dumb mouse never even saw coming.

SOMETIME DURING DINNER, the sound of thunder rolled overhead like distant drums. With no more notice than that, lightning bolts suddenly ripped the black fabric of the night sky. The lightning smell of ozone was strong in the air.

By the time Gwe came around to collect the tab, which nearly wiped Hobie out because the Red Rock Café didn't accept credit cards, the rain had settled into a steady downpour.

Fat droplets of water ran in rivulets down the plate glass of the windows. Outside, the red dirt path was well on its way to becoming a river of red mud. Clustered indecisively around the door of the café, Hobie's dinner guests weighed their options as if there really were alternatives.

"Well, none of us is made of sugar..." Whitney remarked with the legendary pragmatism of her adopted Yankee forebears. She pushed open the door.

A little rain—or a lot of rain—didn't faze her. Neither did it bother anyone else who lived in the canyon, where there were no hairstyles to protect, clothes to be ruined, telephone lines to be knocked out or roads to be flooded. Rain was as natural and unremarkable as the absence of rain.

"Oh gee," Mimi responded in a petulant voice. "I don't know." She made a sweeping gesture with her hands to indicate the smidgen of gold lamé and the voluptuous body it barely covered. "This dress cost me a fortune—I can't just go out and ruin it!"

Whitney eyed Mimi's attire doubtfully. The woman had a point. Still poised in the open doorway, she was about to suggest that Mimi bunk in one of the booths for the night when Mimi herself came up with a better suggestion. She fluttered her lashes at Jesse. "Maybe that waiter would let us borrow a couple of those plastic tablecloths he had on the tables. Would you mind asking him, Jesse?"

Jesse complied with an eagerness that thoroughly exasperated Whitney. By the time he returned with several red-checkered oilcloths he had requisitioned from Gwe, she had already stepped out into the downpour.

As she waded awkwardly through the mud, it sucked greedily at her huaraches. Her face was lifted toward the invisible sky, luxuriating in the feel of the refreshing rain on her skin.

By the time Jesse shouted "Dr. B! Wait!" she was already halfway across the village square, which was now a muddy, rust-colored pond.

Putting on a burst of speed, Jesse caught up with her. He spread the oilcloth over her head like a tent. The uselessness of the gesture suddenly struck them both as hilarious, and they found themselves laughing gaily, sloshing through the mud, spattering it heedlessly onto Whitney's bare legs and Jesse's boots.

From the shelter of the café, Gabe watched them frolicking—if as dour a person as Jesse Sinyella could be said to frolic—like children. Their arms encircled each other's waists, keeping them as close under the oilcloth tent as if they were joined from shoulder to hip. Idly Gabe speculated whether this was just a companionable, childlike embrace or if it signified something more.

In another moment they and their oilcloth tent, the only bright spot in the dismal landscape, disappeared around the bend in the path that led to Whitney's bungalow.

Through the rain-streaked plate glass, Gabe stared at the village square, now deserted except for a few bedraggled stray dogs. He tried to remember whether he had ever enjoyed the rain. It seemed to him now that it had always been cold and gray and miserable, and that he was always huddled in one doorway or another trying to protect himself from it.

Hobie's peevish voice broke into his recollections. "First thing we're gonna have to build down here is a goddamn sewer system!" Then he sidled a step closer to Gabe. "Keep an eye on the little Chink doctor," he said in a terse undertone. "She's got Sinyella's ear, and I don't think she likes us."

Gabe was irritated by Hobie's ignorant lumping of all Asians in a single broad, inaccurate catagory. "As a matter of fact," he replied coldly, "I don't believe Dr. Barrows is Chinese. I believe she is Korean."

"*Whatever*." The politician's smile had fallen from Hobie's face, his geniality discarded like a costume at the end of a play. He turned his attention to Mimi, whose red-painted lower lip thrust forward in a pout.

"Losing your touch?" he challenged.

CHAPTER FIVE

WHITNEY LAY curled up on the vintage tweed couch in her living room. Although a book lay open on her chest, her eyes were half closed. The drone of the rain surrounded her like a cocoon.

Whitney had never heard sound the way she heard it here. All sounds in this canyon were muffled, caught in the labyrinth of rock formations and thrown back as echoes, with the hard edges worn away. At night, even the silence was a sound. It bounced off the towering walls and then returned to fill the canyon with a thicker echo of silence, so dense that it felt almost solid.

This is what it must be like to be deaf, Whitney sometimes thought—a lack of sound so profound that it seemed to come from within rather than from without.

But tonight wasn't one of those nights. Tonight the steady drum of the rain, the noise it made as it spilled across the tin roof and splashed into the puddles on the ground, made Whitney feel as though she were living underwater. Like a fish, she thought contentedly, turning over and burrowing deeper into the lumpy couch. Or a mermaid....

Suddenly the walkie-talkie on the table beside the couch crackled to life with a burst of static. "Medic Two to Medic One. Do you read me, Dr. B? Over."

Instantly awake—a trick she had mastered during the thirty-six-hour shifts of her internship—Whitney seized the walkie-talkie and extended the antenna. "Medic One to Medic Two. Dr. Barrows here. What have you got for me? Over."

"One of the tourists from the Lodge," the voice on the other end informed her. The voice belonged to Jackoby Watahomigie.

Jackoby was a member of First Responders, a team of human ambulances who transported sick or injured patients to the clinic. The First Responders had a golf cart they used when the weather and terrain permitted, but usually they packed the patient in by horseback or stretcher.

"Looks like . . . leg . . . slipped in the mud and . . . into the runoff behind the Lodge . . . to be . . . lot of pain . . ." Jackoby's voice cut in and out. ". . . Mad as hell. Over."

"Be there in twenty," Whitney replied. "Over and out."

This time, she protected herself from the rain with galoshes and a hooded raincoat—if this turned out to be something serious, who knew how long she might have to work in damp, clammy clothes?

She seized her flashlight and, for the second time that night, plunged into the pouring rain.

ENTERING THE CLINIC through the back door, Whitney shed her muddy boots and dripping raincoat just inside. She slipped into a white lab coat as she hurried down the hall toward the examining room.

On the examination table, where Jackoby had positioned him, lay Hobie Stoner. His left leg was immobilized by two wooden boards wrapped with Ace bandages.

This is the first time I've ever seen him without his teeth showing, Whitney noted as she entered the room.

Instead, his lips were pressed together into a thin, tight line. His eyes shifted restlessly around the room as though searching for someone to blame.

Mimi had stationed herself at the head of the table, tentatively trying to comfort Hobie, who kept swatting her ineffectual fingers away like pesky flies.

Gabe, an Indian blanket draped around his shoulders like a shawl, paced the width of the room with tight, choppy steps. The irritated scowl on his face told Whitney he wasn't particularly concerned about his boss's suffering.

All three were soaked, as were Jackoby and his partner, Son Eagle, but Hobie appeared to be the only one injured. Whitney went directly to him.

"Tell me what happened," she said, placing the stethoscope into her ears as she bent over his prone form. His heartbeat was strong and regular, although fast, and his lungs sounded clear except for a chronic cigarette wheeze. He also reeked of whiskey, which gave Whitney a partial answer to her question.

"I fell off the goddamn balcony at that damn motel—" Hobie muttered evasively.

"He fell off the porch at the Lodge," Mimi volunteered at the same time, "into that...that..." She appealed to Jackoby in the flirtatious manner that seemed to be her primary way of communicating with men. "What did you call it?"

Jackoby was delighted to prompt her. "A wash."

"Yes, that wash behind the Lodge," Mimi continued. "It was full of rocks, and he can't swim anyway, so Gabe jumped in after him—"

"Quiet!" Hobie growled. "Nobody asked you." Mimi shrank backward against the wall, while Hobie turned his attention again toward Whitney. "I think my leg's broken, Doc. Hurts like hell."

"We'll take care of that first," Whitney assured him, feeling compassion for his pain if not for the man himself. "Then we'll get an X ray." She twisted the combination lock to open the narcotics safe and withdrew a vial of morphine. Breaking the seal of a disposable syringe, she thrust the needle through the vial's rubber stopper, and withdrew the appropriate amount.

"You'll feel a little sting," she told Hobie.

"BUT...BUT...BUT you can't do this to me!" Hobie sputtered incredulously. "I belong in a hospital!"

"Yes, you do," Whitney agreed. "That's why I suggest you fly out tomorrow. There's a hospital in Kingman, about one hundred miles northeast. It's the only town on the only road for a hundred miles around—you can't miss it. From there they can get a Lifeflight to take you to Flagstaff."

The X rays showed what Whitney had feared. Though not as bad as it might have been, the injury was not as simple as she'd hoped. Hobie's leg was indeed broken, a spiral fracture of the femur, and it was going to require surgical pinning.

She'd removed the First Responders' makeshift splint and encased the leg in an inflatable cast to keep it immobilized until Hobie could be evacuated to a hospital.

"Kingman? Flagstaff? *A hundred miles?*" Hobie repeated Whitney's words blankly, as though he no longer understood English. Then the key word hit him, and his voice rose several decibels.

"Tomorrow?" he shouted indignantly. "*Tomorrow? What in hell am I supposed to do until tomorrow? What kind of quack doctor are you, anyway? I demand to be put into a hospital immediately!"

"We have no hospital here," Whitney said, biting her tongue to keep from answering him in kind. "I've given you an injection of penicillin, I've given you something for pain, and I've prepared your leg for evacuation. I'm afraid I've done all I can."

She paused, then added, with just the slightest hint of malice in her voice, "I'm really not supposed to treat you at all, you know. The Indian Health Service is strictly for the Indians. Tourists come down into the canyon at their own risk. Didn't anyone tell you that?"

"No hospital?" Hobie repeated in a strangled voice. It was obvious he'd heard nothing after that. "All right then, I want out. Not tomorrow. Now. Right now."

He flapped the back of his hand at Whitney, as if to shoo her out the door. "Go tell that chief to get on that goddamn radio of his and order a chopper down here on the double! I'll show you who you're dealing with, by God!"

"Sorry, Hobie," Whitney replied calmly. "I can't do that. You could be a lot more seriously hurt than you are—you could be dying—and the helicopter still wouldn't fly in at night. They can't, for it's too dangerous. On your way in you must have seen how narrow this gorge is, and how irregular the mesas are. It's hard enough to maneuver in the daytime—they'd never make it at night."

"Don't give me any of that crap," Hobie warned. He propped himself up on one elbow. "I'm not one of these dumb Indians you can push around any way you want to. This is Hobart Stoner you're dealing with here. I'm a taxpayer, aren't I? I pay your salary, goddamn it! You have no right to do this to me. This is still the goddamn

United States of America, isn't it? I have rights! I'll...
I'll..."

"As a matter of fact, Mr. Stoner," Whitney said, trying to suppress the hint of one-upmanship in her voice, "This is *not* the United States of America."

She paused, giving the words a few seconds to register. "You're in the Havasupai Nation now."

Hobie faltered as if his English had once again deserted him. "The Havasupai Nation...?" he managed to repeat. Then he struck his forehead with one hand and fell back on the examination table. "Oh shit!" he moaned, "I'm a dead man!"

He glowered at Whitney, apparently deciding that she was the one to blame for all his woes. In another moment the glower became an unfocused stare, and a moment after that, the second dose of morphine she had injected took effect and made him dead to the world.

"Take him back to the Lodge," Whitney instructed Jackoby and Son Eagle. "He'll certainly be more comfortable there." And so will I, she added silently. Aloud she only said, "Who will be staying with him tonight?"

Mimi ran her fingers through her limp, wet hair. "I will be, I guess," she said resignedly. The prospect didn't appear to thrill her.

Whitney smiled reassuringly. "Don't worry," she told Mimi, aware that worry was probably not the reluctant blonde's primary emotion. "He's going to be just fine."

Again she unlocked the narcotics safe and withdrew a large bottle, from which she counted out twelve pills and dropped them into a small brown plastic container. "He should sleep another two or three hours. When he wakes up, let him have two of these every two hours for pain."

She wrote the same instructions on the label and then handed the container to Mimi. "And Mimi..."

"Yes?"

"Try to keep him away from the booze."

Mimi nodded bleakly, then turned to follow the First Responders and their unconscious patient out the door.

The entire time Whitney worked on Hobie, she had forgotten everyone else in the room. Now, the unexpected scrape of chrome on linoleum startled her, as Gabe pushed back the chair he had been occupying and stood up.

With a hand on her shoulder, he stopped Mimi before she reached the door. Lifting the blanket from his own shoulders, he draped it around hers. With the blanket he included a sympathetic smile and a companionable squeeze, and then Mimi stepped out into the rain.

They've slept together.

Where the knowledge had come from Whitney had no idea, for certainly there had been nothing intimate about the smile or the touch. But she knew it as certainly as she knew her own name. She considered their coupling with clinical detachment. They were probably very good together, she surmised. Sex was obviously Mimi's stock-in-trade, and Gabe... well, he looked as though he'd be a natural at it, too.

Whitney knew just about everything there was to know about the human body. After all, she was a scientist, and the human body was her specialty. She knew its anatomy, chemistry, physiology and psychology. And she knew the subtle interplay of causes that combined to create the irresistible urge toward reproduction.

The one thing she didn't understand, had never understood, was what the fuss was all about.

After evaluating the situation objectively and scientifically, she had concluded that love in all its aspects simply had never been high on her list of priorities. There had always been one more test to ace, one more petri dish to study, one more 2:00 a.m. in one more deserted hospital corridor.

Even now, when this disturbing man had removed the colorful blanket from around his undeniably attractive shoulders, the first thing Whitney noticed was not the trim physique, but the blood-streaked T-shirt that covered it.

"You're hurt, too!"

Gabe shrugged.

"Just a few bumps and bruises."

"Judging from the amount of blood on that shirt, I'd say a few of those bumps and bruises could probably use stitches. Sit down and let me take a look."

Gabe assumed the arrogant, impatient attitude that was his first line of defense against attorneys for the opposition across courtroom or boardroom. "Look, Whitney, I really don't think this is neces—"

"*Sit!*"

He sat. How she made that sweet, nightingale voice sound like an army officer's command Gabe didn't know, but it crumpled *his* attitude in a hurry!

"So. How did this happen, anyway?" Her back to Gabe, Whitney sorted through various cabinets and drawers to assemble a minor surgery tray—Betadine from one, anesthetic and several disposable syringes from another, suture materials, gloves.

"Just the way Mimi said," Gabe replied. "Hobie... kind of fell off the porch into that wash behind the Lodge, and I kind of had to...get him out. That's all."

"That wash is neither deep nor fast," Whitney observed. "Why couldn't he get himself out?"

Gabe was silent.

"He was drunk, wasn't he." It wasn't a question. When Gabe still didn't answer, she turned to confront him. "Well, wasn't he?"

"He'd been drinking, yes," he admitted. "But Whitney, he didn't realize it was illegal down here." He thrust his hands deep into his pockets and looked at Whitney unhappily. "Not that that would have stopped him. Hell, you're a doctor. You know how it is."

"Yes, I know how it is," she replied coolly. "He's an alcoholic, like a great many of the people down here. However, unlike the people down here, he's white and he's rich, so he doesn't have to suffer the consequences."

Turning her back again to Gabe, she leaned over the sink, twisted the hot-water handle and proceeded to scrub.

"Take off your shirt, please," she said in a crisp, efficient tone, switching gears so quickly that Gabe was caught unawares.

"Whitney!"

"Come on, Mr. Blade!" she snapped impatiently. "If you don't let me attend to those injuries, you're liable to have a few very uncomfortable days ahead of you!" She jabbed the handle with her elbow to turn the water off, then jerked a disposable towel from the dispenser over the sink.

"Good grief," she chided, pulling on the pair of sterile gloves. "It isn't as though I'm asking you to strip naked!" Briefly she wondered why the word "naked" seemed to occur to her so frequently in regard to this particular man.

Still scolding, she turned to fix Gabe with a withering eye. *A grown man, as shy of uncovering his body in front of a doctor as a gawky adolescent!* He wouldn't hesitate to reveal it to Mimi Samples, she thought with some annoyance.

Her train of thought was abruptly broken by the realization that Gabe was in the process of complying, albeit reluctantly. And the shirt had just passed the washboard-rippled muscles of a torso that looked to her about as perfect as a Greek sculpture.

Not completely perfect, she noticed upon closer inspection. Several scars, like scratches on marble, marred the sculpted surface without detracting from its artistry. The scars were peculiar, though, and there were enough of them that Whitney thought it appropriate to question him.

But then the shirt rose higher, baring a broad, well-muscled chest, and her mind was emptied of the questions she had been about to ask. His skin was copper-colored, and, typically for an Indian, there was no hair on the chest and only sparse dark wisps under the arms.

Her eyes were drawn to the nipples—small, tight circles the size of pennies and with the same dark coppery luster. Totally superfluous for a man—an evolutionary oversight—yet attractive and somehow oddly sensual. Like magnets they drew first her eyes, and then her hands.

She reached toward the flat copper penny on the left. It puckered involuntarily under the heel of her hand as, with trained and skillful fingers, she touched the eight-inch gash that split the flesh just half an inch above it.

"Those were some mean rocks you ran into," she observed.

Gabe winced. He lowered his arms, straightening the glasses on his nose with an automatic motion of his thumb and forefinger. Trying to appear nonchalant about the whole situation, he fixed his eyes on an invisible spot on the wall several feet above Whitney's head, self-consciously wadding the blood-streaked shirt into a ball between his hands.

Not that he was ashamed of his body. He wasn't. He was proud of it, in fact, having put a lot of time and effort into building its well-defined contours out of the skinny, starveling body he'd grown up with.

He didn't mind being looked at by women when their eyes were clouded with passion, by candlelight, or firelight, or moonlight. But being evaluated in this laboratory, under this harsh, fluorescent light, by this bossy little doctor whose eyes he could hardly even see, made him feel unusually self-conscious. Made him feel vulnerable.

Without looking up from her examination, Whitney reached down to take the shirt out of his hands and toss it peremptorily onto the table. "Please hold still," she requested in a voice that broached no argument.

"Whitney, it's fine, really!" Gabe argued nevertheless. "Just give me a couple of bandages and I'll be on my way—"

Ignoring his protests, she moved her eyes and fingers to his face, to a lesser cut just above his left eyebrow.

"Take off your glasses, please," she instructed, moving a step closer to examine the laceration. "Yes, I think we can use a couple of butterfly clips to close this one."

Then she took his chin between her thumb and forefinger and twisted his head this way and that. There was a scrape along the left side of his face from cheekbone to jaw.

"And all these abrasions need is a little cleaning up. But that pectoral laceration is going to require a scrub-down and sutures." She scanned him thoroughly from the front, finding nothing else of note, then circled behind his chair to continue her inventory.

Her hand flew to her mouth. Shocked, she fought the churning stomach she thought she had left behind in anatomy class with her first slice into a cadaver.

The scar that ran the full length of his back and came dangerously close to his left kidney was vicious and deep, though it was old enough to have faded to a thin line several shades lighter than his skin. Whitney realized that it had to have flayed his flesh wide open, past the layers of skin and muscle to the very bone. Here Whitney's instincts and training told her that the wound had been intended to be a fatal one. Who, she wondered, had hated him enough to try to kill him?

She cleared her throat several times. "That's an ugly scar you've got there," she said finally, forcing her voice back into the straitjacket of professional objectivity. "And I've spent enough time in trauma centers to know that it's a knife wound. So are the ones on your stomach. Knife fights, am I right?"

Keeping his eyes fixed on the invisible spot on the wall, Gabe quickly ran through the list of stock phrases he used whenever anyone, usually women in the artificial intimacy of afterglow, asked him about the scar. He could find nothing appropriate to this situation, so he simply shrugged. "It was a long time ago," he replied.

He was right, of course. Whitney knew that. They were very old scars; there was no reason to open them up again now. Anyway, what business was it of hers? The man was trouble, and obviously he had been trouble for much of his life.

She tore open an alcohol swab and wiped down the skin around the eight-inch laceration on his chest. Then she picked up the vial of Xylocaine and a syringe, and withdrew several milliliters of the anesthetic.

"You'll feel a little sting...." she said.

CHAPTER SIX

"EVERYTHING LOOKS GOOD, Winnie." Whitney patted the broad back of the Indian woman beside her. The maternal gesture looked odd, considering that the woman, even if she had not been extremely pregnant, was easily three times Whitney's size.

"We'll fly you up to Phoenix in two weeks, maybe a little sooner with your history of early delivery," Whitney continued. Then mentally she crossed her fingers. "Have you found a place to stay yet?"

"Yes," the big woman replied in her slow, second-language English. "My aunt. The one I stayed with last year."

Whitney breathed a heartfelt sigh of relief. Some pregnant women looked forward to spending a little time uptop, but many more refused to leave the canyon. They had their babies at home, delivered by tribal midwives. Which worked fine most of the time. But Whitney lived in constant fear of a childbirth complication or a neonatal emergency that she was ill equipped to handle. Especially at night, when the helicopters couldn't fly in.

"Is your aunt expecting you again so soon?" she teased Winnie with a smile. Winnie shrugged and shook her head.

"Shouldn't you get in touch with her? What if she's away?"

Winnie's heavy face looked mildly surprised. "Where would she go?"

Where indeed, Whitney thought. She often doubted whether the Indians who lived in this deep narrow fissure in the earth's crust had any idea of the size of the world beyond the rim of their canyon. Many had their first experience with the larger world at the age of eleven or twelve, when they went away to the Indian Boarding School in Phoenix. After that, they came home only in the summertime.

Naturally, it was a difficult transition for a child. Most never made it. Ten out of every eleven children dropped out before finishing junior high. Like Winnie, whose entire universe consisted of the Grand Canyon and the city of Phoenix and the hundreds of miles of desert in between.

Whitney handed Winnie a refill of prenatal vitamins, reminded her of her next appointment, and watched her shamble ponderously out the door. She flipped Winnie's chart onto Chili's desk. "Who's next?"

Chili lowered her reading material, this time a confessions magazine with a man and woman on the cover, twisted into an embrace so awkward it looked painful. She jutted her chins toward the waiting room.

"Him," she said succinctly, then went back to her magazine.

Whitney peered around the corner. "Him" turned out to be Gabriel Blade, seated in one of the clinic's cheap plastic chairs, holding Hobie's borrowed crutches between his legs. Upon catching sight of Whitney, he stood.

"You deliver babies, too, I see," he said, smiling.

"Only in an emergency. Actually, we try to send our mothers-to-be up to Phoenix at twenty-eight or thirty weeks, so they can deliver in the Indian Medical Center. They usually move in with friends or relatives, or else we have a network of foster homes where they can stay."

It occurred to her that a simple "yes" or "no" would have sufficed. Slipping belatedly into her medical mode, she spoke briskly. "Now then," she said. "What can I do for you?"

"Thought you might be wanting these," Gabe replied, extending the crutches.

"Thanks." Whitney propped them against the wall. "Well, did Hobie get off all right?"

Actually, she already knew that he had. Earlier, from the clinic window, she'd watched his halting progress across the muddy village square, flanked on one side by Jesse and by Gabe on the other. Several Indian boys loaded with luggage brought up the rear.

Hobie made his exit on a high note, smiling and waving to the onlookers gathered at the helipad like a prize-fighter who had just staggered manfully to his feet before the final count. Of course, Whitney knew, the painkillers she'd given Mimi had a great deal to do with that.

Still, the man surprised her. He was hobbling on crutches borrowed from the clinic, which had to be returned as soon as he was loaded aboard the helicopter because they were the only set the clinic owned, yet managed to combine his smiling and waving with a terse and uninterrupted monologue directed toward Gabe.

"He got off just fine," Gabe replied. "Sinyella made arrangements for an ambulance to meet him at the top and take him right to Kingman."

"What about you? And Mimi?"

Gabe shrugged. "We have our rooms at the Lodge 'til Sunday, and Hobie was scheduled to appear before the

Tribal Council on Saturday. We figured there's no reason why I couldn't present the proposal for him. And, uh...Mimi?" He hesitated. "Well, Mimi'll be...uh, handling the paperwork for me," he finally said.

The words sounded false, even to him. And that surprised him. Usually he could prevaricate—he wouldn't go so far as to say *lie*—with the best of them. But there was something about this outspoken little woman, now eyeing him skeptically, that made him want to be as frank and forthright as she was. *Better watch it, Blade,* he warned himself ruefully, *or you're gonna find yourself in some serious trouble when you get back into a courtroom!*

"Mimi has her orders, too," he amended more honestly. "As a matter of fact, Hobie sicced her on Sinyella. He knows Sinyella's undecided about this development project, and he figures anything Mimi can do to soften him up will be...helpful."

Whitney drew herself up to every inch of her barely five feet. "I'm afraid you've misjudged Jesse," she informed Gabe coolly. "Nothing would ever persuade him to do something he didn't think was right for the tribe."

"Oh? He looked pretty susceptible last night, I thought."

"He was just being polite. Jesse's like that."

"I'm sure," Gabe replied noncommittally, an innocuous choice of words that nevertheless managed to convey just the opposite opinion. "Well, I won't take up any more of your time. Unless..."

"Unless?"

"Well, I was just wondering if you'd be interested in grabbing a bite to eat later, at the café?" The words rolled out in a rapid jumble, and Gabe found himself waiting with more than his usual chronic impatience for her answer.

"Thanks, Gabe, but I'm afraid I have a house call to make, and it'll probably take all afternoon."

His face fell. "What do you know!" he exclaimed with forced joviality. "This is probably the last place in America where doctors still make house calls!"

"Don't forget, this isn't America," Whitney reminded him tartly. "Actually, I'm just going to look in on one of my patients who has a hard time getting around."

"Let me come with you," Gabe said, suddenly inspired. He gave Whitney a disarming grin. "I haven't been anywhere besides the Lodge and the café. I'd like to see more."

"Why?" she asked bluntly.

"Well...uh, we're hoping to build a multimillion-dollar resort complex down here, that's why," Gabe temporized, trapped by his own glibness into actually examining his motives.

Which, he already knew, really didn't have much to do with Hobie's resort complex.

How could he admit that he had absolutely no interest in exploring the canyon? That he had been here less than a week and already he was bored out of his mind? That the remaining days until the Tribal Council meeting on Saturday stretched out before him like a prison sentence?

How could he admit that the only thing that interested him at all was the diminutive physician whose feisty personality was like a sore tooth his tongue couldn't leave alone?

"It'll take most of the afternoon," Whitney warned. "I'm sure you're much too busy—"

Busy? Gabe thought. Any busier and he'd probably be snoring! "Oh, I've got a few hours to spare," he said.

"Well then," she agreed reluctantly, "I suppose there's no reason why you couldn't come along...."

FOLLOWING THE ROCKY, irregular streambed of Havasu Creek, Gabe automatically took Whitney's elbow to assist her over the rough terrain. Another of those totally unnecessary gallantries from the uptop world, she reminded herself, but this time, for reasons she chose not to examine too closely, she didn't shrug his hand away.

After walking for nearly an hour, they arrived at the small clearing that housed Billy's shelter. There, lying in the hammock stretched between the two huge cottonwoods, was Billy, waiting out the heat of the day in the shade of the old trees.

He tried to rise to greet his guests but, to Whitney's dismay, could not. Then she saw the mason jar in his hand, half-filled with an amber-colored liquid that looked like tea but undoubtedly wasn't.

Billy was both discreet and considerate about his drinking. Not wanting to put the tribe's two policemen in an awkward position, he drank his whiskey from a mason jar so that no one would see the label on the bottle and feel constrained to do something about it.

Her dismay turned to irritation. Mentally she ran through a list of likely suspects, trying to determine which well-meaning but misguided friend had most recently returned from uptop and brought Billy his current supply of cheap booze.

No, you will not scold him today, she reminded herself before she could work up a really righteous anger. *Not in front of a stranger.* Just to be on the safe side, she added, *you will not nag, remind, hint, or even suggest.*

"Billy Hamadreeq, Gabriel Blade," Whitney said, nodding to each in turn. "Gabe is the newcomer . . . one of the newcomers I told you about."

Billy lifted his hand in acknowledgment. Then he peered at Gabe. "It was you running up Wii'baaq'a yesterday at little light?"

Totally confused, Gabe glanced at Whitney for an interpretation.

"Yes, Uncle," she interposed, not surprised that Billy knew this about Gabe, even though Wii'baaq'a lay in the exact opposite direction from Billy's down-canyon home. The rocks at Wii'baaq'a probably told him, she thought, and found that she half believed it herself. "It was he. At least when I saw him, he was heading in that direction."

Vividly recalling the frank appraisal she had conducted while watching him run through the gray of little light, she gave Gabe a sheepish smile and shrugged apologetically. "I was going for a run myself," she said by way of explanation. "You went right past my house."

Billy's forehead was furrowed into a road map of lines. He looked almost as puzzled as Gabe. "You ran toward the rising sun," he said slowly, as though trying to sort it out in his own mind. "How did you know that old trail?"

"There was no trail," Gabe said stiffly. "I simply—"

"There *was* a trail," Billy said in a sharp voice, sounding just for an instant like the powerful and respected song shaman he once had been. "There has *always* been a trail." He squinted more closely at Gabe. "You are Havasupai?"

"No!" Gabe replied quickly, then added, "I don't know. But my father was white."

His answer surprised him. It had been years since he'd bothered to make that distinction. He only did it now because he was repelled by the unkempt old man, and reluctant to admit to even the slightest suggestion of a tie between them.

Shabby, scruffy, and obviously soused, Billy personified every taunt and insult and slur that had been hurled at Gabe all his life regarding his Indian blood. He made Gabe remember, with humiliating clarity, all the reasons he'd ever had to be ashamed of that blood.

"What was your mother's tribe?"

"I don't know."

It took Billy a long moment to digest this. "Your mother never spoke to you of this?" he asked finally.

"My mother was never sober long enough to speak to me about anything," Gabe replied, amazed at the bitterness that rose like bile in the back of his throat, even after all these years.

What was it going to take, he wondered savagely, to put all that behind him? How many expensive suits and silk shirts and electronic toys? How much money? How much prestige? *How long?*

"The tribes have lost many to the cities of the *hay gu,*" Billy acknowledged. "When the blood is mixed, it is hard to tell one from another."

He pursed his lips and studied Gabe more closely. "You are not of the water people, though you live in their lands. You are not as tall as the people of the plains, but you are bigger than our brothers, the Hopi. You might be Navajo. Your skin is pale, as ours is because we have lived since the Beginning Times with so little sun. You *could* be Havasupai, or you could show the color of your *hay gu* blood." Billy looked away from Gabe's face and went on. "But it is impossible to know for sure. I can say what you are not, but I cannot say what you are. I cannot tell you what tribe you belong to."

I belong to no tribe, Gabe wanted to protest, but something stopped him. It wasn't courtesy. It was the startling realization that, for the single, silent moment that Billy had been studying his face, Gabe's heart had inexplicably tightened with the irrational hope that the old man would be able to tell him who he was.

He felt the onslaught of a rare headache. *It's this infernal heat,* he said to himself. No one could exist in this hot, dry climate for any length of time. Obliquely he studied old Billy who, according to Whitney, had existed here for maybe one hundred years, maybe more.

Gabe's eyes began to ache along with his head. Reaching behind his glasses, he massaged the lids gingerly with thumb and forefinger.

To Whitney it looked like a gesture of irritation. "Gabe is from Seattle," she interjected hurriedly, trying to change the subject he apparently found so distasteful.

Billy, or the whiskey he'd put away, allowed himself to be distracted. "I know Seattle," he said after a moment. "I had a daughter once. I heard she went there. Maybe you knew her. Mary. Her name was Mary."

Gabe started, then looked at Billy warily, as if he suspected the old man of some kind of trick. "My mother's name was Mary."

"Seattle's a big city, Uncle," Whitney interjected. "I'm sure a lot of women named Mary live there."

She gave Gabe a conspiratorial wink. "Don't let him throw you," she said in a low voice meant for his ears alone. "Every other woman on the reservation is named some variation of Mary."

Leaving Gabe's face, Billy's near-blind eyes became even more unfocused as they traveled upward to the rustling leaves of the old cottonwood tree. The individual leaves were only an undulating mass of green to him, but the rustling was the same familiar song it had always been, since his mother had rocked him in a hammock very much like this one, and his several wives had rocked his own babies.

"She was a restless woman," Billy said thoughtfully, the words slowing down, the guttural voice more gravelly than usual. "Restless."

He propped himself up on one elbow to take a soothing sip of the warm whiskey, then wiped his mouth with the back of his hand and sank back into his woven cocoon. "She followed the left-handed way—a solitary walker, never at peace. It is a lonely path, especially for a woman. I heard she had a son. Then the agent up at Peach Springs told me she died. Whiskey and tuberculosis, he said."

There was another thoughtful pause while the old man examined this memory. "I did not look for my grandson. Wherever he was, it was better than here."

Billy's eyelids closed once, twice, and finally stayed shut. A gentle snore issued from between his lips.

Whitney reached across the hammock to touch her palm to his forehead, then the back of her hand to his cheek. His skin was neither clammy, to suggest hyperglycemia, nor dry, to suggest a diabetic coma. His breathing was deep and regular.

"Well, it's not a problem with his disease," she announced, relieved. "He's just asleep. Or passed out." She relaxed her shoulders and shook her head ruefully. "I *knew* I should have gotten here earlier."

Taking the mason jar out of his hands, she set it on the ground, resisting the impulse to pour its contents into the dirt.

Gabe looked down at the old man's slack face with both distaste and pity written on his own. "What's wrong with him?" he asked.

"He's a diabetic," Whitney replied, in the concise terms of a medical diagnosis. "He's nearly blind from diabetic retinopathy, and he has vascular blockages in his extremities. He's also an alcoholic, and that complicates everything."

"Is he going to die?"

"Not if I have anything to say about it." Whitney leaned over and again felt Billy's cheek with the back of her hand. "But I'm very much afraid of gangrene in his feet. And if his feet have to be amputated, I just don't know how he'll get along down here. I've been trying to convince him to let us relocate him up to the Indian Nursing Home in Phoenix, but he won't hear of it. He wants to die among the human beings, he says."

In sleep Billy looked defenseless, and Gabe turned his eyes away from the old man's face. In a way he couldn't have explained, staring at Billy without his knowing it seemed somehow disrespectful. "He looks older than God," he said, as if thinking out loud. "Maybe you should just let him."

"What? Let him die?" Whitney straightened up, her narrow eyes flashing dangerously. "Is that what you're saying? You've been down here—what, three days?— and already you have an answer for everything?"

Gabe backtracked furiously, startled by her vehemence. "No, no, I didn't mean that exactly. I only meant that... Well, hell, it's none of my business, Whitney...."

"You're right about *that*," Whitney snapped. Her sweet voice sounded as chilling as fingernails on a blackboard. One more quick look at the snoring Billy and she executed a sharp about-face on the heel of one dusty, red-stained sneaker.

"We'd better be getting back," she said curtly. "It'll be dark soon." She marched through the weed-choked garden toward the purling stream that led back to the village.

Gabe's own quick temper flared. With a few long strides he was behind her. "Come on, Whitney. Look, I'm sorry, okay? I don't know the first thing about medicine. If you think he's going to be all right, then I'm sure he is. Whitney, wait."

He didn't know why he was even bothering to apologize. It wasn't as though he really *cared*. This place had nothing to do with him, and neither did these people, except as pawns for Hobie's plans and Gabe's own ambitions. Nevertheless, he caught Whitney's elbow and turned her around to face him.

"Look, I didn't mean to offend you..." he began impatiently, then his voice trailed off. Looking down, he saw tears glistening in the corners of her almond-shaped eyes.

Uneasy in the role of comforter, especially with a woman he suspected was just as likely as not to spit in his eye, Gabe put his arm around her shoulder and patted it awkwardly. The right words, so easy to come by when he was manipulating business deals, were much harder to find when he wanted them to be sincere.

He tried to think of something sensitive and perceptive, and finally came up with "What is it, Whitney? Is it me? Is it what I said?" The words were not scintillating, maybe, but the voice was gentler than he'd known he could make it.

Embarrassed, Whitney brushed the tears from her eyes, but she didn't pull away, nor did she spit in Gabe's eye.

"No, not really," she replied despondently. "It's just Billy. He's so frustrating, that's all. There's so much I could do for him, and he just won't cooperate." She blew her nose on a tissue she fished from her fanny pack.

"Look at this place," she continued, with a sweep of her arm that took in the entire scene. In the twilight, Billy's wickiup had become only a dark silhouette rising like a giant anthill in the center of the clearing. All its details were lost in the gathering dusk.

Even Billy himself had disappeared among the shadows spreading like a canopy beneath the old cottonwood trees. "He shouldn't be living out here, all alone like this."

What was Billy to her, anyway? Gabe wondered, but didn't ask. The old Indian was as sere and brown as the last leaf on a winter tree—he was practically mummified already! What on earth could she do for him except to make him comfortable for whatever time he had left? He didn't ask that, either. It was already crystal clear to him that Whitney tolerated no argument on the subject of old Billy Hamadreeq.

"It *does* look like a miserable way to have to live, in that filthy little hut," Gabe agreed, eager to find a subject on which they both saw eye to eye.

Whitney shrugged and shook her head ruefully, as if Gabe's comment proved her point. "As a matter of fact, he has a house in town. The tribal government built it for him years and years ago. It's not much more than a shanty, but at least it has plumbing and electricity."

She spread her arms helplessly. "But he won't *live* in it! He wants to stay in the house where he was born, and where his own kids were born."

Gabe glanced back in amazement at the conical earth-and-twig shelter.

"You mean that ... giant *beaver dam* is—?"

"—well over a hundred years old," Whitney finished. "Hard to believe, isn't it?"

Her brisk lilting voice softened. "It's been there since before white men came into this canyon. It survived the Great Flood of 1910, when almost the entire village was washed away."

"You don't like me much, do you?" Gabe said suddenly.

Whitney glanced at him in surprise. "Now why would you think that?" she exclaimed.

"Well, just because of the way you talk about the Indians. And the way you act with Billy. You have a wonderful bedside manner. But last night at the café you were hard as nails with me." He smiled to let her know he was teasing. "Why do you suppose that is?"

"Is it required that everybody ... like you?"

Damn right! After I worked so hard to transform myself into the charming and congenial sophisticate you see before you today, everyone damn well better *like me!* It wasn't a flattering image, and Gabe shrank from it.

"No. But I'd like it if you did."

"Why?"

Gabe groaned with exasperation. "Does there have to be a reason behind everything I say? I'd like it if you did, that's all." He paused. "*I* like *you,*" he offered.

"Why?" she repeated forthrightly, then laughed. "I like you fine, Gabe. I just don't like the company you keep."

It was Gabe's turn to ask why, but he didn't. "Hobie," he said.

"Hobie," she agreed. "I don't like him, Gabe. I don't like what he's come here to do. I have a hard time believing—" *That someone like you would be associated with someone like that,* she started to say. But that was ridiculous; what did she really know about people like him? "—that you would sell out your own people."

Gabe's jaw clenched. "They are not my people," he said coldly. "And even if they were, I'd still believe Hobie's project is the best thing that could happen to them."

"Sure," Whitney said sarcastically. "If you think wiping them out is the best thing that could happen to them." Angrily she kicked a red rock that had the temerity to place itself in front of her foot.

"Hobie isn't going to wipe out the Havasupai," Gabe protested. "He expects to involve them in all phases of the development. And when the resort opens, he expects to hire them to work in it—"

"I can't argue that they'll probably be better off economically. But it'll destroy their culture. The waterfall where you'll decide to locate your hotel, if you have any sense at all, is their most sacred place. And you'll have people walking all over their burial grounds, and chipping pictographs out of the caves. The entire history of their people, everything they *are* is in this canyon. And if you destroy that, you destroy them. Surely you can see that?"

"Well no, as a matter of fact, I can't. All I see is stagnation. All I see is a zoo, and the Indians confined like exotic animals so some misguided do-gooders can pat themselves on the backs for preserving a slice of the wild West." His voice, unlike Whitney's, was dry and dispassionate. He sounded, she realized with extreme annoyance, exactly like a lawyer.

"You're half-Indian, Gabe," she persisted. "How can you feel that way?"

Gabe's smile was cynical. "The half of my blood that's Indian is just an accident of birth, Doctor. It has nothing to do with me."

"But don't you ever wonder about your background? Your roots?"

"Never. I don't know where my white blood comes from, either. And if my mother knew, that's another thing she never told me. I have no roots, and I like it that way. It's that simple."

"But don't you ever feel . . . like a piece of you is missing?" she persisted. "Wouldn't you like to know where you came from? I mean, even if it's impossible, don't you at least *wish* you could?"

The intensity in her voice made Gabe frown. He adjusted his glasses and looked more closely at her. He had the uneasy feeling that they weren't talking about Indians anymore.

"No," he said, but he said it lightly, trying to back down from another heated debate. No matter how diplomatic he tried to be, he thought in utter frustration, their encounters always seemed to end in arguments. "I don't wish anything of the kind. What little I *do* know about my background leads me to believe that I wouldn't want to know any more!"

They hiked the rest of the way in silence. Gabe left Whitney at her door, choosing to forget his curiosity about her, choosing to forget his earlier invitation to get something to eat, forgetting everything except his urgent need to get away from her before he said something he'd *really* regret!

Still seething, Whitney watched him walk toward the village. Her lips were pressed into a stubborn line. What was he but an insensitive boor, a person who understood nothing of the important things in life—history, for one thing. Tradition, for another. A man who was going to be out of her thoughts and out of her life soon. And the sooner the better!

RETURNING TO THE LODGE after a quick greasy hamburger and a lukewarm iced tea, Gabe found the door wide open between his and Mimi's adjoining rooms.

"I hope you don't mind, Gabe," Mimi's voice announced into the semidarkness from the vicinity of his bed.

"What are you doing here?" His voice was tense. *Now what?* he thought with brusque irritation. He switched on the ceiling light and watched her blink into the sudden brightness.

"I got lonely."

"I thought you'd be with Sinyella."

"I was. All afternoon." She slid gracefully off the edge of the bed and stood, a full three inches shorter than usual, and Gabe saw that she was barefoot. He also saw, with a feeling of relief, that she was dressed.

She wore cutoffs that were belted just beneath her navel and a sleeveless white shirt knotted below her magnificent bust. Her blond mane was caught back in a careless ponytail, her face scrubbed clean of makeup. Obviously Mimi was off duty for the night.

"I don't like this, Gabe. I don't like it one bit!" Her pale lower lip, lipstick-free, thrust outward in an appealing and practiced pout.

"What's the matter, Mims?"

"It's Hobie," she said sulkily. "Maybe he's right. Maybe I *am* losing my touch."

She sidled toward Gabe, her pelvis thrust forward in an exaggerated wiggle designed to cause a testosterone rush in a dead man. Upon reaching him, she wound her arms around his neck and pressed herself against him. "It's been such a long time, Gabe," she purred, snuggling closer.

"Mimi, don't." Surprising even himself, he seized her wrists and removed her arms from around his neck. "Too long," he said flatly. "Besides," he added. "I thought you were supposed to be working. What's going on with Sinyella?"

Mimi eyed him angrily, then sauntered back to the bed where she struck a seductive pose aimed at making Gabe regret his rejection. "I'm not getting anywhere with him," she said with a pout, "and God knows I've tried. I hung out at his office all afternoon, and I felt like a fool, following him around like a puppy!"

"He ignored you?" Gabe asked, somewhat surprised at Sinyella's stamina. He knew how persuasive Mimi could be.

"Worse. He was *nice* to me. *Nice!* I was humiliated!" Mimi threw herself dramatically across the faded chenille bedspread. She propped her chin in her hands and regarded Gabe dolefully. "What do you think? You think I'm losing my touch, don't you? You think I'm getting old." Fearfully she patted the flesh under her chin with the back of her fingers, reassured for the time being not to feel a ripple there.

Gabe crossed the room, then sat down beside Mimi and began kneading the tense muscles of her shoulders. "Try another approach," he suggested. "Try playing hard to get—"

"I don't have time!" Mimi protested. "The Tribal Council's going to decide about Hobie's proposal on Saturday. Besides, I don't think that's the problem."

"Oh? What is it, then?"

"I think it's someone else. I think he's in love with that little Korean doctor. You've seen how he lights up when she's around, or even just when her name comes up."

She twisted her head to look up at Gabe. "Can you believe it? A skinny little thing like that?"

Gabe's eyebrows knit together into a single black line. His tongue probed the sore tooth again. *Sinyella and Whitney?* His hands were still for a moment, then began to massage Mimi's shoulders again with the same deliberate pressure.

"Yes," he said slowly, thoughtfully, "I can believe it."

"Oh, she's nice enough," Mimi went on, soothed by the back rub into purring, feline contentment. "And she's probably awfully smart...."

"Yes," said Gabe again.

CHAPTER SEVEN

WHITNEY GROANED and burrowed her head into her pillow. When the knock came again, she groped for the alarm clock, snatched it off the nightstand and peered at it grumpily. If it could wait this long, she silently growled to the perpetrator of the knock, why couldn't it have waited just a little longer?

She swung her legs over the edge of the bed, yawned, then donned the terry-cloth robe lying at the foot and shuffled barefooted to the door.

"Yes? What is—?" she began, suppressing another yawn. Her eyes widened, then immediately returned to their usual slant. "Gabe," she said coolly.

He stood in the doorway, jogging in place. Behind him, the gray haze clung to the sides of the cliffs, deepening to slate at the base. Around him, the breeze carried the leathery scent of expensive men's toiletries and the faint odor of sweat which evaporated as soon as it reached the surface of the skin.

"What are you doing here?"

"You said you're a runner," he said, straightening his glasses on the bridge of his nose with thumb and forefinger. An unmistakable challenge glinted in his eyes. "Let's run."

With a put-upon sigh, Whitney folded her arms across her chest and slouched against the doorjamb. "I don't think so," she said crossly. "I was up half the night—I'd just as soon sleep a little longer."

Instantly contrite, Gabe stopped his jogging. The challenging expression vanished from his eyes. "I'm sorry. Was it anything serious?"

Whitney sighed again and shifted her weight to her other foot. "No, just snakebite in the campgrounds. They'll be bruised for a while, but they'll be fine. It was that group of kids that flew in with you, as a matter of fact—one of them asked about you."

"Oh?"

"He said something like 'whatever happened to that uptight suit from Seattle? Did he ever get with the program?'"

Gabe grimaced. "Ouch! What did you tell him?"

"I said I had no idea."

"You might have said 'yes,'" Gabe pointed out. "I *am* dressing down these days."

Whitney gave his spandex an exaggerated once-over. "I guess I'd have to go along with that."

"Well, Doctor, if you're not up for a run, I'll just let you get back to bed. Sorry I woke you." Gabe raised his hand in a quick wave, then turned to go.

Whitney thought his choice of words sounded patronizing. *Not up for a run, huh?* He made tracks only as far as the hitching post before she decided that a trek across the canyon floor during little light was exactly what she needed.

"Wait just a minute, Gabe," she called, trying to maintain the aggrieved tone in her voice. "I'm awake now. You might as well come in and have a cup of coffee while I get dressed."

THE LITTLE DOCTOR looked more childlike than ever, Gabe thought, running beside him in shapeless gray sweats that concealed her subtle curves like a tent. That she was having a hard time keeping up with his longer strides was obvious; that she was not going to admit it was also obvious. Feeling chivalrous this morning, Gabe slowed down.

"You look warm in those clothes," he commented. The weather was always a good opening gambit.

"Yes, well, you look chilly in those shorts," she returned in a voice as impersonal as if she was delivering a lecture. "It's all in what you're used to, I suppose."

Gabe gave the matter of small talk some serious consideration. He finally came up with, "Tell me about your—emergency last night." He timed his words to the rise and fall of his measured breathing.

"Oh, those kids!" Whitney gave a rich, bell-toned chuckle. Gabe was gratified—he'd landed on a topic that sparked her enthusiasm.

"I knew they were tenderfeet the minute I saw them . . . get off the helicopter," she said, still chuckling, regulating her words to her own measured breaths. "They were packing enough equipment to survive on a desert island . . . for the rest of their lives! Apparently a blacksnake . . . got into one of their sleeping bags . . . and the kid panicked, and the snake bit him.

"The other kid . . . heard the first one yelling *snake* . . . and figured, the way a kid would, that of course it could only be . . . a rattlesnake. Tried to beat it to death with . . . a frying pan . . . poor terrified snake bit him too!" She chuckled again.

Gabe, who suspected that if he saw a snake slithering along in this wilderness he would undoubtedly take it for a rattler, too, looked askance at her. "And you found that funny?'' he asked between breaths. "Doesn't sound very compassionate, Doctor.''

''Well, not funny, exactly,'' Whitney panted. "But it *was* only a blacksnake! And those kids . . . if you could have seen their faces! And . . . heard them, chattering like a couple of hysterical squirrels! Poor old blacksnake . . . quite peaceable, actually. He'd really just as soon have crawled off . . . into the sunset, if they'd given him half a chance.'' She grinned up at him.

Gabe liked her grin. He liked the way it made her chin point downward and her cheekbones point up, emphasizing the piquant heart shape of her face. He liked the way her delicate brows winged upward as her eyes disappeared into tilted slits. Whimsically, he wondered if she could see through those eyes when she smiled?

Someday—it would have to be between now and Saturday, he realized with an unexpected twinge of regret—he would have to ask her.

A FEW STRAY DOGS scratched energetically in the dirt. Other than that, the village was still sleeping when Gabe and Whitney reached it. Not even the old men who spent their days dozing on the benches in front of the trading post had taken up their positions yet.

At the other end of the village, the path became nothing more than a tangle of vegetation. It almost disappeared in some places, crowded by jutting walls that forced them to run single file. But watching Gabe thread his way through the cactus and sage and twisted piñon trees, Whitney saw that the winding route he followed must indeed once have been a continuation of the trail.

After a time, Whitney realized that they were running up a slight incline. She began to wish she'd worn something lighter than a sweat suit. Her own idea of a morning run was a leisurely jaunt around the village, but the challenge in Gabe's voice—"If you're not up to a run..."—made her loath to admit it.

Unclamping her water bottle from her fanny pack, she sucked down a good half of it. At least he wasn't having that easy a time of it, either, she noticed with perverse satisfaction. He was running hard, too.

Beneath his T-shirt, Whitney could see the thin, sinuous outline of the scar on his back. She was more curious than ever about it—it could so easily have been a fatal wound—and wished she'd asked him about it when she'd had the chance. Now all she could do was to watch it writhe, snakelike, under his shirt, and wish in some totally illogical way that she could have been there to help him heal.

A series of hairpin turns took them higher. Suddenly a high red bluff loomed before them, and on it, the mysterious red sandstone pillars of Wii'baaq'a. No one could fail to be awed by them, and by the raw forces of nature that had sculpted them through the ages, carving them, millenium by millenium, out of solid rock.

Finally Whitney's body refused to go any farther. Breathing hard, legs as shaky as string, she sat down on a smooth flat-topped boulder to catch her breath. Propping her arms behind her on the rock, she threw back her head and drew in great gulps of air.

"What's wrong?" Gabe called down to her.

"You go ahead," she returned, panting, waving him on. "I'll wait for you here."

Lifting her face skyward, she let her eyes travel up the full length of the colossal pillars. At this time of morning they were still only black silhouettes against the lightening sky, and then unexpectedly they were joined by a third silhouette.

Gabe. Dwarfed though he was by the soaring pillars, his shape stood out against the sky with the same sharp black clarity. There was strength in the long clean lines of his runner's body, just as there was in the ancient and monumental lines of Wii'baaq'a.

And there was something else.

He didn't look like a sophisticated big city attorney, Whitney thought vaguely. His styled haircut and his blue spandex and his gold watch were invisible in the silhouette he presented, and he looked like an Indian—a man of the Havasupai, maybe, paying homage to the sun the way men of the Havasupai had always done.

Or further back than that. A man of a tribe even older than the Havasupai's seven hundred centuries. An Anasazi—one of the Ancient Ones, going so far back in time that no one was sure who they were. But they had lived in this canyon. And very likely they had scaled these same red walls, to commune with this same rising sun, as it came over the tops of these same awe-inspiring pillars.

Whitney leaned back on her elbows, stretching out full length on her boulder as if it was a sandy beach. She should keep moving, she knew, keep her heart rate up. But instead she let herself relax into the rock, like a lizard waiting for the sun.

Watching Gabe's black silhouette bend over, hands on his knees, while he caught his breath, Whitney settled herself more comfortably into the rock. It was cool against her overheated skin, much cooler than it would be at the sun's zenith, when it would blister human flesh on contact.

This particular boulder seemed custom-made for Whitney. It had a depression at her hips, a shallower one at her shoulders, and lacing her hands behind her head made a perfect pillow.

A short time later, Gabe came loping down the trail. He found Whitney curled into the rock, sound asleep. In an automatic gesture, he brought his hand to her cheek and felt its warmth. Whitney blinked sleepily, looking as rosy and dewy as a child waking up in her own bed.

"Good morning, Sleeping Beauty," Gabe said softly. "I guess you *did* have a rough night last night." Smiling, he smoothed back a wisp of hair that had fallen across her forehead. "Are you ready to go back to the castle?"

THE SUN WAS ALREADY heating up the canyon floor. Soon it would be an inferno.

After their run, Whitney had invited Gabe in for a pick-me-up glass of water before he continued back to the Lodge. Now, her elbows propped on the Formica counter in the kitchen, she watched Gabe drain his glass and shamble awkwardly toward the door.

"Well, the clinic is closed on Saturday, so I probably won't see you again." The words in Whitney's mouth felt as cold and unappetizing as lumps of greasy fry bread left to congeal on a plate. "You're expecting a pretty hectic day tomorrow, I'm sure."

Tomorrow morning was the Tribal Council meeting. And tomorrow night he would be back in the real world—*his* real world—of gray skies and airplanes and traffic noises and skyscrapers. When his jet roared overhead on its way north from Flagstaff, she wouldn't even hear it; and he probably wouldn't think again about the people living in the tiny subterranean world directly below.

"Yes, I expect we'll be in meetings most of the day, ironing out the details. Hobie Stoner's not one to sit on a project. He'll want all that settled right away."

"Sure, I know. I guess by this time on Monday, you'll be an official partner in . . ." She searched for the name.

"Parkhurst and Brandenberg," he supplied.

"Yes. It's too bad that you didn't see the waterfalls while you were here. . . ."

"I'll see them once the resort is built."

"It won't be the same."

"Look, Whitney," Gabe heard himself burst out unexpectedly. "If it were up to me, well, I might do things differently. I'm not sure, but I might. But I work for Hobie Stoner—it's my job. . . ."

"I know." Would he ever come back, she wondered? If he did, it wouldn't be to the rustic Havasupai Lodge and Gwe Watahomigie's Red Rock Café.

It would be to plush guest rooms and room service, beautiful people, beautifully dressed, batting a ball down long green fairways or back and forth over a net, drinking exotic drinks in dark bars. And to the heirs of fourteen thousand years of uninterrupted history in this canyon scurrying behind the scenes like invisible stagehands to keep the whole thing moving.

And if he did come back, would he even remember her?

Gabe continued to back awkwardly toward the door. He took the doorknob in his hand. "Well, say goodbye to Billy for me. I hope he . . . gets better."

"We'll do our best," Whitney said, lapsing into the royal "we" physicians used when trying to distance themselves from situations that threatened to become too personal. Was it her relationship with Billy that she was trying to retreat from, she asked herself? Or the relationship she *wasn't* going to have with Gabriel Blade?

Gabe recognized the ploy. Lawyers used it, too. As she walked over to join him at the door, he also recognized the bright, artificial smile on her face; it was the same one his own face probably wore.

Whitney reached for the doorknob, realizing only after the fact that his hand was already there. She pulled her own away as if it had burned her, but Gabe quickly caught it.

It was so delicate that he could feel all the tiny bones. At the same time he recalled how strong and sure it had been when she cleaned and stitched his injuries.

Unnoticed, the door creaked to a close.

Still holding her hand, Gabe slowly brought his arm straight down to his side. The action drew them closer, until they stood only inches apart. Whitney's face was on a level with his chest.

Her eyes, as she lifted them higher, were suddenly not indecipherable, not mysterious. This close, they read as easily as a child's primer, and Gabe knew that they must mirror the expression in his own. His whole body came to life in sudden, sharp anticipation.

"Whitney, I . . ." he began.

"Yes?"

"I wish we could have met under different circumstances."

Her hand, clasped tightly in his, felt as soft and fragile as a little bird. Into his mind flashed the memory of a bird he had rescued, as a child, from a gutter during a rainstorm. It had been only a nondescript sparrow, but it had felt like a treasure in Gabe's rough hands—as delicate as anything he'd ever touched, and soft and warm when he placed it inside his ragged jacket.

Whitney's hand felt like that now. Soft and warm and yielding. He wanted to say something witty, clever, memorable, but a quick search of his stash of one-liners drew a blank. Instead, by default, he opted for sincerity, not usually his first choice for social interactions. Forgetting about clever, witty and memorable, he drew Whitney's hand up to his chest and clasped it between his two bigger ones, the way he once had the baby bird.

"I wish that, too..." she started to say, but before the words had left her mouth, he lowered his lips to hers, half expecting her to pull away and wither him with a few well-placed barbs.

But she didn't. And when he felt her lips open beneath his, inviting him in, he entered with a gentle chivalry totally at odds with his usual style.

Her lips were sweet. Her mouth was sweet. His whole body vibrated, and his breath came faster than when he'd run to the top of Wii'baaq'a. Then he surprised both himself and her by lowering their clasped hands and releasing her.

Whitney fell back a step and swallowed convulsively. Gabe wondered for an instant if he'd cracked that stubborn Yankee reserve, if her body was quivering the way his was. Except for the involuntary working of her throat, she gave no sign of it.

"Goodbye, Gabe," she said. Her cool, musical voice was as calm as ever.

Her mouth looked soft and damp and rosy, ready to be kissed again. And that's exactly what Gabe wanted to do. Already he regretted his well-bred, gentlemanly restraint. He was *not* well-bred, and certainly, beneath his well-engineered facade, no gentleman.

He was just a streetwise punk who had conned a bunch of gullible do-gooders into giving him a chance, giving him a law degree, and letting him wear suits and live uptown. But inside he was still a half-civilized 'breed who, having fought and clawed his way to the top, was now fighting and clawing to stay there.

No, he was no gentleman; but strangely enough, for the brief moment he'd held Whitney in his arms, he'd felt like one.

"Goodbye, Whitney," he said reluctantly. He focused on her face in a last effort to stall for time. And then he opened the door and walked through it.

CHAPTER EIGHT

"GODDAMN IT, SINYELLA. I thought we had a deal!"

"I don't know why you thought that, Mr. Blade," Jesse said mildly. "You knew it was going to have to clear the Tribal Council."

"But it was *supposed* to be cut-and-dried! We spoke to every one of those council members at one time or another, and they were all in favor of the concept. What made them balk *now*?" A frustrated and furious Gabe paced back and forth across Jesse's cluttered office.

The black wool suit he'd worn to emphasize the significance of the occasion was rumpled, the jacket thrown carelessly over a chair, the pleated trousers pulled low on his hips by his hands thrust deeply into the pockets. With an angry jerk, he loosened the knot of his tie, noting grimly that he was as hot under the collar now as he'd been the first day he plummeted into this godforsaken rabbit hole.

"Well, you know how it goes, Mr. Blade," Jesse said with a philosophical shrug. "Sometimes the whole turns out to be more than the sum of its parts. . . . "

Gabe turned on him suspiciously. "Just what in the hell is *that* supposed to mean?"

Seated behind his desk, his feet propped on top and his hands folded comfortably over his stomach, Jesse shrugged again. "Only that individually, every council member may have thought it was a good plan. But col-

lectively, maybe they didn't think it was in the best interests of the tribe."

Gabe's eyes narrowed. "You sure you didn't have
something to do with this, Sinyella?"

Jesse's voice was as mild as ever. "You might want to
remember who you're talking to, Mr. Blade," he said in
a conversational tone. "I can get you thrown off this
reservation so fast your shadow'll be running to catch
up."

Gabe suspected that the man wouldn't hesitate to
carry out his threat, and furthermore, would probably
enjoy doing it. "What's the problem here, Sinyella?
What'd I ever do to you?"

Jesse looked at the face so like his own. He disliked
the man, it was true. Disliked his high-handed attitude
toward the Indians, as if he were a superior creature
simply by virtue of—what? His half-white blood? His
law degree? The reflected glory of his association with a
rich and successful white businessman?

But it was more than that, Jesse had to admit to himself. He couldn't control the instinct that made his
hackles rise whenever the 'breed lawyer was around. He
recognized his hostility as prejudice, irrational and illogical, and he had always despised people who indulged in that kind of sloppy thinking.

He despised himself now, as, pursed-lipped and
shamefaced, he sidestepped the whole issue.

"No problem, Mr. Blade. I just don't much care for
people messing with things they know nothing about."

"And you don't care much for 'breeds either, am I
right?"

"You said that, Mr. Blade, not me."

Gabe felt his fingers straining to ball into fists. Instantly he was a boy again, squaring off over some in-

sult to his mother, or his ancestry, or his legitimacy. He could almost feel his hand go to the knife he no longer carried in his belt.

Then, just as quickly, he let the anger go. He fought with different tools now—in a courtroom or in a boardroom, which often could be bloodier than street fighting, and he fought for different goals. His present one, a partnership in Parkhurst and Brandenberg, was almost within his grasp, and he'd be damned if he'd let some insignificant Indian chieftain get in the way of that.

"Well, lucky for both of us, I'll be out of here tomorrow," Gabe replied. The forced twist on his mouth bore no resemblance to a smile.

"You will be back," Jesse prophesied, still pursed-lipped, still no expression on his fleshy face. "Once the *hay gu* decides to take something from the Indian, he never gives up."

So now I'm a white man, Gabe thought with bitter irony. Aloud he only said, "Dammit, Sinyella, why can't you understand? Stoner Resorts doesn't want to take anything! We want this project to be good for both you *and* us—"

Unlike Gabe, Jesse didn't even pretend to smile. "Save that for the talk-around, Mr. Blade."

A voice on the wireless interrupted the tense exchange. "Peach Springs KZQ72489 calling Supai KKW45687. Jesse, you on the horn? Over."

Jesse dropped his feet to the floor, walked around the desk and sat down in front of the radio. "This is Supai KKW45687. What have you got for me, Vacey? Over."

"Got your Seattle call, Jesse. I'm patching him through now. Over."

Jesse extended the heavy, old-fashioned microphone to Gabe. "Press here to talk," he said, indicating a button on the stem, "and release it to listen."

"Gabe, my man!" Hobie's bombastic voice filled the tiny office. "How'd everything go? Got a date for the ground-breaking yet?"

Sprawled in the depths of a cracked vinyl chair, Gabe reached under his glasses to massage his eyelids with thumb and forefinger.

"Not exactly," he said into the mike. In a few brief sentences he related the events of the Tribal Council meeting. He could imagine the furious sputterings going on at Hobie's end, and when Hobie took over the transmission, Gabe was not surprised by what he heard.

"Whaddya mean, 'further study'? Didn't you show 'em the sketches? Didn't you show 'em the brochures from the other resorts?" The pitch of Hobie's voice rose with each question. "Didn't they have the engineers' reports? Whaddya mean, 'reconsider it at the next meeting'? And *what* the hell is a *talk-around?*"

Wearily, Gabe took back the transmission. "I showed them the reports, Hobie. And the brochures. They were more worried about the resort cutting into the services they already provide to the tourists. And they had some other concerns as well.

"A talk-around—according to Sinyella, it's like a powwow, a big meeting where everyone in the tribe gets together and puts in their two cents worth. Then the Tribal Council will meet to discuss all the various recommendations and let us have their okay at the next meeting. Maybe."

"Whaddya mean, *maybe?* You mean there's a chance the vote could go against us?"

Gabe continued to massage his aching eyes. "There was always that chance, Hobie," he said tiredly.

"Well, Gabe, my man—see, that's where *you* were supposed to come in, remember?" Hobie's voice dripped sarcasm. "It was *supposed* to be up to you to see that the vote went our way. Hell, you're the one that's *supposed* to be able to work with those people—that's why I *picked* you for the job! Now, if you can't deliver..." He left the sentence dangling on the implied threat.

"I can deliver."

"You're sure, Gabe?" Hobie prodded, his voice oozing friendly concern. "Because we can't afford any mistakes here. If you're not sure..."

"Goddamn it, Hobie," Gabe snarled. "I *said* I could deliver, didn't I?"

"Sure, Gabe, sure," Hobie said soothingly. "I know you can. Never a doubt in my mind. Okay, so tell me when this talk-around powwow thing is supposed to happen."

"Two or three weeks, Sinyella says. As soon as they can contact all the members of the tribe."

"And the next council meeting is a month from now, right? Well, I don't see any way around it, Gabe, my man. You're just gonna have to stay there 'til this thing is settled. Mimi, too. I've got too much time and money invested in this project. I can't afford to take a chance on something going haywire—"

Gabe pressed his microphone button testily. "I can't stay here for a month, Hobie!" he protested. "I've got other clients. I've got court dates pending! You can't expect me to just pick up and disappear off the face of the earth for an entire month!"

"*Other* clients, Gabe?" Hobie's voice fell, becoming deceptively gentle. "What *other* clients do you have who can do for you what I can do?"

Gabe heard the click that ended Hobie's transmission. He could feel the other man waiting, obscenely certain of Gabe's reply. The silence lengthened awkwardly. Gabe pulled his glasses off his nose and tossed them on the table with a rigid flick of his wrist, then began to rub his eyes in earnest.

He pressed the button on his mike with a vicious thumb. "Okay, Hobie. You win. I'll stay."

"Good man," Hobie returned smugly. "Now look, don't let those people get the best of you again. Paper the place with those brochures. Tell 'em how many jobs we're gonna create. Tell 'em how rich they're gonna be. Charter another chopper to bring in a load of ice cream the day of the powwow. You know, schmooze 'em. Get Mimi to schmooze that big, dumb chief, too..."

Cringing, Gabe sank deeper into his chair.

"...not gonna be able to keep it in his pants forever! That's the name of the game, Gabe, my man. That's what business is—ten percent fact and ninety percent schmoozing! I'm surprised you've been running with me all this time and you haven't learned that yet!"

At last Hobie hung up, and Vacey at Peach Springs Station signed off. Slowly Gabe returned the mike to the table. Even more slowly he retrieved his glasses and slid them back on his nose, and then, slowest of all, he turned around to face Jesse.

"Look, Sinyella, he didn't mean that," he began, embarrassed. "He—"

"Forget it," Jesse said gruffly. "I figure we're about even."

Watching Gabe head out the door, he felt a grudging sympathy for the hapless 'breed who had sold his soul to a land shark and was slowly being devoured by him.

GABE SPENT THE REST of the afternoon staring out the plate glass window of the Red Rock Café, sucking down cola after cola, wishing the caffeine was alcohol.

Alcohol. One of the amenities he would be doing without for a while. Not that he minded all that much. He did enjoy a good wine with an equally good dinner, but he had pretty much given up everything else at about the age of ten, when he realized liquor dulled the split-second timing that often made the difference between freedom and incarceration.

Mimi had joined him for a late lunch, ordering only a can of diet cola, as much lunch as she ever allowed herself. A practiced pout graced her perfect features, but as Gabe reported the details of his conversation with Hobie, it quickly turned into an uncharacteristic frown.

"How dare he say that!" she exclaimed, slamming down the diet cola with such force that foam flew from the tab opening. "How dare he humiliate me in front of Jesse that way!"

"I don't think he humiliated you, Mims," Gabe offered unconvincingly. "I think he humiliated himself. Besides, in all fairness, he couldn't have known that Sinyella was in the room."

"Actually, it doesn't matter, Gabe. Hobie manipulated me into staying when he left—he told me he *needed* me down here, can you believe it?—but he's not going to get away with that again."

She shook her head decisively, as if to suggest that this was her final word on the matter. "I'm not staying,

Gabe. I wouldn't, even if Hobie *hadn't* made the whole thing impossible.''

Gabe threw Mimi a skeptical glance. He had known her to rebel before, but always accompanied by tears and followed quickly by a change of heart. This time there was a determination in her eyes that he couldn't remember ever having seen there before. What had accounted for the change?

''Who've you been talking to, Mims?'' he asked curiously.

''No one,'' she pouted. Then she ducked her head almost shyly. ''Well, Jesse, a little. But it's *my* idea. He just told me . . .''

''Told you what?''

'' . . . that he believed I could do it.''

After Mimi had returned to the Lodge to pack, Gabe directed his abstracted gaze out the window, but his thoughts centered on Jesse Sinyella. How, he wondered, had the unprepossessing chief managed to persuade Mimi Samples, who didn't even respect herself, that she could make a man like Hobie Stoner respect her?

He raised his empty glass at Gwe Watahomigie, who eyed him resentfully.

Gwe was lucky his Red Rock Café had no competition, Gabe's sour thoughts continued. Come to think of it, just about everybody down here was lucky there was no competition for jobs—that big, gum-cracking, tabloid-reading receptionist in Whitney's clinic, the even larger, even more indifferent secretary in the Tribal Office, the ample woman who ran the post office and the one who sat behind the desk at the rudimentary gift shop, who could well be her twin.

These large, oddly regal but hopelessly taciturn people were like a herd of dinosaurs trying to survive in the middle of Central Park, lumbering slowly, ponderously, but inevitably toward their own doom. They were all going to have to undergo a complete attitude adjustment, Gabe's logical lawyer's mind reasoned, if they expected to work for Stoner Fantasy Resorts International.

Like the twinges of a bad conscience, the words he'd thrown so automatically at Sinyella kept echoing in his head, the words that had become a slogan in this ad campaign to sell Hobie's resort proposal to the Indians: *We want this project to benefit you and us.*

Well, that was true, as far as it went. If the Indians were smart, they'd adapt. If not, then they were going to find themselves replaced in the resort jobs by vivacious, bright-eyed and bouncy all-American kids doing double duty as resort personnel and window dressing. And what would that do to the economic future Hobie Stoner so glibly promised them?

But realistically, Gabe rationalized uncomfortably, how long could a dinosaur expect to survive in the middle of Central Park?

Between the Lodge and the café, the trail through the village widened to form the village square, the crossroads of this subterranean canyon world. If someone sat long enough at the window of the Red Rock Café, Gabe mused, eventually the entire population of this world-in-microcosm would probably pass by.

He had been here only a week, and already he saw faces he knew.

He saw the same old men that he saw every day, dozing on the benches in front of Jasper's trading post.

He saw Jesse Sinyella amble across the square with
another man Gabe recognized as a tribal council member, then saw the two of them turn and enter Jesse's office.

He saw the Headstart teacher from Flagstaff stroll
past the clapboard duplex that housed the Tourist Enterprise.

Then he caught sight of Whitney, and he realized it
was she he had been waiting for all along. She was riding across the dusty village square directly toward the
Red Rock Café, posting like a classically trained eques-
trian on a raw-boned Indian pony.

She brought the horse to a halt beneath the cottonwood trees, then, positioning one booted toe in the stir-
rup, slid to the ground.

Gabe noticed with his connoisseur's eye her enchant-
ing little backside as it slid down the saddle. He also noticed that the seat of her jeans was branded with a
delightful U-shaped imprint of ground-in red dirt.
Above the jeans she wore a flowered bikini top, covered
by a gauzy white shirt knotted just above her midriff.

Seeing him smiling at her from across the café, Whitney picked up a glass of tea from Gwe and joined Gabe
in his booth. Her skin was glowing, and she smelled of
leather and horses and fresh air. *Country smells,* Gabe
thought. Earthy. And on a woman whose usual scent
was a combination of soap and antiseptic, incredibly
intimate. Bits of white fluffy seeds from the cottonwoods trailed like feathers through her hair; without
thinking, Gabe reached across the table and brushed
them away. Her hair was smooth and heavy. It was also
damp.

"Been swimming?" he said.

"Yes. I rented one of Jasper's horses and went down to the falls. I like to get away on my days off." She smiled wryly. "Although never out of range of my hand-held, of course."

"Maybe you'd like to show me those falls," Gabe said, his voice deceptively casual. "Maybe on your next day off?"

Whitney looked at him dubiously. "You're coming back next weekend? But why? Not to see the waterfalls, surely?"

Gabe shook his head. His face threatened to break into a full-fledged grin. Ever since his totally unsatisfactory conversation with Hobie, the thought had been lurking in the back of his mind that spending another month in the canyon might definitely have its compensations. "The council postponed discussion of our project until the next council meeting."

"Oh, Gabe, I'm sorry!" Impulsively Whitney reached out and clasped his hand on top of the table.

"Actually, I figured you'd be pleased."

"I'm not sorry about the delay," she said honestly. "But I *am* sorry that you had to be disappointed. I know how much this resort thing means to you."

Riding through the village on her way back from the waterfalls, Whitney had overheard scraps of gossip as thick on the air as the drifting cottonwood petals, but because she spoke very little Supai, she hadn't really understood. Now, suddenly, she did.

"So that's why the people were so excited when I came through town," she exclaimed. "Jesse's going to call a talk-around, isn't he?"

"So he said. But what exactly *is* a talk-around?"

"It's one of the few times a year when everyone gets together. For ceremonies, like the Crying Dance, when the whole tribe meets to mourn everyone who's died in the past year, or sometimes to discuss important tribal issues. It's like a—"

"Powwow?" Gabe filled in the missing word.

"Yes. Or a fiesta," she finished. "Food, dancing, catching up on family news, that sort of thing."

Whitney frowned. "And so that means you're going to be staying on until the next council meeting?" She didn't seem particularly pleased with the whole idea.

Gabe was stung by her lack of enthusiasm. Immediately he went on the offensive. "Unless, of course, you don't want to play tour guide. That's okay, too. Actually, I'm not going to have that much free time anyway."

Gabe didn't like surprises. He didn't like being caught off guard, and now this woman had done that to him not once, but twice. The first time had been on the previous day, when he'd bent down to give her a peck on the cheek and found himself being sucked into a vortex of desire; the second was now, when she acted as though the vortex had never opened up beneath them at all.

What had happened between yesterday and today? he wondered in confusion.

Whitney also remembered yesterday. After he'd gone, she'd convinced herself that it was a totally natural reaction, under the circumstances—the circumstances being two people with healthy physical appetites, at least one of whom hadn't indulged that appetite for a very long time. She also remembered her stern Yankee conscience ordering her to forget all about it, which was going to present a problem if she had to deal with this man on a daily basis for another month.

"No, no, that'd be fun, Gabe," she said, suddenly tired of her conscience. "I could show you a little about your Indian heritage. The waterfalls, the pictographs, the caves."

"Remember what Billy said," Gabe pointed out. "This isn't my heritage. I'm not Havasupai."

"He said *probably* not," she corrected him. "But it's still a possibility. Not that it matters—all the tribes have a great many things in common. It'd be interesting for you to learn something about your roots. What do you think?"

What did he think? He thought he was going to take her up on the offer, simply because, roots or no roots, any time he spent with Whitney Baldridge-Barrows was bound to be interesting, though not necessarily for the reasons she had stated.

Across the booth, Whitney glanced past Gabe's shoulder and out the café window. Suddenly her shoulders slumped and she gave a long-suffering sigh. "Oh, dear," she said, half under her breath. "I almost forgot. It's Saturday night."

"Why? Is Saturday night any different from any other night of the week down here?" Gabe asked wryly, already sure of the answer. He turned to see what Whitney was looking at. "Billy?"

"Billy," she sighed. The old storyteller was riding toward the village on his equally old gray somnolent mule. Billy was slumped over the saddlehorn, not even reining the animal, while the mule moved at a snail's pace, weaving to one side and then the other, instinctively keeping his rider balanced.

You couldn't tell the man from the mule, Gabe thought, watching their leisurely approach. Old faded clothes, old faded saddle, old faded flesh draped on old brittle bones. He glanced up in surprise as Whitney suddenly pushed herself out of the booth and threw two quarters on the table.

"I have to go, Gabe," she said distractedly, and before he could ask her where or why, she was exiting the café. "I'll see you around," she called with a hasty smile and a wave as the screen door slammed behind her.

Gabe watched her mount her big bony horse and rein it in beside Billy's mule. Billy's misshapen straw sombrero dipped in greeting, and the two continued down the path toward the village.

A month's stay in this strange land that time forgot wasn't going to be as stupefyingly dull as he'd feared at first, Gabe thought cheerfully. He lifted his glass again toward Gwe.

CHAPTER NINE

Coyote is both the wise man and the clown of the desert. He is the maker and the breaker of all our taboos. He reminds us that the celebration of life goes on unceasingly and invites us to join in the dance.

Those whose abilities are far above others—the fastest runner, the person of superior eyesight—those are called members of the Coyote Clan. But Coyote himself belongs to no clan. He is a traveler, always seeking to become one with the heart of the desert. But because the desert has no heart, no beginning, no middle and no end, he is forever alone.

Before the time of the People, Coyote wept in his loneliness, and the whole desert filled with his tears and became an inland sea. You can still see the bones of ancient fish trapped in the stone cliffs. That is why the People do not eat fish—because they live in the tears of Coyote. And that is why Coyote is such a prankster. If he were not, his tears of sadness would drown the world.

STANDING UNNOTICED in the doorway of Whitney's office, Gabe nevertheless knew that Billy was aware of him. The old man's bright, nearly sightless eyes drifted past Whitney's shoulder, where she sat curled up in her big desk chair with a pocket tape recorder in her hand. He nodded almost imperceptibly at Gabe and continued with his story.

I am of the Coyote clan. When I was young, I could see farther than any of my initiation brothers. With my sling I killed squirrels and rabbits that others could not see. The one who was song shaman before me prepared me to take his place. My eyes were so superior, he said, that I would be able to see from the present into the future. At my initiation I knew that the words he spoke were true, because in the sweat lodge Coyote came to me, and all the way up Wii'baaq'a, when I ran to greet the rising sun, Coyote stayed with me.

But it became harder to sing my dreams. I dreamed a long time passing. I dreamed a time when young warriors no longer ran toward the rising sun. Then I dreamed the People gone from the canyon. Not even the howl of Coyote echoed through the great cliffs. These were signs and omens that the elders could not understand, and after a time they no longer trusted my songs.

It is a terrible thing to know the ending time, and to know it alone. That is why I never looked for my grandson. I knew there was no future for the People. I knew that whatever future he might make for himself among the hay gu, *it could not be worse than here.*

There was pain in his voice. It was an old pain, and almost welcome because it was familiar, like meeting an old enemy when there are no old friends left. Billy took a slow drag on the cigarette he held in one hand, then breathed it out in a long, wheezing sigh.

Now I am not sure. It could be that there is a future, but it is revealed in signs that I do not understand. No more do I see with the eyes of Coyote. Now I only see what has passed.

Billy's gravelly voice trailed off. He sighed again and closed his eyes.

Whitney switched off the tape recorder. She rewound the tape, then reversed it and began to speak, keeping her voice low to avoid disturbing the sleeping old man.

"Recorded July 1993, at Supai Village, the bottom of the Grand Canyon. My informant is Supai Billy Hamadreeq, who says without documentation that he was born in the year the first white schoolteacher came into the canyon to teach the children how to live like the *hay gu*. The year would have been 1900.

"These are the recollections of Supai Billy about the mythology that was still commonly known at that time."

She was puzzled. In all the taping she had done with Billy, never before had he mentioned that Coyote was his spirit animal. The identity of his spirit guide was something no warrior ever revealed. It was like giving away a part of yourself, Billy had told her once, and left you prey to all the evils that travel with men: illness and discontent and death.

Maybe Billy was giving a bit of himself to the future, Whitney thought. Or maybe he simply forgot about the tape recorder.

Whitney hadn't heard Gabe come into the clinic. It was only when Billy had finished speaking and she had added her commentary that she looked up and saw him standing in the doorway. Carefully, she slipped the forgotten cigarette from between Billy's fingers and dropped it into a paper cup on her desk. Then she walked to the doorway where Gabe stood, a suitcase in either hand.

"Why is Billy here?" Gabe said in a low voice. "Is he worse?"

"Not this time." Keeping her own voice to a whisper, she ushered Gabe out the door and gently pulled it closed behind her. "The tribal police picked him up last night. Drunk and disorderly."

Gabe raised a skeptical eyebrow. "Drunk and disorderly?" he repeated incredulously. "You could pick him up for being drunk any day of the week. But disorderly? Billy?"

"Well, they need a reason for taking him in, that's all. It's really for his own protection. Then they bring him to the clinic and I put him to bed for the night. It's more comfortable than the lockup."

She smiled, the piquant smile Gabe liked so well. "And the next morning I can get some good food into him and maybe a good story *out* of him."

Belatedly she noticed the bags Gabe had deposited at his feet. Her voice rose several decibels. "Where are you going?"

"I guess I'm going to have to take a rain check on that sightseeing tour, after all. I've come to say goodbye again, Doctor."

"But ... you changed your plans? Why?"

"I didn't. Ms. Joyful Noise informed me last night that I can't stay. The Lodge is booked solid a year in advance."

Joyful Noise was another one who was going to have to undergo a complete attitude adjustment if she expected to work for Hobie Stoner. She must have been a disappointment to the optimistic parents who named her, Gabe thought, because she was neither noisy nor joyful.

When Ms. Joyful Noise said there was no room at the inn, there was no point in pleading, cajolery, flattery, temper tantrums, or even bribery, all of which Gabe had tried. A stubborn and aggravating woman, he'd concluded in anger; but no more stubborn and aggravating than everyone else he'd met in this obscure, insignificant little hole in the ground.

Including this tiny doctor, who had insinuated herself so completely into his mind in just three days that he was sorry he wasn't going to have the chance to get to know her better, after all.

"I knew about the limits on tourists here," she told him. "The canyon's so small that the tribe keeps track of every single one. But somehow, I thought you might have been able to pull a few strings."

"Not with Ms. Joyful Noise. She wasn't the least bit impressed by Stoner Fantasy Resorts International."

Having tossed and turned half the night, worrying about how she was going to endure Gabriel Blade's disturbing presence on the reservation for an entire month, now Whitney had a whole new problem: how would she manage without him?

He wore the same suit he had been wearing when he arrived, red silk tie knotted like a choke collar under his chin, and he looked just as hot and uncomfortable as he had that day. The expression on his face was the same, too—like a man on his way to an ulcer.

Gabe picked up his suitcases. "Well goodbye, Doctor."

Impulsively, Whitney placed her hand lightly on his shoulder. "'Bye, Gabe. It was nice meeting you, in spite of the reason you came." Then, balancing on her toes, she stretched upward and kissed him. The kiss landed on his chin, making him regret the luggage that occupied both hands, which prevented him from reaching down, putting his arms around her and making the kiss into the kind he wished he had given her last time.

"*Bqi'gthegee.*" Billy's voice quavered out into the hall.

Whitney glanced at her watch. "Do you have time to say goodbye to Billy?" she said.

"I think so," Gabe replied, not caring for the moment if he made the helicopter or not. He dropped the suitcases and followed Whitney back into her office.

Billy was tottering beside his cot. When he heard her come in, he pursed his lips in her direction. "It is time that I left," he said.

"Your mule is outside, Uncle," Whitney said, quickly glancing out the window to double-check. Horses were like buses; if someone needed one, they took whatever horse happened to be nearby. If its owner needed the horse and couldn't find his own, he would simply use another one close at hand. By nightfall, all the horses found their own way home for supper.

No one borrowed Billy's discouraged old mule, though, because it had only one speed, and it was slower than most people could walk. Besides, Billy's mule wouldn't go anywhere else, anyway, except down to its master's wickiup.

Together, Whitney and Gabe helped Billy mount. The mule stood patiently as Billy made several false starts, then finally slid one leg over its back, gripped the saddlehorn with one elbow and pulled himself upright.

Whitney handed him the reins. "I'll come to see you tomorrow, Uncle," she promised.

Billy grunted, then patted her hand. "Thank you, *bqi'gthegee*," he muttered. "And you, *n'home'e*. You will come as well, eh?" Without any signal other than the feeling that its owner was secure on his back, the old gray mule began to shuffle away.

Gabe watched them as they ambled off, Billy cradled as snugly as a child in the hollow between the mule's bony rump and bonier withers.

"Is he going to be all right?" he asked uneasily.

"He has been so far," Whitney returned, looking none too certain herself. "If he loses his balance that old beast will just sidestep to catch him."

"What was that he said at the last?"

"He called you 'grandson,'" she said with a pointed smile.

The word, mere courtesy though it was, touched Gabe. She smiled again. "Maybe you're the age he imagines his grandson might be. Or maybe he'd like to imagine his grandson grew up to be a fine upstanding man like you."

Gabe shot her a surprised look, but he saw that she didn't appear to be voicing her own opinion; she was seeing him through Billy's eyes.

"But his grandson, if there even is one, could be ten, or he could be, oh, fifty or sixty. Or he could have *lots* of grandchildren. We're not even sure of Billy's age, since we have no documentation of Indian births that far back, and there's no one alive who remembers. He says he was born the year the first white schoolteacher came here, but it could have been his *father* who born that year and Billy's just gotten his generations mixed up."

Gabe went inside to get his suitcases, then turned in the direction of the helipad. Whitney fell into step beside him.

"It's too bad things didn't work out at the Lodge," she said.

"You bet," Gabe retorted. "I'm not looking forward to explaining all this to Hobie when I get back."

"He certainly can't blame you...."

"Sure he can. He pays the bills, so he can blame anyone he wants."

Whitney didn't like the cynical tone in his voice. "If you don't like working for him, why don't you quit?"

"I don't have to like working for him, Whitney. He's just a means to an end, that's all. Once I'm a partner in the firm, once my name's up on the front of the building so clients won't look at me and think their case has been palmed off on some two-bit junior law clerk, I can tell the likes of Hobie Stoner to go to hell. But until then I have no choice."

"Yes you do," Whitney replied without a shadow of doubt in her voice. "If you're good at what you do, you don't need someone like Hobie Stoner to open doors for you."

Suddenly the clear, cultured voice with the Eastern prep-school drawl grated on his ears like fingernails on a blackboard.

"What do you know about it?" he said irritably. "You were born with a silver spoon in your mouth. Your father is a doctor, your mother probably stayed home and took care of you and dressed you up in cute little dresses and sent you off to one expensive school or another! What would you know about people hating you just because you're diff—"

He stopped in midsentence. Incredibly, he had forgotten. Looking down at her exotic face, her slanted eyes suddenly grown narrower with surprise, he knew that, silver spoon or not, being different was something she understood at least as well as he did.

"Whitney, I'm sorry. I had no right to say that. Somehow I just *forgot* that you're kind of an outsider, too."

Whitney chuckled, her gay musical laugh that sounded like birdsong. "Don't worry about it, Gabe. It happens all the time. Sometimes I'm not sure myself whether I should call myself Korean or American."

"Maybe you should try a hyphen. You know, African-American. Italian-American. Native-American." He paused. "Half-breed."

She shook her head, smiling. "I don't think that'd help. It's really a psychological problem. In my own mind I'm as American as Little Orphan Annie. But I know when other people look at me, they see something else. Sometimes when I look in a mirror, I even surprise myself!"

Overhead, the purposeful chop-chop of a helicopter rotor, still unseen above the mesas, sliced into the background hum of insects and birds. Like the Pied Piper's flute, the sound summoned children from all over the village and lured them to the helipad. The dogs began to bark.

Shielding her eyes with one hand, Whitney glanced up at the narrow strip of sky. It was empty. In the next moment, the helicopter dropped below the last mesa like an awkward bird of prey, its skids like claws spread for landing. The sound of its rotor filled the canyon world with echoes.

"Gabe," Whitney said impulsively, stopping dead in her tracks. "Stay!"

Gabe stopped too, and set his bags on the ground.

"Stay," she repeated. Already the word sounded shaky, almost drowned out by a chorus of second thoughts.

"What do you mean?" he asked, baffled.

"Well, you might as well stay here for the month, and do everything you can to get a fair hearing on your proposal. And you shouldn't miss the talk-around—it'll be the only chance you'll get to explain it to the whole tribe at once.''

"Whitney," he said patiently. "I certainly agree with all that, but—"

"I mean, I'm against this whole resort thing. But it's not my decision, is it? The Havasupai are going to have to decide. With communications as slow as they are down here, and you having to fly in and out all the time, and the council being so cautious anyway, it could take months to settle this thing!"

"Months," Gabe agreed.

"Years, even!"

"That's true," Gabe agreed again.

"That could be very divisive for the tribe."

"Uh-huh."

"Well, there's no sense postponing the inevitable. I think you should stay. Give it your best shot, and get it over with, once and for all."

"Sounds like a plan to me, Doctor," Gabe said patiently. "There's only one thing."

"What's that?"

"Where would I stay? Remember?"

The helicopter set down in a whirlwind of red dust. It blew Whitney's hair across her face, and she reached up with one hand to hold it down against her neck.

She looked at him, taken aback by the question.

"Why, with me, of course." She raised her voice to cut through the sound of the rotor. "Didn't I say that?"

CHAPTER TEN

"NO," GABE SAID loudly, cupping his hand between Whitney's ear and his mouth. "As a matter of fact, you didn't!"

"Well, sure, Gabe, I mean, why not?" she shouted in return. "A lot of docs who come down here bring their families, so the house has an extra bedroom. One of you will have to sleep on the couch, of course, but I'm sure that won't be a problem—"

"Wait a minute, Whitney. *One* of us?"

"Well, yes. You or Mimi."

"Mimi has no intention of staying," he said carefully.

Whitney's mouth fell open. She stared at Gabe blankly. Then she sucked in a deep breath, accompanied by a mouthful of the gritty red dust that swirled through the air from the helicopter's wash.

Coughing and sputtering, she groped in her fanny pack for a tissue, then occupied herself with regaining her breath as well as her composure. Behind his dust-coated lenses, Gabe's dark eyes danced with amusement.

"Was it something I said?" he inquired solicitously.

"No, not at all." Whitney coughed, playing for time while her mind rapidly weighed her options. She realized that without Mimi, her oh-so-practical plan took on other, more disturbing possibilities. In fact, the idea of spending that much time alone with Gabriel Blade created many more disturbing possibilities for Whitney than she would have thought possible.

She wondered why she had even made the offer in the first place?

In her opinion, if the whole idea of a resort in Havasu Canyon fell apart, it would be a good thing. These large, silent, dignified Indians had adapted to many changes in their long history, but somehow Whitney couldn't picture them allowing themselves to become characters in a theme park.

And if they refused to adapt to Hobie Stoner's fantasy, then what?

Whitney knew that this particular development project was only the most current of the many that had been proposed in the past, and the many more that would come up in the future. The uptop world wasn't short of get-rich-quick schemers who saw a gold mine in the hidden canyon that thousands of visitors from all over the world had christened "Shangri-La."

The tribe had just defeated a proposal calling for mining uranium on the Kaibab Plateau directly above them. That would have meant uranium tailings poisoning the creek that rushed through the canyon and created its magnificent travertine waterfalls. And it would have meant not just the end of tourism, but the end of the life itself that had occupied this canyon for over fourteen thousand years.

It had taken years of resistance to prevail against the determined mining interests; and Jesse had confided that he felt they hadn't defeated the mining industry, but only delayed them while the falling world-market price of uranium made mining the canyon unprofitable.

Whitney hated to throw Hobie Stoner—and by association, Gabe—into the same category as the mining interests. Certainly Hobie's plans were more benign. He intended to commercialize the canyon, not destroy it.

But in the end, wouldn't it amount to the same thing?

The roar of the rotor slowed and then stopped. Its echoes ricocheted off the walls for another minute, and then only silence vibrated through the air.

"Not at all," Whitney said again, more quietly this time. She plucked a bit of gravel from the tip of her tongue. "We might as well get this resort thing settled," she added, in as nonchalant a tone as she could muster, "or it's going to keep the tribe members at each other's throats until it is."

The ramifications of Mimi's absence were not lost on Gabe, either. He wanted very much to stay. When Hobie had first brought it up, Gabe had been dead set against the idea, but he had adjusted his attitude in view of the fact that Hobie had left him no real choice. It certainly *would* expedite the progress of the resort proposal, and it would avoid a messy scene with Hobie once Gabe got back to Seattle.

But those weren't the only reasons, and he was honest enough to admit that to himself.

The lovely Korean doctor intrigued him. She had intrigued him ever since he had heard her crisp, out-of-place Yuppie drawl issuing right from the middle of a group of barefoot Indian kids.

Who was she? What was she doing here? Did she have a life beyond the bustling, efficient twenty-four-hour medical care she delivered to these people?

But he couldn't help realizing that Whitney had made the offer expecting Mimi to be included. Now she was faced with a situation that some—possibly even she, herself—would call compromising. Probably she wished she'd never brought the whole thing up, but she was too polite to retract the offer once she'd made it.

For the second time in as many days Gabe found himself going against all his natural, predatory instincts. "It's very kind of you to offer," he said. "But I think it's best that I go." Then quickly, not knowing where this gentlemanly behavior had come from, nor how long it would last, he picked up his bags again.

"Well...well, wait a minute now, Gabe," Whitney said reasonably. "You could still stay. If you want to, I mean. If it would help settle this resort business once and for all..."

Gabe set down his suitcases again and took a deep breath. "Look, Doctor," he said in his most objective courtroom voice. "I'm not the kind of person you apparently think I am. I'm not a nice guy. I'm a user, Doctor, and I'm a taker. I'm not proud of it, but I'm not ashamed, either—it's just the way I am."

His black eyes glowered at her, warning her away. "But I don't want to use you. And I will, if I stay." His voice fell to a reluctant whisper. "Please. Don't let me use you."

Whitney shrugged as if the whole thing was of no consequence to her, as though her heart wasn't jackhammering in her chest. "For heaven's sake, it's only a place to stay, Gabe. And it's only for a few weeks."

"Whitney," he said, with as much formality as he could muster, "it would be very helpful to me if I could use your place as a base of operations for the next few weeks. What I need to know is whether this is going to create any problems for you?"

"Not at all. The house is plenty big enough, and I'm away all day. We'll both have our privacy. We probably won't even see each other except at night." Bad choice of words, she realized belatedly.

"What I'm asking you is," he said, in the same emotionless tone, "do you want me to stay?"

"Yes," she said truthfully.

"It's a deal then. Let me go tell Mimi about the change of plans, and I'll be right back, okay?"

Very okay, Whitney thought as she watched him jog away. The other times she'd seen him cross the helipad, his body language had been stiff, uptight. Now his steps were less militaristic, his posture almost relaxed. It didn't take a psych rotation at Harvard Medical to know this change was a good sign. *Very,* very *okay!*

WHEN SHE OPENED the refrigerator, a refreshing blast of cold air met Whitney's face. Examining the contents took no time at all.

"A pitcher of ice water. Peanut butter. Strawberry jam. A package of hot dogs. Hm-m-m..." She removed the plastic wrap from a bowl of something she vaguely recognized as having once been tuna salad, and without comment, deposited it on the counter behind her before continuing her inventory. "Eggs. Cheese—a little dry around the edges..."

She had told Gabe that she had enough food at home to whip up a meal, but that didn't appear to be the case. "Margarine. Tomatoes. Kind of squishy—never mind! A head of lettuce, pretty decrepit, too. That shoots salad. Oh, well, there's only a smidgen of dressing left, anyway.... What's this?"

She turned over half a loaf of dry bread that had been hiding behind the egg carton, and flipped it onto the counter. "Peanut-butter-and-jelly sandwiches?" she suggested brightly.

Gabe leaned on one hip against the sink, arms folded across his chest and an amused expression on his dark face. "Don't you *eat* down here?"

"Sure I do," Whitney answered. "At the Red Rock Café."

She spread her hands helplessly, denying any responsibility for the barren condition of the refrigerator. "The I.H.S. people told me to bring as much packaged food as I could carry, and my folks send me care packages every so often, but Gwe's been my main source of nourishment. I'll tell you—" she smiled ruefully "—I've developed a real taste for Indian fry bread, but there are times when I'd sell my soul for a Big Mac!"

Gabe jutted his chin, almost Indian-like, toward a framed photograph hanging on the wall. "Your... parents?"

"Yes. That was taken last year, on their fiftieth wedding anniversary."

The couple in the photograph were not Asian. White-skinned, white-haired and distinguished-looking, they seemed more like grandparents than parents.

"That's true," Whitney told Gabe when he said as much. "I was kind of a change-of-life baby, you might say. They were in their late forties when they adopted me."

They'd always wanted a baby, her mother used to tell Whitney, but God had never sent them one. They waited and waited, and they never gave up hope. But then they got too old to care for a baby, so they began to think about having a child instead of a baby; and then they heard about Whitney and saw a picture of her, and they knew that she was the little girl God meant for them. God works in mysterious ways, her mother often told her.

It was the fairy tale Whitney had been raised on. In a way, it was her own origin myth, since she had no other. Even after four years of medical school, she always pictured a womb looking vaguely like the interior of a Boeing 737, and birth as walking down a long, dim jetway, opening out from the stomach of a great, silver bird.

"And next to your folks—what are those?" Gabe set his glasses higher on the bridge of his nose and peered across the room. "Your Medical Diploma. Harvard, no less. And your Residency Certificate, also from Harvard. I have to admit it, Doctor. I'm impressed!"

He looked at her curiously. "With credentials like those, how in the world did you end up working for the Indian Health Service in this godforsaken part of the world?"

"I didn't exactly 'end up' here," Whitney corrected him tartly. "I chose to come here. My father's speciality is diabetic research, and I'm doing field work for him. Believe me, there's no place in the world with more diabetes and diabetic pathology than an Indian reservation. Especially this one. It's like a huge, self-contained laboratory. And in a year, when I've collected enough data, I'm going to go back to Boston and work with my father."

She paused, and her clear, forthright voice became a little...*wistful*, Gabe might have said, if he didn't know that was totally out of character for her. "I'll miss it, though. Clinical medicine, I mean. I've learned that I really enjoy dealing with people. When Little Mary Manakaja comes into my clinic hardly able to breathe, and I can send her out looking and feeling like a normal little girl ... well, I'm going to miss that."

"If you feel that strongly about it, why don't you stay in clinical medicine?"

"I intend to come back to it someday. But right now—" She raised and then lowered her small shoulders. The shrug was almost as wistful as her voice. "I owe it to my dad. He's expecting me to come back and go into practice with him."

Gabe started to say something scathing about family ties that turn into chains, but held his tongue. In the short time he had known Whitney, he had already learned that roots and tradition were sacred things to her. No sense going out of his way to antagonize her, especially when she'd very kindly opened up her home to him.

Listen to me! Gabe thought in cynical amusement. Seldom in his life had he avoided a confrontation, whether with petty criminals like himself in his youth, CEOs in boardrooms who tried to tell him how to do his job, or women after he'd slept with them and promised to call but didn't.

In fact, sometimes he sought out friction just for the fun of it, just to hone his wits and get his adrenaline running.

But he found that he didn't want to match wits with the likes of Whitney Baldridge-Barrows.

For one thing, he suspected she'd get the better of him in any battle of wits. And for another, he sure didn't need to provoke her to get his adrenaline flowing—just thinking about her did that, only Gabe didn't believe it was adrenaline that rushed through his blood when he thought of her. More likely, she herself would define it as hormones.

"I suppose that's how parents are," was all he said in a neutral tone. "I wouldn't know anything about it." He returned to the subject at hand. "Okay, so we know that your refrigerator's bare, Old Mother Hubbard—what about your cupboard?"

Whitney threw open one of the whitewashed kitchen cabinets and stood on her toes to peer into its farthest recesses. "Powdered milk," she itemized. "A dozen packages of ramen noodles. Oh—" she turned around brightly, a previously unsuspected jar of pimiento-stuffed olives in her hand "—a real treat. Olives, left behind by a former occupant, no doubt a person of gourmet tastes."

She twisted open the cap, plucked an olive from the jar, and popped it into her mouth. "Not bad," she said, nodding her approval as if judging an olive contest. Then she plucked out another and offered it to Gabe.

Leaning forward, he took it from her fingers with his lips. The simple gesture was intended to be playful, but the sudden tightening of muscles deep in the pit of his stomach turned it into something shockingly intimate.

Shaken, Gabe quickly changed the subject. "I saw a trading post in the village," he began, in a voice as rough as Billy's. He could feel the softness of her fingers still pressed against his lips, and the sweet-and-sour taste of her fingertips lingered on his tongue long after the olive was gone.

Whitney gave an inelegant snort. "Canned food and breakfast cereal, and a few fruits and vegetables no better off than mine! And everything marked up about 140 percent of the price you'd pay uptop."

"Sounds illegal. Or if it isn't it should be."

"Well, Jasper has to pack his stock in by horseback, just like everyone else."

"I'll check it out tomorrow, while you're at the clinic," Gabe decided. "Meanwhile..." He reached into the refrigerator and brought out several of the items Whitney had rejected.

She watched curiously as he lined them up on the counter. "Do you cook?"

"No," he replied, "but obviously, neither do you. One of us is going to have to give it a try."

IT WAS WHITNEY'S TURN to be impressed. She and Gabe sat on the top step of the porch, eating unexpectedly good eggs scrambled with sliced olives and cheese, and toast-and-jam squares with the dry crusts cut off. The eggs, Gabe said, had started out to be omelettes until they stuck to the pan.

"To make a real omelette, you need an omelette pan," he informed Whitney. "Or at least a pan you don't use for anything else. Otherwise they stick."

"I think you lied," she said, eyeing him suspiciously. "That sounds an awful lot like cook talk to me!"

Gabe grinned. "If owning an omelette pan qualifies me as a cook, then I guess I'm guilty. I *do* have a couple of specialties that I trot out on occasion, but it's pretty much macaroni-and-cheese, TV dinners, that kind of thing. Like you, I prefer to eat out."

"Oh," said Whitney, trying to phrase the question as though it was nothing more than idle curiosity. "Don't you have anyone to cook for you?"

Gabe looked at her closely, surprised by the question but definitely not displeased. "Like a housekeeper, you mean?"

"Well, yes." With great concentration Whitney picked at a slice of olive on her plate.

"Or like a roommate, maybe? Or a wife?"

"Yes," said Whitney, still studying her plate.

"No," said Gabe. "How about you?"

"I had a ... roommate, but we broke up a long time ago."

"That's too bad."

"Not really," Whitney said frankly. "It was completely a matter of convenience. We were just helping each other get through medical school. We shared living expenses and textbooks. As well as a bed. It saved us both the time and trouble of hanging out at bars when we needed a little ... um ... *companionship*. After we graduated, we went our separate ways without a second thought."

She paused again, trying to interject something personal about the man with whom she had lived for four of the most hectic years of her life. She could hardly remember his face. "He's a pediatrician now, up in Vermont somewhere. Skis a lot."

"I had a wife once, too," Gabe said abruptly. "But she was into causes—I think that's why she married me. I didn't want to be a cause. And then I was into money, and she didn't think that was appropriate for a Noble Savage. She's probably out saving the rain forests in Brazil now."

"Doesn't sound like such a bad thing to me," Whitney murmured.

"The rain forests need to be saved," Gabe replied. "I didn't."

He gathered up their plates and took them inside, returning in a few minutes with two glasses of iced tea. One he handed to Whitney, and the other he nearly emptied in a single long swallow, while he slouched on one hip against the banister. Silently he gazed upward at the majestic twin monoliths of Wii'baaq'a and Wii'bqi'i, where they overlooked the canyon from their own separate section of red sandstone.

"Those rocks look as though they could topple over any second. I wonder how long they've stood there like that?"

"Always, the Indians say. The spirits of the gods live there, and as long as Wii'baaq'a stands, the Havasupai will continue to be."

Gabe looked down at Whitney and smiled. "Sounds like one of Billy's stories."

"It is. Wii'baaq'a and Wii'bqi'i. 'Man-rock' and 'woman-rock,' he calls them. They figure in most of the Havasupai myths, just like our origin myths about Adam and Eve. And they're just as old as our myths— maybe older. After all, this is a world where the Apache and the Navaho are regarded as newcomers because they only arrived within this millennium!"

"Well, then, I wonder what they think about us?" Gabe said thoughtfully.

"By 'us,' I take it you mean the dominant white culture, not specifically you and me?" She laughed. "The Havasupai believe, as many Indian tribes do, that the presence of Europeans is a temporary aberration, and that the survival of the world depends on them preserving their ancient wisdom until it's needed again."

"Good luck," Gabe muttered under his breath. But as far as myths went, he supposed it was a comforting one.

The fading sun had slipped behind the canyon walls. Its last rays were absorbed by the red sandstone of the two great pillars, turning them deep purple in the lavender air of the long, slow twilight.

"This must be a nice place for lovers," Gabe said, still gazing up at Wii'baaq'a, "with the days so short and the nights so long."

Whitney glanced up at him, surprised. "Do I detect a note of romanticism beneath that cynical exterior?"

"Oh, I don't know," Gabe replied sheepishly, not at all comfortable with the side of himself that just being with Whitney seemed to bring out. "There's magic in the night for some, I guess."

After a few moments of silence, Gabe pushed himself away from the banister. "I'll just go wash up those few dishes. I want to earn my keep around here."

Whitney stood and followed. "I'll dry."

CHAPTER ELEVEN

"I DON'T LIKE IT, Dr. B. You don't know anything about this man. He could be anything—a rapist, a murderer, a thief—"

"Come on, Jesse. He's an attorney, remember?"

"Like I said," Jesse mumbled.

"Or more to the point, a half-breed?" Whitney retorted sharply. "Shame on you. Roll up your sleeve, please."

Dutifully, Jesse rolled it up. With an alcohol swab, Whitney sterilized an area the size of a nickel on his upper arm, then injected his morning dose of insulin. Jesse rolled his sleeve back down and buttoned the cuff, but still stood as if he had something more to say.

"This Gabriel Blade, I've seen his kind before. He takes advantage of people. He *uses* people. And when he's got what he wants, he's gone—"

"I know that, Jesse."

"You do? How?"

"He told me." Annoyed though she was at Jesse, she almost smiled at the surprised look on his face. "But it doesn't matter. All I'm offering is a place to stay for a little while. He wants to get this resort thing settled, and isn't that what we *all* want? Your people don't need to have it hanging over their heads for years, like that uranium mining fiasco."

She placed her hand lightly, sweetly, on Jesse's arm. "You're not going to give me any trouble about this, are you, Jesse?" She smiled persuasively, knowing very well that he could, if he chose.

The chief groaned inwardly, but no emotion showed on his stoic face. His dark eyes were as inscrutable as her own. "No, of course not, Dr. B. Truth be told, I guess we should all be thanking you instead." He pushed himself away from the examination table where he'd been leaning. "Meet me for lunch?"

"Oh, Jesse, I can't today. I promised to show Gabe the waterfalls this afternoon. Maybe later this week?"

"Sure, Dr. B," he replied. He walked toward the clinic door, his raven's wings dragging glumly through the film of red dust on the floor.

THE TRAIL THAT LED down to the falls was three miles long, and steep and rocky. It was also very narrow, flanked on one side by the wall of a cliff, and on the other by a deep, sandy arroyo. As long as he didn't look down, Gabe found himself doing all right.

"This might be a bad time to tell you this," he'd mentioned earlier, as he'd watched Jasper saddle the two unnecessarily large horses out behind the trading post. "But I've never been on a horse before."

"Well, it's a beautiful hike down to the waterfalls, if we had more time. But some areas down-canyon are out of range of my walkie-talkie, so I need to be able to get back fast in case of an emergency."

"Oh, I don't mind," he'd hastened to assure her, "as long as someone tells this horse that he's dealing with a total novice here!"

"There's nothing to it," Whitney had replied in her no-nonsense way. "Just give him his head. He'll follow me. These horses know exactly where they're going."

Gabe wasn't quite sure what "give him his head" meant, but he was more than happy to let his horse follow Whitney's. Riding behind her, he could drop his gentlemanly facade and allow himself to get a kick out of watching her tiny rump bounce up and down in the saddle.

Havasu Creek rippled along beside the trail for a short time, then forked off to the left. The right fork continued on the ledge between the high bluff and the deep arroyo. Farther along, the trail wound down narrow banks of talus and around the bases of huge broken red-and-gray rock formations. Clouds of sand, stirred by the afternoon breeze, gusted upward and then dispersed in the hot dry air.

Whitney turned in her saddle. "That's Navajo Falls down to our left," she said, sounding very much like a tour guide. "Some people think it's the most beautiful of all the falls, maybe because it's so isolated. I'm afraid we won't have time to go there today. We'll have to wait till next time, I guess."

So hidden in its jungle of tangled greenery was Navaho Falls that Gabe couldn't see it; he could only hear the great roar of the water as it rushed over cliffs and boulders. Closer than the roar and much more significant, he heard Whitney's gentle, musical voice. *Next time.* It sounded like a promise.

The sun beat down like a living flame. The dryness sucked moisture out of Gabe's body like a sponge. His eyes ached, his nostrils were sore and his mouth felt like cotton. The borrowed cowboy hat shaded his eyes, but made his head feel as though his hair were on fire. The borrowed jeans were stifling over his spandex running shorts.

They would swim in the pools at Havasu Falls, Whitney had told him, and right now, that was the only thing that kept him going.

That, and the beguiling woman in front of him.

Gabe really had little interest in seeing these waterfalls she was so eager to show him, but it was a new experience for him, having someone do something solely and wholly to please him. He was enjoying that part of this trek immensely. And when they got to these waterfalls, he'd deliver the requisite "oohs" and "ahs," and enjoy every minute of that, too.

If he didn't drop dead from heatstroke first.

Two miles below the village, the trail rounded a huge bluff of red sandstone and confronted Whitney and Gabe with a rock wall. It was covered by a dense grove of cottonwoods and willows, the greenery so thick and high that the sun hardly penetrated it.

It was the head of Havasu Falls.

Tying the horses to saplings off to the side of the trail, they unpacked the picnic lunch Gabe had provided and completed their descent on foot.

Huge boulders had tumbled down from the cliffs on either side of the falls, and from between these grew mosses, graceful drooping willows and giant ferns. They formed a sort of grotto that hid the falls as effectively as a wall. Gabe could see nothing until they had climbed all the way to the bottom of the grotto on the irregular steps hacked into the red ground.

The first thing he saw were the pools. He hardly believed they were real. Then, climbing down the last few haphazard steps, he came face to face with Havasu Falls, and he knew without a doubt that he had stumbled into some sort of incredible and exotic never-never land.

Great circular pools, perfectly symmetrical, fanned out from the single, vast and deep pool at the bottom of the falls, creating a mass of spray and foam and mist. Sparkling blue water flowed from that deep pool into the lower ones that circled it, and each one of those overflowed with perfect symmetry into the ones below them like a champagne fountain.

Rainbows on top of rainbows circled the crashing waterfall, and the colors flowed from one colossal champagne cup to another like liquid crystal.

The water was full of lime, which accounted for its brilliant blue, and the entire cliff behind it was plastered with mineral deposits patterned into giant, fantastical semi-circular shapes cascading down the rock face. The lime spray coated every root and branch in its path, turning them to solid, silvery stone. Even leaves were coated with stone, each serrated edge, each tiny vein clearly evident in the silvery filigree.

It wasn't what Gabe had expected. Three hundred feet high, it certainly was impressive. But it was something else. It was also delicate, as ethereal as a soap bubble blown through a child's wand.

He had never seen water so crystalline, shining in the bright sunshine like a faceted diamond, nor anything in nature so perfectly formed that it seemed to be an intentional design.

It looked enchanted, as if any instant the bubble would burst and it would be gone.

Gabe reached for Whitney and hugged her close, needing to share this strange moment of pure, unadulterated delight.

"Like it?" Whitney asked as they walked around the lowest, outermost cups of the glittering champagne fountain. "Of course you do—I knew you would!" she crowed in answer to her own question, as pleased as if she'd created the whole magnificent scene just for him.

Then, ever practical, she added, "Would you like to eat first or swim first?"

"Let's go in the water," Gabe replied, "before the whole thing floats up into the sky and disappears."

"It won't do that," Whitney said with a laugh. "It's been here since the Havasupai came, and they say they've been here always. And it'll probably still be here long after there's no one left to see it!"

While she spoke, Whitney had been nonchalantly unbuttoning her shirt. Though he knew that she must be wearing a swimsuit, the gesture seemed shockingly intimate to Gabe. He was almost disappointed when she shrugged off the shirt and revealed not the golden-skinned illusion his mind had conjured up but a flowered bikini bra.

Gabe felt like a fool, but not so foolish that he didn't observe with interest the rest of her disrobing.

She removed her boots by propping each foot on the opposite thigh and pulling, hopping up and down with an appealing awkwardness to keep her balance. Tossing the boots onto the grass, she bent to climb out of her jeans. When she stood, she saw Gabe gazing at her with avid eyes.

It had been many years since Whitney had been bashful about the human body—her own, or anyone else's. In fact, she hardly noticed bodies at all anymore, except to take note of some pathology. Now, with Gabriel Blade's unprofessional but undoubtedly experienced eye surveying hers with unabashed pleasure, she felt suddenly self-conscious.

"Well, come on," she demanded in a voice more assertive than she felt. "Take your clothes off, too. I don't want to be the only one naked around here!"

Her body was perfect, Gabe thought. So delicate, so diminutive that it was almost as though she was of another, more refined species. Her legs were long in proportion to the rest of her, and well muscled like the runner she was. Her shoulders were broad for her small stature. Her hips were small but womanly and so was the rise of her chest, while the midriff between them, revealed by the miniscule bikini, was taut with muscle.

In her daily uniform of white shirt and wide-legged khaki shorts, she was cute, almost boyish if one didn't take the time to notice the subtleties of her form. But in the as-good-as-nonexistent bikini, she was all woman. The instant, instinctive response of his own body left no room for doubt about that.

"Watch it, Doctor," Gabe warned with a strained laugh. "This isn't your office, you know. You'd better be careful about ordering strange men to take off their clothes. Besides—" he gave her a suggestive once-over "—you really aren't naked. If you were, believe me, I would've noticed."

Gabe kicked off his sneakers and unzipped his jeans. They fell in a heap at his feet.

How sacrosanct were the rules of civilized behavior, he mused wryly, as the two of them turned to the water and waded into the first ring of pools. Just a few insignificant wisps of fabric, which really served to emphasize the body parts they were intended to disguise. Just a few wisps of fabric between them, yet they were as inviolate as a suit of armor.

AFTER LUNCH, leaving their horses tied at the top of Havasu Falls, Whitney and Gabe hiked down to the even less accessible Mooney Falls, so deep in the canyon that not even mules could make the steep descent.

Early prospectors had named it after one of their own who had fallen over it to his death. The Indians called it "Mother of the Waters."

Through low tangled forest they climbed, slid and grappled another mile, until they heard, long before they could see, the roar of another waterfall. It echoed like thunder all up and down the narrow chasm.

An opening in the forest took them to the head of Mooney Falls.

Here, a curtain of water crashed over a wide ledge higher than Niagara Falls. The water plunged in an unbroken sheet into the deep blue pool at the bottom, and sent clouds of spray far into the dark green chasm below. Thick, mysterious folds of mist churned up from the pool, creating the same circling rainbows they'd seen at Havasu Falls.

It must be the clarity of the water that created those rainbows, Gabe thought. Or the minerals in it. Or the sun, shooting through the overgrown foliage, burnishing the sheet of crystalline water now golden, now silver, now a pale pink reflecting from the red sandstone walls.

Gabe stared at the falls with an awe entirely different from the enchantment he'd felt at Havasu Falls.

This falls was not as beautiful, not as soft, not as gentle, not as fairyland-like; but it was something else. It was dark, wild, mysterious.

Where Havasu Falls, with its perfect, round pools and its silver-painted, travertine-coated roots and trees, looked as though it was painstakingly designed by a whimsical and delicate cosmic hand, this falls looked as though it had been hacked into the living flesh of the earth by some savage primitive force and then just left to bleed.

The blue water flowed like the earth's lifeblood from this vicious, violent, magnificent wound. Gabe sensed emotions for which his logical mind had no words. It was terrible. It was chaos. It was the most beautiful, awe-inspiring thing he'd ever seen.

"The Indians don't come down here," Whitney said, as she and Gabe stood side by side, enveloped in the mist that sprayed from the deep dark basin. "It's a sacred place to them—it's where they used to cremate their dead. They still believe that the spirits of their ancestors sometimes float up and down on the mists and the rainbows."

"If spirits were going to hang around anywhere, it'd be here," Gabe agreed. In the interplay of shadow and sunlight on the giant dripping ferns, the thick, haunting mist, the strangely dark rainbows, he could almost see spirits himself.

"We can't stay too long," Whitney said in her sensible way. "My hand-held doesn't receive this far down."

Gabe laughed. "I thought *I* was driven! But you make me feel like I'm standing still! Don't you *ever* slow down?"

"Well, sure! But not in places where my walkie-talkie doesn't reach!"

He turned to look at her. Half-hidden by a veil of mist, dark rainbows circled around her through the spray. She looked for a moment as ephemeral as the soap-bubble beauty of Havasu Falls.

Gabe couldn't help himself. He reached out to seize her small shoulders and pull her closer. She came willingly. He knew he should make no demands on her. He knew he should be grateful for what she had already given him. But something inside wanted more, much more. And this primeval grotto with its crashing, churning waterfall somehow made both civilization and consequences seem very far away.

What Gabe wanted was to lay her down in the wet tangled grass and make love to her until both their bodies were limp with exhaustion. But he didn't. It's her life, he thought, and it was happy and successful before I came along. Who am I to drop in for a little while and try to change it?

Instead he held her by her shoulders, smiled down into her eyes, and said, "Thanks for bringing me here."

"I knew you'd like it," Whitney replied, sensing his withdrawal, though not the cause of it. She had been prepared for a kiss. When it didn't come, she fell back a few steps and ran her fingers through her damp hair.

"Maybe we ought to get going," she suggested uncertainly. "My hand-held—"

"Your hand-held doesn't reach this far. I know!" Gabe finished her sentence with a mocking laugh, directed more at his own indecision than at Whitney. He put his arm around her waist and swept her toward the steep rocky path that led up the canyon.

NO SOONER HAD THEY retrieved the horses and started back to the village than Chili's monotone crackled weakly over the walkie-talkie.

Whitney pulled it from her fanny pack and threw up the antenna. "Medic One here. What do you have for me, Chili?"

"Been calling you for an hour," Chili said, neither accusation nor criticism in her flat voice. "Winnie Putesoy is here. Says the baby is coming."

"How far apart are her pains?" Whitney asked, hoping against hope that Chili, whose main qualification for her job was that she was willing to show up for it every day, knew enough to count contractions.

"Says she doesn't have any pains. Says she never does."

"I'll be there just as soon as I can," Sidney returned, then dropped the hand-held into her fanny pack and turned to Gabe.

"I'm going to have to get back a lot quicker than we came down," she told him. "But don't worry. Joker will take you right back to Jasper's."

"What do you mean, Joker will take me?" Gabe echoed indignantly. "I'm coming with you."

Whitney nodded brusquely. Clicking her tongue and giving the reins a smart snap, she wheeled her horse around and urged him into as fast a gait as she dared on the steep trail. Gabe and his mount followed as close behind as the red gravel flying from her horse's hooves would allow.

CAMPBELL'S TOMATO SOUP, one of Gabe's culinary specialties—with handpicked wild chives and peppers that Jasper had told him where to find—was chilling in the refrigerator against Whitney's return.

Gabe knew little about birth and babies—only what he had picked up from movies and snatches of overheard conversations—but he did know that it could take hours, maybe even all night.

He also knew, because Whitney had told him, that mothers-to-be were usually flown out of the canyon long before their babies were due. For Whitney's sake, even more than for the mother's and the baby's, he hoped there wouldn't be any problems.

He settled in for a long wait, but it was only two hours later that he heard Whitney at the door. She looked tired, but in the deepening purple shadows, he couldn't make out her expression.

It was hard to live with a physician, he thought unexpectedly, studying her face, looking for subtle clues as to her frame of mind. You had to wait and follow their lead before you even greeted them at the front door. Had they had a good day, or a bad one? Had they saved a life, or lost one? This was brand-new territory for Gabe, who had never before in his life considered anyone's moods but his own.

He met her at the door with a tall glass of iced tea. "How did it go?" he asked warily, after she had drunk half of it down without a pause.

Whitney walked into the living room, plopped wearily onto the couch and gave Gabe a proud, pixieish smile.

"Great! I was really worried because the baby was a month early, and I don't even have an incubator down here. But the whole thing went so easily that Winnie could almost have done it herself—if she could have reached to catch it, which is about all I did! She rested for an hour while I gave the baby a physical, and then she took it home. Amazing!"

"Why did she even bother to come to you?" Gabe asked, ladling the chilled soup into plastic bowls.

"Winnie had some trouble with her first pregnancy," Whitney replied. "The cord was wrapped around the baby's neck. Whatever the problem was, she knew the baby would have died if it had been born down here. But it was born uptop, at Phoenix Indian Medical Center, and the doctor saved it. Now she makes sure all her babies—I think there are nine of them—are delivered by real doctors. It's become kind of a point of pride for the whole family."

Her pixie smile tilted higher at the corners. "The baby is a girl. And guess what? She's going to name her after me!"

Gabe grinned in return. "Whitney. Quite a moniker for a little Indian kid."

"Not Whitney," she corrected him. "Doctabee!"

CHAPTER TWELVE

"THE INDIAN HEALTH SERVICE was established in the early 1800s," Whitney told Gabe, "when Army doctors tried to fight smallpox on the frontier. Health care's been written into land exchanges and treaties ever since. The docs are overworked and underpaid, but there's not a more dedicated bunch of people in the world!"

The Havasupai Reservation, she went on to say, was designated as hardship duty by the IHS, and was served strictly on a volunteer basis.

Still doctors came—sometimes for a full year, more often for a week, or a month, on their way to somewhere else; but not *really* on their way to somewhere else, because Supai *wasn't* on the way to anywhere else. It was only a tiny green island amid hundreds of square miles of parched sandy seas.

Gabe looked dubious. "Why do they bother?" he asked.

"Because they're needed. Because they make a difference here."

The corner of his mouth quirked in a skeptical smile. "C'mon, Doctor. I don't believe there are really people like that."

Whitney looked at him for a long moment. "Well," she said finally, "maybe you've just been running with the wrong kind of people."

HARDSHIP DUTY. That part of it Gabe understood. A week was probably about as long as most people could take this place without getting cabin fever.

Once you'd admired the stupendous natural beauty, once you'd seen the waterfalls like stage sets for paradise, once you had marveled that a place like this even existed at all, then you were faced with the fact that there was absolutely, positively not one other thing to do.

This obviously didn't bother Whitney. She was so busy with both her medical practice and her research work that she didn't have a moment to flirt with boredom.

Neither did it bother the Indians. They lived as they had lived for centuries—cultivating their gardens and their orchards scattered throughout the canyon, and tending their small herds of cattle up on the plateau.

But for possibly the first time in his life, Gabe found himself with time on his hands.

Even schmoozing, as per Hobie's orders, didn't occupy much of his time. Schmoozing didn't work with these people, he learned very quickly. They weren't into small talk. If they had something to say, they said it; if not, they said nothing.

Most days he sat on the wooden deck of the Red Rock Café in the shade of the old cottonwood trees, and watched this tiny world revolve.

It occurred to him, now that he had time to sit still and think about it, that he had spent his whole life on the run. Sometimes from the other occupants of the streets where he had grown up hard and fast, sometimes from the law, but always from the seemingly inevitable fate that was forever hot on his heels, waiting, waiting for him to stumble.

Now, after thirty-five years of hard running, he had these few days to slow down and catch his breath. The only running he planned to do for the next four weeks was his morning run up Wii'baaq'a.

The rest of his time he planned to spend sipping Cokes on the wooden deck in front of the Red Rock Café, following the shade as it shifted from table to table, running from nothing more than the hot sun moving across a cloudless blue sky.

Only it occurred to him, now that he had time to slow down and think about it, that his success felt a little... hollow.

Perversely, now that he'd covered his tracks so well that no one even suspected where he'd come from, nor would dare suggest it if they did, there was no one in the world who understood the full measure of his success. There was no one with whom he could dare share those early years.

There was no one who gave a damn.

His mother was dead. He'd never given her much thought when she was alive—he'd understood very young that she knew nothing about survival. But lately he'd begun to wonder, now that he had time to wonder, whether she would be proud of him.

What about Rear Admiral and Mrs. McDaniel, who had employed his mother as a cleaning lady during those increasingly infrequent periods of time when she went on the wagon? The kindly McDaniels, who had come looking for her when she didn't show up for work and found, instead, him?

They gave him a job and a makeshift apartment over their garage, and tried to persuade him to go to school. They showed him another kind of life, a life he became determined to have for himself.

And when he left, he took everything they had.

Oh, not quite everything. Not the enormous amount of memorabilia the admiral had accumulated during his naval career, which collected dust on every surface of their home. That restraint had pissed off Chino the Fence and owner of the truck, who was sure they could get a good price for the admiral's past.

Nor did Gabe take Mrs. McDaniel's jewelry, which he thought might be the kind of things handed down in families, and which Chino the Fence insisted would be worth a fortune.

Although they would never know it, it had been the McDaniels who had unwittingly given him his first and only lesson in ethics, who had made an honest man of him in spite of his past.

From them he'd learned that he couldn't handle the guilt. After twenty years, he could still imagine how they must have felt when they learned that the boy they'd befriended had turned out to be just a punk, after all. It still shamed him to think about it.

He had used the money to go to school, as they'd wanted him to do; but somehow he was sure that the rear admiral and his wife would not be proud of him.

Gabe threw some change on the table, shoved his hands into the pockets of his khaki shorts and left the Red Rock Café, feeling about as restless as he'd ever felt in his life. He decided that contemplating one's own psyche, like contemplating one's own navel, was a distinctly overrated activity.

In desperation, he dropped in at the clinic, where a blank-eyed Chili had lowered her tabloid long enough to inform him that the doctor was with a patient.

Finally he headed down-canyon to hike to the energy-charged yet peaceful waterfalls. He wished that he too could find some balance between energy and peace.

Instead he found his feet taking the left fork of the trail and following the creek toward Billy's wickiup. He found himself crossing Billy's neglected garden, scratching the head of the dust-colored dog who slept in the shade, and then, not sure how to announce his arrival, coughing loudly and artificially, the way Whitney had.

And now he found himself inside the dim mud hut, sitting on a dirt floor beside a flickering firepit, on a day hotter than he'd ever known days could get. The mud-and-wattle shelter smelled of earth and smoke, but not the foul, gamy smell Gabe would have expected in a 150-year-old sod house. The dirt floor was hard-packed and swept clean.

On the opposite side of the firepit sat Billy, his bare feet practically roasting in the fire, smoking a cigarette with great concentration, as if relishing every last trace of nicotine.

"I'm surprised you have a fire on such a hot day," Gabe commented.

Billy dug his toes into the warm dirt at the edge of the firepit. He made a sound somewhere between a grunt and a cackle. Gabe surmised it was intended to be a laugh. "My body does not work as well as it once did. Often I am cold when I should not be. Especially my feet."

Gabe noticed that the old man's feet, half-buried in the warm dirt, were indeed precariously close to the fire. In this dim light, they looked bluer and more mottled than the last time Gabe had seen him. "Maybe shoes would help," he suggested tentatively.

"I wore boots when I worked in the uranium mines. But a man cannot live as he should if his feet do not touch the life-giving earth. And you can see that I have lived for a very long time." He glanced at Gabe's high-tops and again gave his high cackle. "You would do well to take off your rubber shoes when you run toward the rising sun. You would learn more quickly that way."

Gabe looked at him curiously. "Learn what?"

Billy shrugged. "Whatever you wish to know," he said.

Gabe was glad Billy didn't ask him what that was, for he had no idea. He was also glad that the old Indian didn't ask why he had come, for he didn't know that, either.

What am I doing here? Gabe asked himself, feeling foolish and also feeling tense, and yet, in some inexplicable way, feeling more peaceful than he had all day.

Billy waited. He knew the young *Hai'ko*—the American—would speak what was on his mind in his own time. Besides, it was not the Havasupai way to make a guest feel he needed a reason to sit at your fire.

Reaching into his vest, the old man brought out a pint bottle of Everclear. Politely he tipped it toward Gabe, who declined, then angled back his own head and took a gulp.

"I've never been inside a place like this," Gabe ventured. The shelter was dim, the only light coming from the low doorway and the smoke hole in the roof. From the lintel below the roof hung a few pieces of clothing, a small assortment of cooking pots and utensils, and a number of woven fiber bags that Gabe guessed, from their lumpy shapes and hard edges, contained a supply of canned goods.

Other than that, except for a stack of blankets and a cot covered by a sleeping bag, the wickiup was bare.

"That is because there is *not* another place like this," Billy replied with incontestable logic. "I was born here. My children were born here. My father was born here. It may be that my grandfather was born here, also."

"Whitney—*Dr. B,*" Gabe corrected himself with the name the Indians used for her, "tells me it's 150 years old. Your family must have been very good builders."

"Not good builders, I think, but maybe good at choosing a place to build. One winter before I was born—in those days we always spent the winters up on the plateau—the *hay gu* came into the canyon. They burned all the places where we lived so that we could not return. But they did not burn this one. It was so far from the village that they did not find it."

Billy took another drag on his cigarette, ruminated a bit longer, then continued. "The canyon is different in the winter. It is cold and damp. It is a time of long darkness, for the sun comes only a few hours each day. All the birds disappear but the ravens, and they wait in the bare branches of the trees, fighting over what they find dead or forgotten in the gardens."

The droning voice made a captive audience of Gabe. He wasn't sure whether this story was about Billy's grandfather's time or the present. It didn't seem to matter. Billy changed tense at will, making yesterday and today appear to be all part of one timeless panorama.

It was only the tomorrow that was unclear, Gabe thought. Would it be part of the same, seamless cloth that Billy wove?

And what, he wondered with black humor, would Hobie Stoner do with his guests during the winter, while starving ravens perched, vulturelike, in the trees?

"We never left the canyon after that winter. We were afraid the *hay gu* would not allow us to return. We could no longer hunt game on the plateau, and now we live on canned meat and government cheese. *Pah!*"

Billy slipped the bottle from inside his vest, and downed another mouthful. He smacked his lips and closed his eyes as a shudder of bitter pleasure went down his throat.

"Why are you telling me all this?" Gabe asked when Billy had lovingly stored the pint back in his vest. "You should be telling it to Dr. B, so she can tape it."

"I tell you this because it is something you must know. The little *bqi'gthegee* should know as well." He opened his eyes and his nutlike face broke into a grin. "*You* could tell her," he suggested, and cackled gaily. "Tell her it is a message from Supai Billy. Then she will listen. And while she listens, you can say to her the other things she wishes to hear you say."

Gabe enjoyed the animated expression that wreathed Billy's face. This is a red-letter day, he thought—the first time I've seen one of these people smile!

"What other things does she want to hear me say?" he bantered back.

"Do not tell me that the *hay gu's* blood has diluted yours so much that you do not know what a woman wants from a man! Even I have not forgotten that!"

He cackled again. "The little *bqi'gthegee* would know the meaning of my words. Why do you not know?" He made a sound of tongue clicking against teeth. "*Tsk tsk,*" he scolded, "it is truly a sad day when a woman is wiser in the ways of a man than a man is in the ways of women! She has opened her home to you. Do you not see that she wants to open more?"

"Not so, Billy. What makes you think that?"

"The little *bqi'gthegee* is no ordinary woman. She is of the Coyote Clan. Oh, you did not know that? Yes, she is *bqi'kathatka nave*—taught by Coyote. She is one of those who practice Coyote medicine—like those doctors you have uptop, especially for the mind?"

"Psychiatrist?"

Billy nodded. "Yes. A doctor of the mind."

"She is an internal medicine doctor, Billy. She treats your diabetes."

"That may be," Billy said, pursing his lips, Indian-style, "but she also heals with Coyote medicine. She goes right through your flesh and bone and walks around in your mind. That is what she has done with me. She has made me remember that I am a song shaman. That is why I tell stories I have not remembered for more than half my lifetime. Coyote has sent her to record my stories on her machine, to show me that the future of my people is safe. Soon I can die in peace."

"I don't think that's her intention, Billy," Gabe said wryly. "I think she intends to cure you."

"*Pah!* The only cure for old age is death. The *bqi'gthegee* knows, only she will not allow herself to accept it. But Coyote is wise, and he gives his medicine only to others who are also wise. When the times comes, she will also learn acceptance."

GABE WASN'T HOME YET. Dinner hadn't even been started, so he obviously had been gone a long time. Whitney was frantic. He wasn't an outdoorsman. He didn't know his way around the canyon. Where could he be?

The moon, when it did come up, would be full, but it wouldn't rise for hours, and he hadn't even taken a flashlight. Meanwhile he could be lying broken and bleeding on some trail leading nowhere, or fallen down a wash, or snakebitten and helpless!

Pacing to the window, she pulled back the Indian blanket that covered it and peered outside. From where she stood, she could see an occasional square of light shining through the foliage and the darkness that was quickly closing in. They were the windows of houses scattered in the hills, but they were so very few and far between, and the trails leading to them as rocky and treacherous as the overgrown trail to Wii'baaq'a!

The piping voices of a billion insects pierced the thick night silence only faintly. In the distance, Whitney heard a coyote. It was a yip-yip-yip, then a long, melodious howl that echoed like the cry of a lost soul through the labyrinth of rock, then disappeared into the empty desert sky.

Mooncallers, Billy called them. Their cry was such a lonely one. Was that just a human interpretation, Whitney wondered? Or was it, as Billy said, the essential longing of a creature condemned to be always alone?

Gazing anxiously out her window, Whitney felt a little that way herself right now. With no telephones, no vehicles, no way to get in or out, no help except what she alone could provide, she felt as much at nature's mercy as though there were really nothing at all beyond the borders of these canyon walls.

Then she saw a beam of light zigzagging through the shadows. She ran to the door, threw it open, and barely skimmed the porch stairs as she took them two at a time.

"Gabe!" she cried, running toward the light. Her little leather huaraches flapped madly at her heels, echoing like clapping hands in the still night air. Upon reaching the dark figure holding the flashlight, she flung her arms around his neck, laughing and crying and scolding all at the same time.

Gabe was laughing, too. "Wait a minute, wait a minute!" he exclaimed, catching her around the waist as she flew at him. "What if it *wasn't* me out here?"

"I knew it was you!" she returned tartly. "I've been watching for you for hours! Now put me down!"

Reluctantly he released her. She'd felt like no more than a wraith in his arms, but when she slid to the ground, she felt solid and warm and womanly against him. Gabe felt his body stir.

"Where have you been, Gabriel Blade? I could just—" He felt her small hands grip his elbows and try to shake him angrily. "I've been worried sick about you! Where have you been? And where did you get that flashlight?"

"As a matter of fact, it's Billy's," he told her. He draped one arm across her shoulders, and they followed the flashlight's beam home.

He told her he was sorry he'd upset her.

But he wasn't. To have someone worry about him, to have someone care about his comings and goings... well, it was something he had never experienced before in his life, and he found it incredibly sweet.

CHAPTER THIRTEEN

"THE CHOPPER IS a nice touch," observed Jesse.

He was sitting on the bottom step of the Tourist Enterprise, with his stocky legs stretched out in front of him, crossed at the ankles. A straw sombrero was pulled low over his disapproving eyes. "I wonder if he's going to start kissing babies next?"

"He will if he thinks it'll help." Whitney smiled. "Succeeding with this resort means a lot to him."

Somber-faced, Jesse regarded the activity on the helipad. Censure was plain in his usually stoic expression.

A half dozen Indian kids were unloading three times that many coolers from the hold of a Grand Canyon Helicopter Tours aircraft, then dragging them through the dust toward the trading post. "I think he's going to find that the Havasupai aren't that easily bought."

"I'm sure not," Whitney replied soothingly. "But still, they'll enjoy the ice cream."

"Is Billy going to be here today?"

"I don't know, Jesse. He's hardly getting around at all these days." She met Jesse's solemn eyes. "We're going to have to make a decision soon."

"Billy's already made his decision, Dr. B," Jesse said gently. "I think you know that."

Whitney felt Jesse's quiet empathy, but was somehow unable to accept it.

Where Billy was concerned, she sometimes wondered whether she had lost her medical objectivity. If a situation like his had occurred in her training program, she would have presented the facts to the patient, as she had to Billy; explained the course of medical treatment, as she had with Billy; and then accepted the patient's decision, whether she agreed with it or not.

Working on the reservation was so frustrating, she felt, and often so pointless. All her special clinics, in which she had taken so much pride, initially—the well-baby clinic, the prenatal clinic, the diabetes education clinic, the Friday night A.A. meetings she held at the clinic with an alcohol and drug abuse counselor who flew in from Flag—were poorly attended, unless she badgered people into coming.

Preventive medicine was not in the Indians' vocabulary. Neither was nutrition. Unless they were actually ill, or bleeding severely from some injury or another, or had a bone sticking through their skin, they didn't concern themselves with health.

And sometimes it seemed to Whitney that all the aggravation of working with the Indians, all the disappointments, all the sense of frustration and failure, had somehow become inextricably bound up in this one intractable and uncooperative old man, whom she had grown to love.

It didn't have to happen. At least not yet.

But it appeared that Billy had made up his mind to die.

Whitney's eyes hardened. "I won't accept that, Jesse. And you shouldn't, either." Her voice became shrill. "With care, he could have a lot of good years ahead of him. If he would just live in his house instead of that...that damned *wickiup!* Or if he'd go to the Indian Nursing Home!''

Jesse sighed. This was territory they'd been over before. He appreciated everything Whitney tried to do for his people—he sometimes feared that he was even beginning to love her for it—but he knew this standoff with Billy was going to end badly for one of them. And, since Billy himself was completely at peace with his decision, Jesse was very much afraid it was going to be Whitney.

''Would you like me to go bring him up for the talkaround?'' Jesse offered, hoping to get off the treadmill that discussing Billy's deteriorating health had become.

''Oh, Jesse, would you? That'd please him so much, to know that you thought of him!''

''I'll do it,'' Jesse decided with the somber smile that never quite reached his eyes. ''As soon as everything's under control here, I'll go.''

''Hey, you kids,'' he shouted suddenly in the direction of the trading post, where several little boys were taking turns giggling into his microphone. ''Cut that out now!'' He hauled himself to his feet, pushed his straw sombrero to the back of his head, and headed off to deal with the latest trouble spot in his world.

FROM WHERE SHE SAT in front of the Tourist Enterprise, Whitney continued to watch Gabe orchestrate the unloading of the ice cream.

He was surrounded by a mob of children, in whom the only signs of excitement were the shy smiles on their round faces and the eager shuffling of their feet in the red dirt. There were a fair number of adults, too, even more reticent than the kids, but just as pleased about the unexpected treat.

Gabe looked as though he enjoyed the role of Santa Claus. Whitney wondered if he truly did, or if he was just politicking? With Gabe, it was hard to tell.

He'd been living in her house for nearly two weeks now, and still she wasn't sure. So often he seemed like a carbon copy of Hobie Stoner—fast-talking, impatient and irritable. But there had been other times when she'd caught a glimpse of a much different person behind the slick facade.

Like when he'd kissed her goodbye, for example, when he'd expected to leave the next day. It had turned out not to be goodbye, after all, but the kiss hadn't happened again, much to Whitney's secret disappointment.

She thought about that kiss a lot—how unexpected it had been, yet how welcome; how tentative, yet how urgent; how much more she had wanted, yet how quickly he had ended it.

Every evening after she went to bed, when she could hear his breathing on the other side of the flimsy single-board wall, she thought of it too, and tried not to fantasize about the other ways it might have ended. Not that she would have gone along with those other ways, she assured herself—those other ways that she couldn't stop imagining. She was a doctor. She knew what was going on here.

It was that copper-colored skin, and that body taut with muscles, and the suggestion of how those muscles might be used. It was that hawklike Indian face that expressed a gene pool determined to survive, always a good choice in natural selection.

It was pheromones. It was hormones. It was chemistry and physiology and survival of the species, and it called to every living creature on earth. But she understood it, and so she could resist it. Although she had, on occasion, responded with enthusiasm when her hormones began to surge, it had never been something she had taken seriously. And she didn't take it seriously now.

She and Gabe spent every evening on opposite ends of the couch, he with his briefcase and a laptop computer spread out before him on the coffee table, and she with one of the novels in her small stack or else a medical journal propped open but unread on her chest.

Outside, the thick, muffling silence filled the canyon like cotton. Often Whitney wondered if the absence of sound bothered Gabe the way it had her, when she first came here. If so, he gave no sign of it while he concentrated so completely on the tiny click-click-click of his keyboard.

"WELL, WHAT DO YOU THINK?" Gabe's cheery exclamation broke into Whitney's reverie. He plopped down on the bottom step and reached up to hand her an ice-cream bar. "Look at 'em!" he demanded. "Think they're having a good time, or what?"

"Yes, they're definitely enjoying themselves," Whitney agreed. "Thanks," she added, unwrapping the bar he'd given her and nibbling fastidiously around the edges.

Gabe looked very pleased with himself. "Can you imagine a kid growing up without ice cream?" he said almost indignantly. "Even *I* had ice cream—though of course I had to steal it!" He didn't look the least bit abashed by the admission. "But these kids—there isn't even any to *steal*." He shook his head pityingly. "Shame, that's what it is."

"If those kids could vote, I think your resort would be a shoo-in."

Gabe looked at her, surprised. "Well, yeah, sure," he said haltingly, as if he had forgotten his original purpose in importing the ice cream, "but I figure the parents like to see their kids having fun. And anyway, those adults are no slouches when it comes to ice cream, either!"

"I bet this is costing Hobie a fortune."

Gabe shrugged. "He can afford it. Besides, the whole thing was his idea." His eyes twinkling, he dropped his hand to Whitney's knee and tickled it with a squeeze. She jerked it away with a most feminine squeal. "It's the *second* chopper that's strictly my *own* idea!" he informed her, with a grin.

MESSENGERS HAD RIDDEN all through the canyon, summoning even the most isolated of the tribe to the talk-around, and the village was full of people, many of whom Whitney had never set eyes on before.

Most brought food to contribute to the potlatch, so that the blankets spread beneath the cottonwood trees were loaded with store-bought provisions as well as traditional Indian fare.

Small children were assigned to stand guard against the slinking dogs that were as drawn as everyone else to the appetizing odors filling the air.

Groups of women worked together over charcoal braziers, which substituted for old-time firepits, fresh roasting corn, wild nuts and sunflower seeds. There were also pots of strong hot coffee, which the Indians seemed to relish even on this hot summer day.

As Whitney had told Gabe, a talk-around was as much a fiesta as an exercise in democracy. Together, they worked their way through the crowd to the food area, to partake of specialties they knew they would never have a chance to taste again.

They sampled jerked rabbit, venison stew—undoubtedly fresh, so undoubtedly poached—little green watermelons, sliced and sprinkled with lemon juice, freshly roasted piñon nuts, still so hot that the heat penetrated the little rolled paper cones in which the nuts were served, and burned their fingers.

The words that filled the air around them were Supai. The language had a soft, rapid, flowing sound, like the rushing water of the legendary stream that had taught the People, back in the dim reaches of time, how speech should sound.

There were few *hay gu* in attendance—only a band of hikers who had wandered up from the campground, the alcohol- and drug-abuse counselor from the Bureau of Indian Affairs at Flagstaff, Gabe, and herself.

Although not really herself. After all, she was not *hay gu*. She felt the old and disconcerting realization that she didn't know quite *what* she was.

Unlike for Gabe, it wasn't the simpler matter of mixed blood and mixed cultures. It wasn't her blood that was mixed, Whitney often thought—it was her mind. Physically she was Oriental; psychologically she was white. And the doorway between the two was the seven years she had lost. Who was Quan Jwa Gee, and why wouldn't she give even a clue to Whitney Baldridge-Barrows about the child she once had been?

AFTER THE ARRIVAL of Gabe's second chartered helicopter and the consumption of its cargo, and after the last crumbs of the feast had been devoured, Whitney watched Jesse mount the steps of the trading post.

A microphone and speakers had already been set up on the porch, which was to be used as a grandstand.

Jesse tapped the microphone a few times with one finger, then tried a few tentative "testings."

"Greetings, my people," he finally began in Supai. The crowd of Indians came together in the square, squatting on their heels or sitting cross-legged on the ground. There was the rustle of several hundred people settling down to pay attention.

"Welcome, my people," Jesse said, speaking in English for the benefit of the man whose presence had brought about this talk-around. "We of the Tribal Council are faced with a decision that must be considered by all of us. It is like the uranium mining, in that once in place, there will be no turning back. The changes on our land will be irreparable."

"Damn it, Sinyella!" Gabe, standing in the shadow of the eaves, hissed under his breath. He was angered by Jesse's association of the resort project with the uranium mines.

"However," Jesse continued, "the proposal you're going to hear today is one that, unlike the uranium mining, will have some benefit to the tribe as well."

"Thank God," Gabe muttered feelingly.

"With us is a representative of the backers of this proposal. He will describe to you what they have in mind to do, and then you may ask questions of him, and make your thoughts known."

Jesse stepped back, and Gabe moved to centerstage. He surveyed his audience with a friendly smile, which he held for a long moment, making sure the people as far back as the steps of the Red Rock Café could sense his warmth and sincerity.

"Well, I hope you all enjoyed the ice cream," he said, and waited for a corresponding ripple of camaraderie. The faces before him didn't change. *Right,* he reminded himself. *They don't like small talk.*

Quickly he revised his approach. "Tourists come down to your beautiful canyon from all over the world," he began again. "In the short time I've been here, I've met people from Germany, Great Britain and New Zealand. Think for just a moment how many *more* tourists would come if you had more facilities. And if you could offer not only more facilities, but more *luxurious* ones as well, you would attract not just tourists who want to hike and camp, but rich tourists with money, who would *spend* their money in your canyon. Now what do you think about that?"

Again he expected a crowd-wide ripple of interest. Again it didn't come. "Okay," he continued doggedly, "—let me show you what Stoner Fantasy Resorts International has accomplished with some of their other resorts."

He handed packets of brochures to a cadre of Indian boys recruited earlier, and they began passing them through the audience.

One of the flyers showed, in five-color glossy pictures, the amenities of Club Valhalla Golf and Tennis Resort on the shores of Lake Winnemeade, Minnesota. Prints of bare-breasted Valkyries in horned helmets hung over every fireplace, and the bathtubs were shaped like tiny Viking ships.

The second brochure featured Las Golondrinas de Capistrano Beach and Tennis Club. It was located only blocks from the historic old mission built by Franciscan friars on the southern California coast. The brochure showed all the amenities available there, including imitation adobe painstakingly hand-antiqued to look authentic, a party room faithfully copied after the original old mission chapel, and a flock of birds circling overhead.

Gabe hoped no one realized that the birds were pigeons.

On St. Joseph's Day—the day, according to legend, when the swallows are supposed to return to the *real* Misión de San Juan Capistrano—the resort staff had orders to release a few dozen pigeons to fly over the guests' heads for a few hours. It added atmosphere, Hobie said, and the resort guests didn't really know whether it was swallows or pigeons crapping on their heads. Or care.

Also pictured in the brochure was a bevy of bikini-clad bathing beauties playing volleyball on the beach. The accompanying copy cunningly suggested that this was a vast improvement over the real mission, which was, after all, nothing more than an old church.

Now Gabe heard undertones of laughter rippling through his audience. Puzzled, he looked closer. He saw that all the old men and the little boys were sniggering at the cluster of bathing beauties pictured at Las Golondrinas de Capistrano Beach and Tennis Club. Others appeared to be scratching their heads over the bare-breasted and horned Valkyries at Lake Winnemeade.

His presentation went downhill after that.

When the time came for questions, the brochures were still being exchanged and discussed gleefully. One old man asked where they were going to get the girls. Another, why the women in the pictures had rams' horns on their heads.

All in all, by the time the Indians who lived farthest away began packing their horses in order to make the trip home before nightfall, Gabe hadn't the slightest idea whether he'd made any impression on them at all.

CHAPTER FOURTEEN

WHEN THE WORLD WAS NEW it was covered by water. As the waters dried and flowed away, the face of the earth became dry and cracked. The land became deserts, and the cracks became deep canyons.

Now the earth was so dry that the People had nothing to drink, and they asked Coyote to take them to the place where the waters had gone. So Coyote led them to the edge of a deep canyon. Far below, at the base of the great rock walls, they could smell the damp of cottonwood trees and willows, and they could hear the rushing of the river and the crash of great waterfalls.

Coyote led the People down into the canyon. The trail was very narrow. In many places there was no trail at all, so that the People had to cling with their hands and feet to the sides of the cliffs. They made handprints and footprints on the walls, and those marks are still there today.

Coyote himself painted pictures on the rock walls, and in the little rock houses high among the cliffs where the People stopped to rest. These were to teach the People about the animals they would hunt, and the plants they would grow, and how they would live. And those pictures still remain. We go to them when we hunt the deer or plant the corn. They remind us of the generations of our lives since the Beginning Time in this place.

THE MOUTH OF THE CAVE was a low arch. Behind it, the high ceiling disappeared into shadows.

The rough walls, lit by what daylight came in through the cave's mouth, were covered with drawings.

The drawings were yellow, red and white—people, unidentifiable animals and birds, and enigmatic, indecipherable symbols. The people were not much more than stick figures with vague suggestions of clothing, but the animals were drawn in lush, vivid detail.

There were also small handprints, palms placed flat on the wall and outlined in white.

The beam of the flashlight Gabe carried created a large circle on one wall. "What do they mean?" he asked. Instinctively, his voice came out hushed, almost reverential.

Whitney's flashlight beam joined his on the wall. "No one is sure," she said. "This one looks as though it might have been a hunting shrine." Her voice was also as hushed as if she was in a church.

"Archaeologists call them pictographs. Picture writing. The Indians say they're messages from Those of the Long Ago. Some experts think they tell the myths of the people who painted them, and battles, and migrations, and plagues. Or maybe it's information for traders crossing the mountains.

"They're many thousands of years old, and the people who study them don't even know who painted them. They attribute them to the Anasazi, the people the Indians call—"

"I remember," Gabe interrupted, disguising the awe he felt with a strained attempt at humor. "The Ancient Ones, which probably boils down to 'Don't ask me, they were here when I got here.'"

"That's exactly what the Havasupai myths say. They believe Coyote painted them, to guide them down to the bottom of the canyon and show them how to survive there."

Whitney shifted her flashlight around the dark recesses of the cave. Every inch of rock was covered by the ancient paintings. Unexpectedly, her beam fell on a long dark crack in the back wall, so inconspicuous that she hadn't even noticed it the first time she'd been in this cave. She walked closer to examine it, and suddenly slipped through the wall and disappeared.

"Hey, there's another cave back here," Gabe heard her call. "When I was here before, I didn't see it."

Her voice sounded thin and faraway, as if it was coming through . . . well, through several feet of solid rock, as a matter of fact! Gabe followed her through the cleft.

The first cave opened up into another room with a lower ceiling. Not even a hint of daylight marked the narrow entrance. Without the flashlights, the interior of the second cave would have been pitch-black.

Like the first one, the walls of this cave were covered with pictographs. The ceiling was smoke-blackened, probably from torches that had served as light for the painters while they worked.

"It seems to go even deeper," Whitney said. She directed her flashlight toward the back of the cave, where there was another breach in the stone. This one was hardly bigger than a crawl space. To Whitney, it resembled nothing so much as a large mouse hole. She shuddered. "Who knows what creepy, crawly things might be in there!"

"Not to mention an old Anasazi or two," Gabe added, then a moment later commanded, "Whitney, come here and look at this."

Standing in the middle of the cave, he had been studying the pictographs when suddenly he brought his flashlight to a halt. It focused on a single section of wall. "What does that look like to you?" he asked.

She came to stand by his side. "Well . . . well, actually it looks like a man and a woman copulating, doesn't it?"

"Look there. And there," said Gabe, moving his light up and down the wall.

The rough stone was covered with figures performing the sex act in every conceivable position. Some of the drawings were sticklike depictions like the ones in the outer cave; others, like the animals, were drawn in loving detail.

The female figures had huge yawning vaginas and the males sported enormous erect penises and testicles that hung between their knees. All were grotesque, their sexual parts crudely enlarged and exaggerated. The female figures in particular were grossly misshapen, with gigantic breasts and buttocks. Some were nothing more than torsos—no arms, no legs, no heads, just basic and primitive depictions of the crux of sexuality.

Some of the female figures were drawn with flexed knees and outspread legs, with a second smaller figure positioned below and between the legs. They were obviously in the process of giving birth.

There were also animals involved in the act of mating, and surrounding everything were stylized drawings that looked a little like centipedes but were actually symbols of corn, the basis of life.

"I can't believe it," Gabe breathed. "Prehistoric pornography!"

Whitney stared at the multitude of tiny copulating figures, speech for the moment eluding her. The grotesque and simplistic drawings seemed to have a lascivi-

ous life of their own. They almost seemed to move on
the stony wall, and had a vitality that took her breath
away.

"This must be a fertility cave," she said finally. "Billy
talked about them. Even in his youth, he said, they were
no longer used, but sometimes women who were barren
would secretly go to one and offer food and prayers to
Kamuiugiuiue'ba—Mother of the Corn—in hopes she
might conceive."

Gabe whistled softly. "So this is a valuable find,
then?"

"Probably not. It's too accessible. The canyon is
honeycombed with caves like this, hundreds if not
thousands of them full of pictographs. This one's probably been entered and mapped by dozens of amateur
archaeologists over the years."

"Too bad. It'd really be something to stand in the ac-
tual footsteps of people who lived thousands of years
ago," Gabe replied, still moving his flashlight beam over
the crude but curiously compelling drawings. "It'd be
like...reaching back through time and actually touching them. Like..." His voice was vague, unlike his usual
brash confidence. "It's hard to put into words," he finished lamely.

Whitney turned in his direction, unable to see his face,
but struck by the reflective tone in his voice. For all his
cynical sophistication, for all his assertions that the past
didn't matter, she was pleased to see that being confronted by that past didn't leave him entirely unmoved.

"I know what you mean," she said. "Even people
who spend their lives exploring places like this have a
hard time putting that feeling into words."

She felt Gabe beside her, the heat of his body, the
sound of his breathing in the otherwise silent cave.

Moving a step closer, she slipped her hand into his. "These could be your own roots, you know."

These were new thoughts for Gabe. He wasn't sure where they fit into his construct of the universe. All he knew for sure was that the little painted figures on the wall gripped him, by the heart and by the soul, as well as by the balls.

They were more sensual than anything he'd ever encountered in the slick men's magazines he'd chanced to read. They were almost comical, like every cartoon he'd ever seen of club-wielding cavemen dragging cavewomen off by the hair. But these were *not* comical. They were almost brutal. They were raw and powerful, stripped of all the refinements of civilization. The sex act—not as a power game, not as a few minutes or a few hours of sensation, but as a law of nature. Immutable. Inescapable.

Gabe felt a shiver run through him, starting somewhere deep in the pit of his stomach and instantly radiating out to every nerve ending in his body. His heart began to pound. These little, ancient figures, copulating with such earnest concentration, stirred him more than he could express.

More shaken than he liked to acknowledge, he squeezed Whitney's hand, still nestled soft and warm in his, and pulled her toward the opening in the wall. "Let's get out of here," he said, in what he hoped was his normal voice.

OUTSIDE ON THE LEDGE, out of reach of the midday sun, Whitney and Gabe shared the provisions they'd carried up in their backpacks. Parching waves of heat reflected off the stone surrounding them.

"Don't drink that so fast," Whitney, munching a peanut-butter-and-jelly sandwich, warned Gabe, who was drinking from his water bottle as if it was a bottomless reservoir. "You'll get a stomachache. And you need to save some for the trip down."

"Yes, Doctor!"

Whitney had made the sandwiches. Gabe contributed a plastic bag filled with homemade trail mix he'd bought from Gwe. Gwe had assured him it was an authentic old Indian recipe—dried peaches grown in the canyon, almonds, piñon nuts, raisins, and other bits of twigs and bark Whitney couldn't identify. She had her doubts about its authenticity—Gwe probably came from a long line of snake-oil salesmen!—but it certainly was delicious.

The view from their ledge was a phantasmagoric landscape of color and chaos. The dark red of the walls was sparsely dotted with piñon, cactus and creosote bushes, so deep a green that it seemed impossible they could have grown out of cracks in this hot, bare rock.

Beyond the red sandstone of the inner gorge, the outer walls were a broken, tumbled wilderness of white limestone. They had been carved by wind, rain and frost into freestanding stone turrets, rocky towers and mystical castle walls.

Heat waves fractured the light like a prism. The fantastical stone formations, shimmering in the golden rays of the sun, looked like an ancient celestial city, hovering halfway between heaven and earth on nothing more substantial than heat waves.

Gabe wasn't sure he liked it. It disturbed his logical mind. He liked order in his life. He liked straight lines and right angles. He liked tall mirrored buildings, manicured trees shaped by gardeners' shears, flowers that bloomed in pots. He also liked sidewalks that went where you expected them to go, and highways that did the same.

There was no order in this bizarre kaleidoscope of broken shapes, this psychedelic paintbox of colors. There was no logic here, no method to the madness of nature gone wild. It was lawless and orderless, Gabe thought, almost indignantly, as if somehow this anarchy should not be allowed to exist.

He found that he couldn't tear his eyes away.

WHITNEY HAD NEVER been to Seattle, but she imagined it was a lot like Boston—wet and green where it wasn't asphalt and concrete, and full of trees, cars and people. Watching Gabe's unblinking gaze as he studied this alien vista, she guessed that it fascinated him the same way it had fascinated her the first time she'd climbed up here. And though he had been born and raised in one of the great metropolitan centers of the country, he nevertheless seemed to blend with this rugged land as if he belonged here.

This land they now sat on had belonged to his people before it had belonged to anyone. Although the tribes had wandered far, their blood was the same. All Native-American roots spread out from one deep taproot, which extended clear back to the Orient.

"What are you thinking about?"

Gabe's voice startled her. "Well, I was just thinking about you, as a matter of fact," she said.

She had been perched on a sloping rock beneath a low-lying piñon tree. Now the movement of the sun across the sky had taken away even that scant shade, so she left her rock and joined Gabe at the shadowed cave entrance.

Sitting down cross-legged beside him, she smiled impishly. "I was thinking that if you go back far enough, you and I could be related!"

"If you go back far enough," Gabe said dryly, "we *all* could be related."

"Maybe. But maybe that's why my work with the Indians fascinates me so much. Indians are really Asiatic, did you know that? The current theory is that they migrated from Asia during the last Ice Age. They came over an ice bridge that spanned the Bering Strait and connected Asia with North America. So, in a way, they're kind of my own people."

Idly, Gabe scooped up a handful of small colored stones and rattled them like marbles in his hand. "You're really stretching a point, Doctor," he said with a wry smile.

"That's easy for you to say! You know who you are, even though you've had to fight all your life because of it. But me? Where do I belong? Who am I?"

"You're an American, of course. You belong right here."

Whitney smiled ironically. "Do I look American to you?"

"Of course you do..." Gabe's black-and-white, right-and-wrong, good-and-bad, legal mind made him reply automatically. "But," he had to admit, after giving the question a moment's thought, "if I didn't know you, that probably wouldn't be my first guess, no."

"But I'm not Korean, either. I know, because I went there. Looking for my roots, as my mother put it."

The expression on Gabe's face made her smile. "Why does that surprise you?" she asked. "I'm not like you—I've always needed to know where I came from. So I went on this Homecoming Tour, the summer between high school and college. It was sponsored by the agency that arranged my adoption. We toured a couple of cities, visited some historical sites and a typical orphanage, and then we went home, each of us carrying a child who was being adopted by an American family.

"The whole purpose of the Homecoming Tour was to be a sort of closing-of-the-circle experience. And it was great, especially bringing back the baby. But... I didn't find any roots. I didn't feel anything. For the first time in my life, I was in a place where everyone looked like me, and still I was a stranger. I'd expected... I'd *hoped* to feel something more."

"But why?" Gabe asked. "You were adopted when you were a baby. Naturally you wouldn't remember it."

"Well, that's the point, I guess. I *wasn't* adopted when I was a baby. I was adopted when I was seven years old. There are things I should remember—people, places. But I don't. Those first seven years are as blank to me as if they never happened."

"You mean you have complete amnesia about the first seven years of your life?"

Whitney nodded. "And if it's true that the foundation of who you are is established in the first seven years of life, then the basis of what I am was formed in Korea, by people and places and things that I don't even remember. I don't know anything about my biological roots, *or* my psychological ones."

She paused. "It's a fourth of my life," she added in a low voice. "It makes me feel like... like part of me is missing."

"Maybe you're lucky. It might be worse if you did remember. Sometimes I think I can remember every single day of my childhood, and every single day was rotten. I'd give a lot to be able to forget the whole thing!'' Even now, the memory of those days had the power to make him feel small and helpless and scared, had the power to make him wake up in the middle of the night in a cold sweat.

If his memories were so bad that he couldn't forget, how much worse might hers be, when her mind wouldn't even let her remember? A totally unexpected wave of protectiveness washed over Gabe, a feeling he had never experienced before in his life except toward his mother, and then only when he was very young and somehow still believed he could change things.

He was again overwhelmed with the almost irresistible urge to put this little China doll in his pocket and keep her safe from all the known and unknown dangers of the world. That he had survived a life on the streets was one thing; that this delicate, beautiful, fragile woman—who must have once been a delicate, beautiful, fragile little girl—might have had to endure that same bitter life was something else entirely.

''For a beautiful woman,'' he said carefully, trying to work away the knot in his throat, ''it seems to me that you spend too much time worrying about the past. I also think you spend too much time with old Indians.''

He aimed for humor, but felt a rising tension in the pit of his stomach that was all too familiar, and not at all funny. His voice became gruffer. ''But spending more time with a...*younger* Indian, a half-breed, maybe, now that's another story. It's not quite the same thing, though, is it?''

He knew he was coming on too strong.

It's this damnable heat, he told himself irritably. He squinted resentfully toward the offending sun, suspended like a giant brass disk in the empty blue sky. By now its rays had reached every nook and cranny of the canyon.

Any minute, he was sure, his brain was going to catch on fire.

"No, it's not quite the same thing," Whitney agreed with a friendly smile. "But I think it's a very good idea."

Good idea? Gabe thought. *The fact that I want to kiss you senseless, tear off all your clothes, and try every single position those old Anasazi suggested in their drawings?* If she knew his true thoughts, would she still consider it such a good idea?

Abruptly he stood and walked to the edge of the stone ledge.

Hunkering down on his heels, he began to pick absentmindedly through the stones in his hand, tossing them one by one over the side. As they bounced off other lower ledges and finally hit the canyon floor, the sounds they made echoed like distant thunder.

Of course, he reminded himself, not many women were as honest and forthright as she was. Maybe being a physician gave her a whole different perspective.... Again he felt the hot pleasure-that-was-almost-pain harden his body.

Closing his eyes against the hot brassy sun, he tried to erase the image of Whitney's small, heart-shaped face, her bee-stung lips, her narrow eyes tilting upward like a cat's. Behind his eyelids he could see the imprint of a multitude of red and yellow and black shapes, writhing together in stony ecstasy.

"And I'd like us to spend a lot of time together," she said to his back. "Quality time, I hope. Even if it's only for a month."

"Not the kind of quality time *I* want," he replied gruffly.

His brain burst into flames, and with it, the civilized, well-bred straitjacket he'd been forcing himself to wear ever since the day he first realized how savagely he wanted her.

He stood, releasing the remainder of the stones he held in his hand so that they fell to the ground, then turned and strode back to the mouth of the cave.

Dropping to one knee in front of Whitney, he took her face between his two hands and kissed her purposefully.

He smelled peanut butter. *Rubbing alcohol, soap and antiseptic, and now peanut butter* some still-unscorched part of his brain noted. One thing was certain—this intriguing woman was certainly expanding his list of sexual turn-ons!

Her eyes fluttered closed, and a dreamlike expression settled over her features. "That's nice," she whispered sweetly. He felt her melt bonelessly into his arms.

Beneath the wilted white cotton of her shirt, Gabe could plainly see the shape of her small, high breasts. He had noticed from the moment they set out on this excursion that she wore no bra—hell, he couldn't help but notice!—and now that they were inches from his grasp, the need to touch them filled his mind to the exclusion of everything else. Only to touch them, only that.

For now.

"It *is* nice," he echoed, his voice thick. "*You're* nice." He took off his glasses and slipped them into his pocket.

Now it wasn't only Gabe's brain that was going up in flames. It was his entire body, possibly even that nebulous nonentity he vaguely thought of as his soul. He kissed her again, more purposefully this time, and suddenly thrust his tongue into her mouth, engaging hers in a writhing coupling every bit as erotic as those depicted on the walls of the inner cave.

Instantly her dreamy expression vanished. She caught her breath, and the yielding became resistance. She braced her small palms against his chest and pushed. Hard. Her narrow eyes looked both shocked and confused.

"This isn't what I want, Gabe," she said breathlessly, in a voice that showed no trace of shock or confusion, although Gabe saw a small contradictory pulse beat rapidly in her neck. "And I don't believe it's what you want, either."

In the reluctant moment it took Gabe to release her, she had become as cool and calm as ever. She sounded so cool, in fact, so sure, that Gabe found himself wondering if he had imagined her passionate response.

"The hell I don't," he muttered in frustration. He felt angry and he felt ashamed, but mainly he felt like a fool, with the proof of his passion still embarrassingly evident in his khaki shorts.

"It isn't that I don't find you attractive, Gabe," Whitney continued in her direct, no-nonsense way. "I do. If I was interested in having an affair with anyone, I'm sure it would be you. But I'm a doctor, and I know how temporary these...urges...are. I make it a point not to act on them. I think we have the opportunity to do something much more important here, and I don't think we should allow ourselves to be...distracted. How often are you going to have a chance like this, to learn something about yourself? To get in touch with your roots?"

"I told you, Doctor. My roots, or lack of them, are of absolutely no interest to me. They shouldn't be to you, either."

"I think there are things you'd like to know, if you weren't so damned obsessed with being a self-made man. And I could help you. I'd enjoy it."

She sounded so prim that Gabe was tempted to take her in his arms again and kiss her until her eyes glazed over.

Since that behavior would likely meet with even stronger resistance, he took his frustration out in words. "In the cave just now," he said crudely, "the only thing I could think about was getting into your cute little pants. That's what I *really* wanted—and I sure didn't see you so eager to help me with *that!* And please don't think I'm bragging when I assure you that you would have enjoyed *that* a lot more."

Whitney wasn't so easily offended. She recognized bluffing when she heard it. "You and I both know that we could get involved in a sexual relationship and it would be . . . fun. But in a few weeks it would be over."

"*Fun,* Doctor?" Gabe echoed disbelievingly. "You have a talent for understatement."

"Well, I'm certainly no prude. Sex *is* fun. I mean, I enjoy it as much as anyone, but there are so many things more important."

"Don't lecture me, Whitney," Gabe growled. "If you don't want me to make love to you, fine. That's your loss. But don't pretend it's because you want to direct all your energy to unearthing my roots!"

THE TRUTH WAS, he scared her to death.

Yes, she knew these urges were fleeting, but she had never before known they were so strong. Yes, she enjoyed sex in much the same way she enjoyed a good meal—a pleasant pastime, but not terribly important in the whole scheme of things.

Deacon had been her only serious relationship, except for the inept fumblings of adolescence, and it had been the same for both of them. For the four years they were together, sex was something grabbed on the run like fast food, a tension reliever at the end of a frenetic day, cheaper than alcohol for students living on a shoestring, and quicker, too.

So many other things came first. As a student, she spent most nights burning the midnight oil until two or three in the morning and then getting up at six or seven for classes. And later, during her internship and then her residency, so few nights were uninterrupted. Sex wasn't even important as a muscle relaxant then. If she ever had the chance to get horizontal for more than thirty seconds, she fell asleep.

It hardly seemed worth the effort.

Until Gabriel Blade had taken off his bloodied T-shirt in her office.

She'd seen more than her share of naked bodies, too, in all shapes and sizes, some possibly even more attractive than his, although just for the moment she doubted it. But none had affected her the way his had.

Why? Whitney had spent a lot of time since that night trying to figure it out. She hadn't come up with a scientific explanation yet. And when he kissed her today, her attitude toward sexuality had undergone an instantaneous transformation.

Suddenly it was no longer fast food, or even a seven-course dinner in a fine restaurant. It became a crust of bread to someone who was starving—not a tempting morsel, but an absolute necessity.

But that hunger surprised and frightened her, so she *had* resisted it. And now, lying alone in her bed, listen-

ing for his breathing on the other side of the wall, she fell
asleep wondering why.

SOMETIME DURING THE NIGHT, the squawk of her
walkie-talkie startled Whitney awake.

"Base calling Medic One. Come in, Medic One."

She grabbed at the hand-held and threw up the antenna. "Medic One here. What have you got for me,
Base?"

"Sorry to bother you, Dr. B," said the voice of one of
the constables. "Just wanted to remind you it's Saturday night, and old Billy's been mooncalling again. You
want me to bring him on over?"

Whitney sighed. "I'll meet you at the clinic, Stu. And
Stu—thanks."

"Figured you'd want to know," said the constable.

CHAPTER FIFTEEN

WHEN GABE WOKE in the morning, he was careful not to disturb Whitney. He'd heard the walkie-talkie go off in the middle of the night, and heard her leave the house. He knew she must have been gone for a long time because it had taken him hours to fall back into his deep and troubled sleep, and still he hadn't heard her return.

It was a stay of execution. There was so much he knew he had to say to her. And since he had no idea where to begin, he was glad for a little more time to think about it. As if the strained three hours hiking back down the mountain yesterday hadn't been long enough; as if the long night hadn't been.

Admit it, he upbraided himself, *you know exactly what you have to say—you just don't want to say it!*

He knew he had to apologize.

He had to tell her that she was the best, the finest thing that had ever come into his life, and he was sorry he'd repaid her kindness by treating her like a very tasty bone he thought he was entitled to just because he wanted it.

And then he knew he had to offer to leave, before she threw him out.

And he sure didn't want to leave.

Suddenly he wanted very much to explore his roots. And ride down to the waterfalls again. He wanted to eat Gwe Watahomigie's greasy fry bread and greasier hamburgers until they came out his ears. He wanted to do

just about anything at all, just so he could do it in
Whitney's company.

And he could think of no reason in the world why she
should give him a second chance.

The smell of the coffee he'd perked wafted through
the house. Pouring a cup, bitter and black to fortify
himself, he waited for the good-morning smell to drift
through the cracks of Whitney's closed bedroom door.
He finished his cup, poured another, and waited a little
longer.

Then, feeling lucky, and feeling guilty because he did,
he set out for his morning run.

The bell from the old Quonset-hut Christian church
was pealing as he passed, but only a handful of church-
goers were straggling in. The village was deserted except
for Big Jim's 'mail train,' a string of pack mules loaded
with creaking leather pouches standing stoically beneath the cottonwoods in front of the post office.

Big Jim was getting a late start this morning, Gabe
noted. Even the Red Rock Café's hand-lettered Open
sign was in place already. Big Jim'd better get a move on,
Gabe reflected as he watched the man double-check his
loads, or he'll be driving those mules the last mile to
Hilltop after dark.

Despite his mood, Gabe chuckled wryly to himself. He
was surprised at how quickly he'd become accustomed
to the rhythms of life in this place. He had learned to
judge time by the opening of the Red Rock Café, the
arrivals and departures of the mail train, the helicopter
schedule, the sun making its abbreviated trip across the
narrow strip of sky.

Of course, it was a very simple life. But there was
peace here, and charm of a sort, and roots so tenacious
that no one knew how deep they went, or how long they

had been growing. That there could be value in peace and charm and tenacity was something he had never considered before—could *that* be one of the things Whitney had wanted him to learn about his roots?

While his mind grappled with this new possibility, Gabe broke into a slow walk, then gradually increased his speed. He passed the post office, the mail train with its stoic mules and creaking leather pouches, and then Big Jim.

Not lifting his eyes from the strap he was tightening, Big Jim grunted a greeting as Gabe power-walked by.

"Morning, Big Jim," Gabe returned.

Being one of the more voluble Indians Gabe had met in the canyon, Big Jim offered a few more grunts. "Dr. B's too busy to run today?"

"I guess so, Jim."

"Not surprised," said Big Jim, still not looking up. "S'up all night."

"You were?" Gabe asked politely. He wondered why the man was sharing this particular bit of information. "Why?"

"Not me. Dr. B," Big Jim clarified in another series of grunts. Moving on to the next mule, he jutted his chin toward the clinic.

Gabe's eyes followed the direction of Big Jim's jaw. Through the haze of little light, he saw that the single window in Whitney's waiting room was lit.

Gabe frowned. A medical emergency? He took off at a slow jog in the direction of the clinic.

Then his frown deepened. If this had been Seattle, or Boston, or any other big city in the real world, there would be cause to worry about a woman who hadn't come home all night. But not here. *Surely* not here?

He broke into a run.

"WHITNEY!"

She was sitting in Chili's chair, her elbows propped on top of Chili's desk, and her forehead resting in the palms of her hands. As Gabe burst in she looked up, only mildly startled by his Rambo-like appearance through her clinic door.

"Are you all right?" he demanded.

She didn't look all right. Her shoulders slumped. Her head drooped as if it were too heavy for her slender neck. And her eyes were swollen—she looked as though she'd been crying.

"Fine. I'm fine," she answered. Her voice was dull and lifeless.

Gabe walked over to the desk. "Whitney, what's wrong?"

She dropped her forehead again into the palms of her hands. "It's Billy," she said in the same lifeless voice.

"Has something happened?" Gabe asked, his own voice suddenly tense. "Is he . . . ?"

"No, he's not dead. But . . . he has gangrene in both feet. We're going to have to amputate."

"Whitney, I'm so sorry."

She sighed wearily. "Well, we've been expecting it," she said. She started to rise, then instead fell back into the chair, and again dropped her head into her hands. "I can't face telling him."

She looked on the verge of collapse, Gabe thought. "You've been here all night?"

Whitney looked around as if she had forgotten where she was, "Yes . . . no . . ." she said vaguely, then noticed the gray daylight beyond the window. "I guess I have."

Gently Gabe took her by the shoulders and helped her stand. "Let's go home," he said quietly.

"No. I can't. Billy's here. He's in the back, sleeping it off. He doesn't know yet. I have to talk to him...I have to tell him." She wiped her fingers across her cheeks, erasing the tear tracks and replacing them with her usual capable expression. Then she turned and headed down the hall.

God, this must be the hardest job in the world, Gabe thought. I wouldn't do it for any amount of money—I *couldn't* do it. That Whitney would, could, and *did* overwhelmed him with admiration. How could she carry around the knowledge of so much suffering, so much pain in that delicate little body, yet give back only skill, and caring, and hope?

Feeling inept, useless, but most of all humble, Gabe followed. At the door to her office, Whitney stopped. Placing one finger against her lips to request Gabe's silence, she cautiously pushed open the door.

Billy was awake. "Good morning, *bqi'gthegee*," he said cheerfully to Whitney. "Good morning, *n'home'e*," he added, looking over her head at Gabe. His voice, raspier than usual, showed the signs of a long night of hard drinking.

The cubbyhole office reeked of stale whiskey. The ashen daylight fell across the old man, the cot he lay on and the heavy woolen blanket that covered him. It gave everything, even the bright red bandanna Billy wore knotted around his neck, a drab gray cast not at all in keeping with Billy's cheerful, broken-toothed smile.

He beamed expectantly. "Is it time for breakfast?"

Gabe touched Whitney's arm. "Why don't I go pick us up something at Gwe's?" he suggested.

Whitney nodded, then took a deep breath, squared her small shoulders and walked into the office.

"UNCLE, PLEASE LISTEN to me! Uncle, you don't have time to think about it anymore. The decision has to be made now, right now, before the gangrene progresses any further."

"*Bqi'gthegee,* I have lived for a very long time. Life must end sometime, and I am ready." The old man's voice was stern but gentle, as if he was trying to comfort Whitney instead of the other way around.

"Uncle," she countered, holding his wrinkled brown hand between both of hers. "Of course life must end, but yours doesn't have to end yet. At the hospital they'll take care of you, and afterwards you can live in the Indian Nursing Home. It won't be so bad, Uncle. You'll have a wheelchair, and you'll probably be getting around better than you do down here with your feet."

"*Bqi'gthegee,* I have had my feet for all of my life. I would miss them too much. Besides, how would I journey to the land of the spirits without them?" Billy smiled gently at his little joke.

"Please don't tease about this, Billy!" Whitney entreated desperately. "I can help you. Please let me try!"

Hearing a sound in the corridor, she turned to find Gabe standing in the open doorway. In his hands he carried several brown paper sacks.

"Ah, *n'home'e,*" Billy said, straightening up in bed and smiling with anticipation. "I see that you have brought breakfast."

WHEN THEY HAD FINISHED the overcooked bacon and undercooked eggs, the cold Indian fry bread and the lukewarm orange juice, Billy leaned back against his pillows, replete with the satisfaction of a full belly, and lit a cigarette. Then he turned to Whitney.

"I would speak with my grandson," he said courteously.

Whitney stood up. Her bowed lips were folded in a tense line, her teeth so tightly clenched the tiny muscles in her jaw stood out.

"Maybe your grandson can talk some sense into you," she said tiredly. With body language as stubborn and unyielding as her voice, she turned and left the room.

From the depths of his pillows, Billy beckoned Gabe into the chair Whitney had vacated. "There was a time when I did not want you to come here—"

"Not me, Billy. I'm not your grandson. You *know* that."

"I saw that our world was passing into time . . ." the cracked old voice continued, as if Gabe hadn't spoken " . . . that we had no place in the new one. I see farther now. I see that much will be different, but much will stay the same.

"No," he admonished, raising one hand to stop Gabe's words before he could pronounce them. "Let me speak. I am going to die. It will be soon. The little *bqi'gthegee*, the little female doctor, she knows much of the medicine of Coyote, but this she refuses to see. You and I must work together. I will not die until I have seen my grandson become a warrior of the Havasupai."

"Look, Billy, I—"

The old man raised his hand again. "Let me speak," he repeated sternly. "It has been many years since we have used *t'olvo*—the sweat lodge—for the rite of manhood, but I and some of the elders who still remember the old ways will teach you what you must know. Your spirit animal will come to you, and then you will run toward the rising sun."

Gabe recoiled. Visions danced in his head of sweaty naked bodies smeared with paint, beating drums around a campfire in the woods, under the influence of peyote, or magic mushrooms, or who knew what strange mind-altering drug.

"But Billy, what makes you think I'm Havasupai all of a sudden?" he protested. "You said before that even *you* can't tell for sure. I can't just...just act a part in someone else's ritual!"

"You are too much *hay gu*—too much a white man. You must learn how to be an Indian. Even when you return to your own place, your spirit animal will walk with you, and remind you of the ways of the Havasupai."

Gabe couldn't go along with the grandson charade, not even to placate the sick, maybe dying, old man. Somehow, he thought vaguely, Billy deserved more than that. "I'm sorry, Billy. I can't do it."

Billy chose not to listen. Sticking his cigarette in the corner of his mouth, he struggled to rise. "I will go now," he said, but found himself unequal to the task. "You must help me, *n'home'e*," he said.

Gabe was unsure how Whitney would feel about this, but the old man had obviously made up his mind to leave, so Gabe prepared to help him get to his feet. He bent over the cot and removed the blanket.

A rancid stench assailed his nostrils. He stumbled backward in confusion and then in horror, trying to keep down the breakfast he had just eaten. He stared at Billy's feet.

The misshapen lumps at the end of the old man's legs hardly resembled feet at all. They were mottled black and purple, and swollen beyond recognition. At the ankles there were several festering, oozing sores, lightly covered with gauze bandages; at the other, toes that looked like dead black twigs.

"You can't get up!" he whispered in shock, covering his nose and mouth with one hand. "My God, Billy, you can't walk on . . . *those!*"

"I can walk. You must help me, my grandson," Billy said again.

"Let's wait for the doctor—!"

"You must help me, my grandson," Billy repeated calmly. He edged the swollen black stumps that had once been feet toward the side of the cot.

Swallowing his bile, Gabe reached under Billy's knees and gently lifted his legs to the floor. Then he supported him by one elbow as the old man got painfully to his feet, retrieved his tattered sombrero and clapped it on his head.

Hobbling slowly, partly under his own steam and partly under Gabe's, Billy got as far as the waiting room before Whitney heard his shuffling footsteps and caught up with them.

"Billy, you can't leave!" she insisted frantically.

"I am not a child," Billy replied with quiet dignity. "I am a man. And I will go home." He turned to Gabe. "*N'home'e,* is my mule outside?"

"It is," Gabe said. Helplessly, he met Whitney's eyes above the old man's head.

Moving with painful slowness, the two made their way to the porch and down the steps, and then Gabe helped Billy get astride his mule.

"You will come to see me tomorrow, *n'home'e*?" Billy asked Gabe. "There is much to do."

"I'll come tomorrow," Gabe promised. "But Billy, I'm not interested in any rituals, or spirit animals—"

"Come tomorrow," Billy said in his rusty voice. "We will talk more. You come also, *bqi'gthegee*. I will dream another story for you."

Then he clucked almost imperceptibly at the old mule, which began to move forward at a turtle's pace. Slumped over the saddle horn, clutching it like a lifeline, Billy looked like a small pile of old clothes with a straw hat protruding from the top. He shifted precariously from side to side with every step the old mule took.

Gabe looked down at Whitney and saw that tears were streaming unheeded down her face. He put his arm reassuringly around her shoulder. "The mule won't let him fall," he said.

CHAPTER SIXTEEN

"WERE YOU ABLE to make any progress with him?" Whitney asked. She sat cross-legged at one end of the couch. At the opposite end, Gabe slouched low on the base of his spine, his feet propped up on the coffee table in front of the couch.

He looked surprised. "What progress was I supposed to make?"

"He wants to believe you're his grandson—I hoped maybe you might have some influence with him."

"I don't understand. Influence about what?"

"Gabe, he won't agree to the surgery." She threw her hands up in a gesture of total incredulity. "He won't let us amputate."

Gabe's eyes reflected her own disbelief. "Won't let you amputate? You mean he's going to live with his feet in that condition?"

"No," Whitney replied, her voice hollow. "No, he isn't going to live."

Comprehension dawned on Gabe. He let his feet fall to the floor and sat up straighter. "Without the surgery he'll die?"

Whitney nodded miserably. "Without the surgery, he has maybe a week, maybe ten days. And it'll be awful, Gabe. It'll be so bad." Involuntarily a shudder coursed through her. "And painful. And there won't be anything I can do for him...."

"And he *knows* this?"

"He knows. He's known it all along. This, and his blindness, are both complications of long-term diabetes, and nobody could ever get him to take proper care of himself. He won't wear shoes, and he's always injuring his feet because he's lost feeling in them. I don't believe he even takes his insulin unless I come by to inject it. And then there's the alcoholism.

"When I first got here I could see he was in trouble. I tried to convince him to go uptop for treatment, but he wouldn't listen. And now it's too late."

"But the surgery would save him?"

"Yes. That, followed by strict control of his diabetes at the nursing home."

"He says he doesn't want to die among the 'non-human beings,'" Gabe began hesitantly.

Whitney cut off his words with a decisive gesture. "Nonsense!" she exclaimed hotly. "That's just an excuse!"

"I don't think so, Whitney. I think maybe it's his way of saying that he doesn't want to live separated from his roots. You, of all people, should understand what that means."

Whitney looked up at him suspiciously. "You sure seem to know an awful lot about Indians, all of a sudden."

"Why should that surprise you? Isn't that what you've been trying to teach me?"

Whitney smiled for the first time that day. It was a tremulous smile, but a smile nevertheless.

"There's something else I guess I should tell you." Gabe looked down to study the nubby weave of the couch. "I'm leaving tomorrow."

Whitney sat up. "Gabe, why?"

"Because of yesterday. Because I acted like a jerk, and I don't want to act that way again, not with you. And I'm afraid the only way I can guarantee it is to stay as far away from you as I can. I only hope Seattle is far enough!"

"But Gabe, why should you go? What about the resort? What about your partnership in..?"

"Parkhurst and Brandenberg," he supplied.

"Yes. And what about Billy? He needs you."

"I've schmoozed about as much as I can on Hobie's behalf, I think. It's all up to the Tribal Council now. And Billy—well, he needs you, Whitney, not me."

"But I don't understand why you think you have to leave. Nothing has changed between us because of yesterday."

"I'm afraid it has," Gabe insisted. Restlessly, he stood and walked to the window, where he pulled back the Indian blanket and slid open the pane. He propped his hands on the windowsill and leaned out. The air outdoors was no cooler than what was inside; but opening the window accomplished Gabe's purpose, which was to stall while he decided how much he wanted to say.

"You're class, Whitney," he finally said out the window. "And I'm not really a very nice person. I've done a lot of things that I'm ashamed of. I got used to taking what I wanted, and I'm still that way. It's a hard habit to break.

"But I want to take something away with me when I leave here. I want to be able to think that, at least once in my life, I acted like class. And I really believed I was going to make it. Until yesterday."

Whitney unfolded her legs and walked to where Gabe stood at the open window. Because his back was to the room, he didn't know she had come up behind him until she gripped his arms with her small hands and turned him around.

"Don't I have anything to say about this?" she demanded. "Please don't leave, Gabe. *I* need you."

Gabe shook his head, determined to do the right thing, no matter how much it hurt. "You've had a rough day," he said doggedly. "What with Billy's problems, and no sleep last night, you need more time to think this through."

"No, please don't think it's because of Billy. It isn't. It's because of you. And me."

She looked up at him ruefully. "Do you know how hard it's been to sleep these past few weeks, just thinking about you on the other side of the wall, just listening to you breathe? I want to have sex with you, Gabe. I think I wanted you the minute I saw you. But yesterday at the caves..." She hesitated and glanced away, suddenly shy.

"What about the caves?" Gabe prompted.

"Well, I don't quite understand it myself. Yesterday, at the caves, you scared me. I scared myself. I never knew I could feel that way, so out of control. I had to stop and think about it."

"That's the thing about being out of control," Gabe said, laughing softly. "You're not *supposed* to stop and think about it. Although it doesn't surprise me that *you* would approach even *that* part of life scientifically."

She wasn't going to ask him to leave. He felt as though he'd been given a second chance. He didn't deserve it, and he would never have dared ask for it, but he wasn't about to turn it down.

Nor would he turn down the rest of what she offered.

The suave, well-bred veneer cracked—he had never felt entirely comfortable in it, anyway. *Punk!* he said to himself, half derisively and half triumphantly as he moved his fingers slowly, caressingly up her back, over her delicate shoulder blades and into her hair.

Cupping the back of her head in his palms, he tilted her face up to his. "Whitney," he said, and his voice was thick. "There's just one thing. Stop calling it sex, okay? That sounds so...*clinical*. Call it *making love*. It's so much more romantic that way."

Gabe felt two sensations at the same time. He felt Whitney's small arms slide around his waist, and he felt something shove against his back. Hard.

Before he could turn to see what was happening, it came again, pushing with such force that he staggered into Whitney, nearly landing them both on the floor.

"What the—?" he exclaimed, instinctively raising his hand to defend himself. He touched something warm, dry, and soft as velvet. Quickly he regained his balance and managed to turn his head.

And found himself nose to nose with a horse.

Its big brown head and neck reached halfway across the tiny kitchen. Its big mouth lipped him gently, looking for a snack. "What the—?" Gabe repeated in disbelief.

He gripped the halter rings on either side of the horse's head and shoved backward. The horse shuffled and blew affectionately into his face from one large nostril. Then in the background he heard soft giggles and high childish voices. At the top of the window he saw two small dusty bare feet dangling over the horse's side. Shoving the animal firmly backward, he craned his neck out the window to peer upward. "What's going on here?"

Whitney joined him, also looking up in the direction of the giggling. "Jeffery! Jeje!" she exclaimed. "What are you *doing* out there?"

On top of the horse, riding bareback, sat two Indian children, hardly big enough to fit their chubby legs over the horse's broad back. "You the man who brought the ice cream?" one of the children called down to Gabe between giggles.

"Yes," Gabe returned.

"Jesse Sinyella says you got a call at the tribal office," the child announced, then wheeled his horse to ride away. By the time they reached the hitching post, the silly laughter had begun again.

"Wait a minute," Gabe called. When the boys returned, smothering their laughter behind their hands, he reached up and handed each a dollar. "Tell him you couldn't find me."

The two children looked at each other for an instant, then burst into fresh titters. "We saw you 'n' him kissing," one of them admitted to Whitney, between shy giggles. "Is he your *swalg'baa'a?*"

"No, Jeje, he is not. Now, how about going straight to Jesse Sinyella and giving him your message?"

The horse wheeled with an abandon that made Whitney's heart stop. The two little boys held on for dear life, the one in front to the horse's neck, the one behind to the one in front.

Gabe lowered the blanket over the window. He reached for Whitney's hands and drew her close, placing her arms around his waist and his arms around her.

"That's probably Hobie," Whitney said.

"Who's Hobie?" Gabe replied. "By the way, what did those kids say to you?"

"They, well, as a matter of fact, they asked if you were my sweetheart."

"And you said no?"

"Well actually, the Havasupai are earthier than that, even the little ones. They asked if you were my bed-sharer."

"That could be arranged, too," Gabe said, his voice muffled as he took possession of her mouth, "if you're really sure it's what you want."

"I'm sure. Let's go in the bedroom."

"Now?" he asked, in a voice almost as raspy as Billy's.

"Of course now. Why not now?" Whitney's words were bright and eager and gay. Her eyes were very bright, too, and so was her wide smile. And as she took his hand and gaily led him toward the back of the house, her steps fairly danced.

The couch would have been fine with Gabe, or even the floor, but the horse's head in the window had already shown him how little the Indians respected privacy. As an afterthought, he reached for the front door and turned the lock.

Gabe was nervous. For the first time since he had learned about recreational sex at the tender age of twelve, from a sentimental old hooker who blearily assured him she was doing him a favor, he understood that the act didn't have to mean anything beyond an animal drive. Now, when he wanted it to mean something, he wasn't sure he knew how to make that happen.

Presumably the first thing, he thought tentatively, would be to get rid of the clothes. He reached for the buttons on Whitney's shirt and slowly began to unfasten them, one after the other. His fingers felt stiff and clumsy. When he had worked the last button, he pushed the shirt back from her shoulders, exposing her slender blue-veined throat and fragile shoulders, and the subtle curves of her breasts. They looked like peaches, new spring peaches, all pink and golden and delicious.

Whitney watched Gabe's fingers moving down the front of her shirt, and waited for the emotions she'd felt at the cave to overwhelm her again. Nothing seemed to be happening.

All she felt was sadness enveloping her like a fog. Her consciousness jumped frenetically from one unrelated idea to another, in spite of her attempts to concentrate on the sexual encounter she had fantasized about for so long.

... time, it goes by so fast... Billy's hundred years probably seem like the blink of an eye to him... too much time in the past... too much time with old Indians... with old Indians... Billy... Billy!

Suddenly her shoulders slumped, her head fell forward and she began to cry. Her arms hung loosely at her sides, and great, wrenching sobs wracked her slight body.

Gabe, somehow, was not as astonished as he thought he ought to be.

He should have known, he berated himself. He should have seen that it was too much—too much gaiety, too much brightness, too wide a smile. She was a lousy actress! And if he hadn't been so full of himself and his own needs, he would have seen it.

She'd had a long and terrible day, and no sleep the night before. She was probably running on raw nerves now. She'd said she'd wanted him since the day they met at the helipad. If that was true, then hopefully she'd want him again.

But it was obvious that she didn't want him right now.

"It's all right, babe," he told her gently. "It's okay. We don't have to hurry."

While he spoke, he began buttoning her shirt back up, watching with hot-eyed regret the small plump breasts he hadn't yet touched disappear beneath it. With a vague sense of surprise, Whitney watched as her shirt closed up like a film running backward.

Gabe slipped one arm around her shoulders and walked her to the bed, where he gently forced her to sit. Keeping his arm around her, he used his other hand to press her face against his chest.

"Go ahead and cry, babe," he crooned, patting her cheek. "You're overwrought, that's all. You're all stressed out. It's probably just sinking in about Billy—just let it all out, and then you'll feel better."

He didn't know where the words were coming from, but they seemed to be the right ones, because she wept into his chest for a long time.

"I'm sorry," she finally gasped, wiping her eyes with the back of her hand. "I don't know what got into me. It *is* Billy, I guess...."

"Of course it's Billy. You should know that. Plus the fact that you didn't get any sleep at all last night and you're exhausted, plus you've probably been working too hard and too long for the entire time you've been down here. I'm the one who's sorry. I never intended to add to all your stress."

"No, Gabe, you didn't. Don't think that. Please!"

"Shh. Don't worry about it. There's plenty of time, we don't have to hurry...."

He made her lie down on the red and blue Indian blanket that covered the bed and plumped up the pillow beneath her head.

"You just rest now." Standing, he reached up and pulled the chain of the ceiling fan. Immediately Whitney felt a rush of marginally cooler air.

"Gabe, you won't leave?" Her normally forthright, confident voice was hesitant and childlike; she sounded half-asleep already.

"Of course I won't leave," he announced, as if the thought had never crossed his mind.

"Now? I mean—now? Will you stay *now?*"

"Are you kidding? Who could turn down an invitation like that? Of course I'll stay. I'll stay as long as you'll let me." He lay down next to her on the bed, and took her in his arms. He didn't know how he could find this platonic embrace as exhilarating as what he had been prepared for earlier, but he did.

God! he thought with a mixture of pride and sarcasm, *if I stay down in this canyon any longer, I'm going to turn into a goddamn* saint!

CHAPTER SEVENTEEN

"COULDN'T FIND YOU, that's what Sinyella said. So where the hell were you?" Hobie's accusatory voice crackled over the shortwave radio. "Oh yeah. *Over,*" he added.

"Hey, you know this place, Hobie," Gabe bantered with forced cheerfulness. "Where am I going to go? Over."

"That's the truth," said Hobie, mollified. "Actually, I expected to hear from you before this. But now that I've gotcha, go ahead, fill me in on the powwow thing. Over."

"Well, it was hard to judge just what they thought, as a matter of fact. They didn't say much. I distributed the brochures, and they seemed interested." Gabe didn't mention it was the old men and little boys who were most interested, and then it wasn't in the architecture.

"There were a couple things they liked," he continued. "The proposed building of a high school went over real well. Over."

"Good, good," said Hobie. "And that'll give us a labor pool of workers to pick from."

"The estimated employment figures impressed them, too."

"Estimated. They understood that? *Estimated?* No guarantees?"

"I think they did. They also liked the idea of getting a better-equipped clinic and a permanent medical staff. Over."

"Damn right! The types of people we wanna attract aren't going to plunk their money down to get the barbaric kind of treatment *I* did, that's for damn sure!"

"One thing they *didn't* like was the plan for building a tram down from Hilltop. It's been suggested before by the mining interests and voted down every time. The Havasupai are afraid it'll interfere with their main source of income, which is the packing services they already provide for the tourists."

"Well, of *course* it will!" Hobie sputtered. "That's the whole *idea!* We might keep a few mule trains around for atmosphere, but they're too slow and inefficient to handle the amount of clientele we plan to move."

"And there's another problem. Alcohol isn't allowed on the reservation, and the people don't want to legalize it. Several women said it causes them enough grief *without* being legal."

Hobie chortled. "What'd they think? That we're gonna build a luxury resort without a bar? Are they nuts?"

"I don't know, Hobie. Some of them seemed to feel pretty strongly about it."

"Well, I don't foresee that as being a problem, Gabe, my man. We all know about Indians and whiskey, don't we?" He chortled again, then his voice took on the silky, touchy-feely tone that Gabe called his Hobie the Cat voice.

"It's *you* I'm a little worried about, Gabe, my man," he purred. "I was hurt that you didn't think it important to call me about the powwow. But when it got to be over a week and I still hadn't heard from you, well, it really started to bother me. And now, when I *do* talk to you, you're full of 'I can't tell' and 'I don't think so' and 'I'm not sure.' That's not like you, Gabe." His voice oozed concern. "What's up? Is there something going on I should know about?"

"Nothing's up, Hobie," Gabe growled. His jaws were clenched so tightly his teeth hurt. "It's just that these people don't do business the way we do. They're hard to predict. From the meetings I've had with Sinyella and other council members, I don't think there's going to be any problem."

"But see, there you go again," Hobie pointed out in his Hobie the Cat voice. "'I don't think.' I don't pay you to *think*, Gabe, my man. I pay you to *know*." Then Hobie the Cat pounced. "I sure hope everything's going all right down there. You really deserve that partnership at Parkhurst and Brandenberg. It'd be a shame to see anything go wrong with it."

"Hobie—" Gabe began angrily, then stopped. The silence lengthened awkwardly.

"Well, look, I got places to go and people to see," Hobie said pleasantly, having let the dead radio air last just long enough to make sure Gabe understood which of them called the shots. "You call me after the council meeting next Saturday, and I'll see you in Seattle on Sunday. Tell you what, I'll send the limo for you and we'll go out and celebrate, huh? Whaddya say?"

"Sure, Hobie. Sounds great," Gabe replied. He wondered why Hobie's veiled threats suddenly irritated him so much. It was Hobie's style of management—crude, but effective, and Gabe knew that. It had never bothered him before.

Was it only that being chastised like an errant child was something he hadn't put up with, even when he had *been* a child? Or was it because of Sinyella, sitting behind him at his desk, undoubtedly enjoying every word that crackled like gunshot across the room?

Or was it something even more basic than that? Was it just that a partnership in his law firm had come to mean less to him? No! It had been his dream since he graduated from Law School and he wasn't about to lose it now. He'd earned it. He deserved it.

But when he *did* get the partnership at Parkhurst and Brandenberg, he wondered suddenly, who was it that would step into the position—himself? Or a clone of Hobie Stoner?

IT FELT LIKE the hottest, driest day of the hot, dry summer. Whitney was grateful that Gabe had rented two of Jasper's horses for the long trek down to Billy's, although she felt sorry for the horses, who plodded alongside the streambed with their heads hanging low.

Gabe. What a strange and remarkable person he had turned out to be.

When he had first arrived here, she had been attracted by his unusual looks, but her razor-sharp instincts about people hadn't been colored by that. She'd quickly seen that he was acerbic, abrasive and short-tempered, with all the psychological trappings of a man who had structured his life so that his vulnerabilities wouldn't show.

Now she thought she might have misjudged him. That, or he had done a complete turnaround in the short time he'd been here. Not even Deacon, who now treated children and their distraught mommies and daddies, could have been kinder, gentler or more sensitive than Gabe had been last night.

Mortified, she recalled how she had led him on, letting him think it was sex—no, lovemaking—she wanted, when really it had been nurturing she craved. But Gabe had understood, even before she understood herself. And even though he hardly knew her, even though he'd be gone in a week and they'd never see each other again, he'd taken care of her, not advantage.

And in the morning, he was still taking care of her.

She had slept straight through until little light in a sleep so deep it seemed drugged. When she woke, it was to the smell of coffee perking, and bacon and eggs frying—all the things a physician would tell her patients to avoid but which on this particular morning were, well, just what the doctor ordered.

Riding up a hillock from a low-lying section of the streambed, Whitney's walkie-talkie went off, picking up in midsquawk as though it had been trying to attract her attention for some time. "... Base calling Medic One. Come in, Medic One."

Quickly Whitney retrieved the hand-held from her fanny pack. "This is Medic One," she said in answer to the barely intelligible summons. "What have you got for me, Base?"

"... got a tourist, drunk and disorderly in the campgrounds," said Stu, his voice cutting in and out. "We had to cuff him, and now he's complaining that his wrist's broke."

"Is it, can you tell?"

"Naw," Stu assured her. "Just swole pretty bad from the fight the s.o.b. put up. Decked Vernon."

"Is Vernon okay?"

"Yeah, takes more than a drunk kid to keep Vernon down. What you want I should do with this guy?"

"Put him in the lockup," Whitney decided. "I'm down at Billy's, and I'm not going to waste my time with some kid who thinks the laws don't apply to him. I'll drop by when I get back up. Over and out."

THEY FOUND BILLY in his usual place, stretched out in the hammock between the two ancient cottonwoods. He was asleep.

Whitney pulled up the wooden bench Billy kept in front of his house and sat beside the hammock. The last few white petals of the season drifted down from the trees to catch in her hair.

"Uncle," she said, gently shaking his arm. "Uncle, wake up. It's Dr. B and Gabe."

The dog snoring fitfully beneath Billy's hammock woke first. He cocked one eye open, thumped his tail a few times in lackadaisical acknowledgment, then let his eye fall closed and resumed his snoring.

Billy woke up more slowly. "Ah, *bqi'gthegee,* it is good you have come," he smiled sleepily. "Has my grandson come with you?"

"Yes, Billy, I'm here, too," Gabe announced as he leaned on one hip against the tree at the foot of Billy's hammock.

Whitney looked up at him, surprised, then smiled gratefully. Only after the fact did Gabe realize he had responded to Billy's question as naturally as if he really were the old man's grandson.

"Are you cold, Uncle?" Whitney asked. The temperature was easily 110 degrees, but Billy was covered by a heavy woven blanket and still he was shivering. Feeling his forehead with the back of her hand, she estimated that he was running a low-grade fever.

"Only my feet are cold." It was phantom sensation, Whitney knew, for Billy couldn't even feel his feet anymore.

She took out her glucose-testing kit, pricked his finger, then put a drop of blood on a test strip and waited for the strip to indicate his blood-glucose level.

"Uncle, your blood sugar is extremely high," she said severely. "Did you take your insulin today?"

He nodded.

"I'm going to give you some more insulin, Uncle, to try to bring that blood sugar down."

"Whatever you think, *bqi'gthegee*," Billy agreed. Whitney drew the clear liquid medication into a syringe, cleaned a small circle on his arm with an alcohol swab and injected the insulin into his emaciated flesh.

Billy patted her hand. Then slowly, painfully, he pulled himself upright, hauling his legs and almost useless feet over the side of the hammock. An empty mason jar clattered to the ground.

Who, she wondered angrily, had brought Billy whiskey, knowing, as the whole tribe did by now, how ill he was? Fortunately, his misguided supplier mustn't have brought too much, because Billy didn't appear to be *very* intoxicated.

The first thing he did was light up a cigarette. He'd begun smoking at about the age of six, he'd told Whitney once. He'd begun drinking whiskey at about the same age. It was a miracle that he had lived so long.

She studied the miracle that was old Supai Billy Hamadreeq, whom she had come to regard as the taproot of his tribe.

Almost one hundred years old, give or take a few. He had been born the year the first white schoolteacher came to live in the canyon, to teach the Indians the ways of the *hay gu*. He had been a man when his tribe was confined to this tiny reservation. He had seen his people dwindle to the verge of extinction, and seen them walk the long road back.

"The fasting is itself not so important in the ceremony," she heard Billy say to Gabe, "except it is the surest way to ask the spirit animal to reveal himself. Maybe we can think of another way. Jimsonweed still grows down-canyon, in the place where the creek joins Hackataia. It is possible—"

Hackataia—"Roaring Noise." The mighty Colorado, Whitney translated without even having to think about it. But fasting? Jimsonweed? Spirit animal? What did those things have to do with Gabe?

And then, suddenly, it dawned on her.

Billy was offering Gabe the rite of manhood. The ritual figured prominently in many of Billy's stories, but it was performed so seldom now that it had almost become the stuff of legends.

"Billy, I wish you'd understand," Gabe said wearily. "I can't do it. It wouldn't be fair to you if I did. I'm not your grandson."

Gabe wondered why he was being so adamant about the whole thing. It would be so simple, really. Chew—or smoke, or drink, or snort, or however it was you ingested jimsonweed—wait until some animal showed up to tell you it was your spirit guide, then go home and forget the whole thing.

He was very tempted to do it for the old man. After all, who could it hurt? But somehow it felt wrong. It felt disrespectful, after the long life Billy had led, the trials and tribulations he had overcome, to let him go out in a fantasyland like one of Hobie Stoner's theme resorts.

He deserved to die with the dignity of the truth.

"If I went through this ritual thing, it'd be a lie, Billy," he reiterated. "You have a grandson out there somewhere, maybe, but it isn't me. I wish you'd understand that."

"I do understand what you say. You are an honorable man. You do not want to take what is not yours. But how can you know that for sure that it is *not* yours? And if you are Havasupai or if you are not, it is still a good thing to have an animal spirit to guide you through your days."

"Look, Billy, I'm real sorry...."

"Do not be sorry, *n'home'e*. Every man can do only what he can do. We will talk more another time." He gave Gabe his sweet, snaggle-toothed smile, then turned to include Whitney in their conversation.

"Jesse Sinyella came to sit with me today."

"Oh?" said Whitney, pleased. "What did he come about?" She hoped that Jesse had been able to sway Billy in the direction of agreeing to the surgery.

"He came to sit with me, that is all."

Whitney knew enough about Indian traditions to know what that meant. Jesse had come to pay his respects. He had come to say goodbye. She had believed that she and Jesse were on the same side. Now she realized, with a sense of outrage and betrayal, that it was Jesse who had brought Billy the whiskey.

How could he *do* that?

Jesse—the most modern, the most educated, the most farsighted person on the entire reservation—breaking tribal law to bring whiskey to a dying old man to ease his journey to the spirit world! Well, she was going to fool Jesse! She was going to fool all of them! Billy was *not* going to die. Not yet, anyway.

The miracle could go on, at least for a little while longer. Who knew how many years he could have ahead of him? Four? Five? Ten, maybe? And they could be good years, peaceful and pain-free, where he would be comfortable and well cared for in the Indian Nursing Home.

"Bqi'gthegee." Billy sensed her inner turmoil and interrupted her peacefully. "Little Coyote Doctor, I am very grateful to you for returning my grandson to me. It is the only medicine I need now. Coyote was wise in choosing you to bear his medicine sticks, for you know much for one so young. There is only one thing Coyote did not teach you, and that is something each must learn alone. He did not teach you about death, which is as necessary to life as birth.

"Do not look so unhappy, *bqi'gthegee.* I have a gift for you. I have dreamed another Coyote story." He smiled sweetly, and gestured courteously toward Whitney's fanny pack, where she carried the tape recorder. "It is a story from the Beginning Time. I have not dreamed it for many years."

Whitney produced her recorder and switched it on.

Sitting at the edge of his hammock, Billy began to rock back and forth, closing his near-blind eyes and directing his thoughts both inward and backward.

The People were sad because those they loved died and went away to the land of the spirits. Everywhere Coyote heard the sounds of mourning....

WHEN GABE PULLED BACK the red blanket that covered his bedroom window, he could see several stars, brighter than any he had ever seen uptop. They seemed closer, too, as if he could reach up and touch each one on its points.

From where he lay in his bed, with his hands folded behind his head, he could see a slice of moon, too, the rest hidden behind a towering red wall. In the distance he heard a coyote howl. The lonely sound echoed through the rocks, returning magnified a thousandfold.

It didn't sound like a coyote, Gabe thought. The echoes of each howl were overtaken by the echoes of the next, and the resulting pulsating din sounded like demons from hell turned loose in the hills.

Gabe was having a restless night, the kind of night that had become more and more frequent lately.

It wasn't the resort deadline that kept sleep at bay, although Gabe knew he should be concerned about that. Despite what he'd said to Hobie, he didn't feel at all confident about the vote, and what's more, he didn't even care very much.

What did keep him awake was the disturbing realization that he was letting a golden opportunity slip away. He'd found a woman he wanted more than any other woman he'd ever known, and he seemed totally unable to make a move on her.

It was the gentlemanly thing.

Tonight, for example. After he and Whitney had ridden up from Billy's and returned Jasper's horses, they'd stopped for a late dinner at the Red Rock Café.

Over fry-bread fajitas, and against his better judgment, because basically he believed that Billy had every right to refuse treatment if he chose, Gabe had come up with another approach Whitney might use to get the old man to agree to surgery.

"Maybe you could convince him that he has an obligation to make sure his stories survive," Gabe suggested. "If he believes he has a purpose to live for, he just might decide to give it a try. And I'm sure there'll be no shortage of anthropology majors at Arizona State who'd be eager to work with him.''

"What a marvelous idea!" Whitney had leaned across the booth, thrown her arms around his neck and attached her lips to his with an enthusiasm that took his breath away. "Now why on earth didn't I think of that?"

"I guess it takes a brilliant legal mind," he replied modestly.

After that, they had strolled home arm in arm through the deepening twilight.

But when they got there, they had seated themselves at opposite ends of the couch, as self-conscious as teenagers with a parent in the next room.

The gentlemanly thing, again.

He should get up and go to her room, he thought as he tossed and turned under the blue starlight. He should get up and go to her room, open the door without knocking...

Then he heard a faint click. It sounded like the spring of his doorknob. Then he heard feet padding across the linoleum, becoming inaudible as they stepped onto the Indian rug beside his bed.

Backlit by starlight and by the sliver of moonlight that streamed through the window, a wraith stood before him. A fairy, an enchanted creature covered by nothing more than a filmy wisp of white.

"Gabe?" he heard Whitney say hesitantly in her soft, fluting voice.

Her diaphanous gown was a simple gauze nightshirt touched at the neck and sleeves with lace, and reaching only to midthigh. The pale light made the thin fabric as sheer as cellophane, and outlined her slender form with unabashed precision.

As though in a dream, Gabe reached out to touch her, tentatively, as if assuring himself that she was not just a figment of his imagination. Delicate though she looked, standing beside his bed in an envelope of blue starlight, his wondering, wandering hand proved that she was solid and warm and real.

He felt like the callowest of adolescents! "Whitney, I didn't plan on this...when I came down here. I don't have any..."

"Protection?" she said matter-of-factly. "Never mind. I do." She gave a quick and silent thanks to Lone Arrow, whose middle-of-the-night visit a month ago had initiated the idea of keeping a supply of condoms in the house.

Throwing back the blanket that covered him, Gabe stood, and wordlessly pulled her against him. He wore only jockey briefs, and there was no hiding the fact that he was instantly, fully aroused.

"You have more courage than I do," he said softly, admiringly. "I was lying here fantasizing about this very thing, and you go and do it."

As she tilted her face upward to request a kiss, her lips were parted and provocative. "Maybe I want you more than you want me," she said, in a voice that held more than a hint of a challenge.

"Not possible," Gabe stated unequivocally.

"Prove it," she challenged again, and this time there was no mistaking the seductive invitation in her voice.

Without speaking, Gabe took her hand and placed it where his proof throbbed, hot and hard and heavy. Whitney's small fingers closed around him. His knees almost buckled. Instead of fighting it, he went with the motion, letting himself fall back onto the bed, pulling Whitney down with him.

Lying on her stomach on top of him, she was light as a feather. Featherlike, too, were her warm lips, as she trailed them from his mouth to his chest.

"I want you so much," she said in a breathless voice, her body in its gossamer covering writhing provocatively against him. "I thought I knew all about it, but I never knew I could want this much."

She was on fire. She had been, even before she came into his room. Gabe wondered if it was possible that she'd been on fire as long as he had? You don't build up a heat like this in one night, he told himself in his last rational thought.

Moving his hands up and down her back in a paroxysm of pleasure, he finally fitted them around her buttocks, pinning her against him so that she felt his hard masculinity waiting between her thighs. With importunate fingers he raised the nightshirt, gathered it up over her thighs and buttocks to her shoulders, then whisked it over her head and tossed it on the floor.

Then with a single, sure twist, he rolled her over. Whitney found herself on her back, with Gabe's hard body beside her. Propping himself up on one elbow, he leaned possessively over her.

"You're so tiny, so perfect," he whispered hoarsely. "Like a little China doll. I'm almost afraid to touch you. I'm afraid you'll break...."

"I'm not a doll, Gabe, I'm a woman. And I won't break." To prove her point, she pulled his head down and met his mouth with a kiss that made his toes curl.

The reality was better than the fantasies had ever been.

Gabe had accurately imagined how her dainty, perfect, golden-skinned body would look, stretched out in his bed. And he had imagined how that body would feel—warm and soft and pliant. Receptive. Yielding. But

somehow he hadn't imagined this kind of passion in her.
He'd thought she was more practical, and that nothing
about the human body would surprise her. But now she
was venturing into uncharted territory, and trusting him
to show her the way. It was an awesome responsibility.
It inflamed him.

When he cupped first one breast and then the other in
his hand, he felt them quiver, felt her back arch with the
instinctive need to get closer. When he took each peak in
turn between his lips and caressed it with his tongue, he
heard the gasp that started deep in her throat and came
out nothing more than a long, shuddering moan.

Moving very deliberately, gauging her every reaction,
Gabe's mouth went lower, slowly skimming her body,
curving in at the indentation of her waist, then outward
again at the slight, female rise of her belly. Inserting one
hand between her thighs, he nudged them open. Then,
with deft, sensitive fingers, he parted the satiny folds of
her vulva and stroked with the tip of his tongue the place
where the fire burned the hottest.

She felt the waves building, like heat waves reflecting
off the glaring white limestone. She felt her hips thrust-
ing upward toward the source of the heat. Taut as a bow,
her body arched, desperate for the waves to crest, needing them to overtake her and wash her away in an ex-
plosive tidal wave of scintillating, shimmering heat.

She was ready. And so was he. Head reeling, pulse
racing, every nerve in his body vibrating, Gabe stood,
hooked his thumbs in the waistband of his briefs, and
pulled them down his muscular runner's legs.

The light that streamed in through the window fell on
Whitney lying across the bed, and on Gabe standing beside it. It played games of shadow and light with the
curves and angles and planes of their bodies, illuminat-

ing the great jutting thrust of him, the throbbing, swollen veins looking even thicker and bluer in the blue starlight.

Tearing open the little foil packet that Whitney had placed on the nightstand, Gabe rolled it on with a determined gesture that made her tremble with anticipation. She stood on the edge of a sheer, hot precipice, and she knew that he was going to take her over. She yearned for it.

With both arms she reached for him, and drew him down on top of her, and took him inside.

CHAPTER EIGHTEEN

WHITNEY'S PRACTICE took up most of her day; but between every tongue she depressed, every pill she prescribed, she thought about the night ahead.

As long as the nights were, in this narrow fissure at the bottom of the world, they were never long enough. She was amazed, even a little embarrassed, by her sudden preoccupation with sensuality.

She had never known such obsession. She had never even suspected that she was capable of it. Her textbooks taught her everything, and yet they had taught her...nothing.

"A little knowledge is a dangerous thing," Gabe teased when she told him that, one night in the afterglow of their lovemaking.

"A *lot* of knowledge is even *more* dangerous!" Whitney said ruefully. "In medicine you have to learn to distance yourself or you wouldn't last a week. Eventually it gets to be such an automatic thing you forget how *not* to do it."

Was it the brain or was it the genitals? she wondered with wry humor. Or was it simply Gabe?

Was it the sometimes fierce, sometimes gentle touching, and holding, the kissing of lips and legs, the shocking, exploring, comforting, learning?

Or was it Gabe?

Was it obsession? Or was it Gabe?

All Whitney knew for sure was that she had experienced these sensations before, occasionally, and with varying degrees of intensity, but never with the force they held for her now. Now she knew that everything before had been only foreshadowings, only experiments, nothing more than rehearsals for the real thing.

The real thing? She sat up in bed and stared in surprise at Gabe's sleeping face on the pillow beside her.

This can't be love, she wailed inwardly. That would be so terribly inconvenient! It wasn't the right time or place! They lived three thousand miles apart, on opposite coasts! And she liked her life the way it was; she had no intention of changing it! Besides, they had nothing in common!

No, she was *not* in love, she concluded, but she was certainly willing to admit she was in lust. Propping herself up on one elbow, she smoothed Gabe's tangled hair, now grown longer and looking much more Indianlike, away from his face. Gently she pressed her lips to his forehead, and then to each of his eyes, in sleep much like hers—dark, fringed lines slanting upward.

They had this much in common, at least.

Then there was the fact that they had both grown up rootless, even though that seemed to bother her a lot more than it did him.

That was another thing.

She leaned forward and gave his mouth a lingering kiss.

Gabe must have felt the tender pressure of her lips, or maybe he just sensed that she was awake, because he rolled lazily onto his side.

"Are you trying to start something?" he asked. His voice was thick with sleep, and with something more.

"Depends. What do you have in mind?"

"Turn over," he said huskily.

He swept her hair aside. Then, nipping at the soft nape of her neck, he pressed her against him so that they fit together like two spoons, and he took her from behind.

Every night was like that.

GABE'S DAYS were different. He spent most of them with Billy. Whitney showed him how to administer injections, and Gabe gave the old man his insulin every day.

Why, he wasn't sure. The insulin was little more than a finger in a dike, Gabe figured. It didn't take a medical degree to know there was probably nothing anyone could do for Billy anymore.

Now his feet were mottled almost black, and the decaying stench from the dead flesh was very strong. He could barely hobble from hammock to wickiup. Soon, it was heartbreakingly apparent, not even amputation could save him.

But for Whitney's sake, and for Billy's as well, he gave it a shot.

His ploy about making sure Billy's stories endured for future generations only made the old man chuckle.

"What use are those stories now?" he said. "They were meant to teach the People how to live. Now they have no purpose. They can no longer teach us anything about our world. Our world has changed, and it requires new stories."

"But people should know their past. They should remember—" It was the Bible, chapter and verse, according to Whitney Baldridge-Barrows.

Billy chuckled again. "Now you sound like the little Coyote doctor. You and I are of this place—we know better. Those stories are living things. They need air and light to survive, not to be shut up in a box and gather dust. Let them die with our gods. They were never meant to exist beyond their usefulness."

He paused for some minutes, his lips pursed. "It is the same for people," he finally said.

"Why do you let Whitney record your stories, then?" Gabe wanted to know.

Billy leaned closer. "I have said that she is of the Coyote Clan," he reminded Gabe in a low, intimate whisper, as if the *bqi'gthegee* might be listening from behind a tree. "She comes to me and asks me about the past, and before I know what is happening, I dream things I had not thought of since I was a young man. She makes me remember that I was once a shaman."

He smiled sagely. "Her Coyote medicine is powerful—but you know that. Didn't she search in my mind to find you and bring you down here?"

Gabe had been about to launch into his customary denial when suddenly he saw, from seemingly out of nowhere, two men standing at the outskirts of Billy's dead garden.

It was obvious that they were Indians, but they were like no Indians Gabe had seen since he'd been in the canyon. One was old, the other middle-aged, but both stood tall, and their bodies were lean and spare. Both carried rifles, and had canteens slung across their chests. They were long-haired, dirty and shirtless, and wore, not the jeans everyone in the village wore but breech-clouts made of something soft and gray like buckskin, and moccasins of the same fabric.

Their faces, marked with a thick red line zigzagging down each cheek, looked wary and hostile as they eyed Gabe from the edge of the garden. They seemed prepared to slip back into the woods as noiselessly as they had come.

The younger of the two men addressed Billy in a low voice, in Supai. Billy spoke in return, also in Supai. Gabe had no idea what Billy was saying, but he did hear the word *n'home'e*.

"What do they want?" Gabe asked in a low voice, not for one moment taking his eyes off the men.

"They have come to sit with me," Billy replied simply. The two cautiously came closer and sat cross-legged on the ground beside the hammock. They lit three cigarettes, handed one to Billy, and proceeded to chainsmoke through half an hour of total silence. But not quite total silence. Every so often one or the other of the wild-looking visitors would rock back and forth and break into a litany of low, guttural chants.

Then suddenly, with no preparation at all, they rose in unison to their feet, slipped silently back into the woods and disappeared. Gabe stared, amazed at how one minute they were there, and the next they were just . . . gone.

"Who are they?" he asked.

"They are the Hidden People. They live in the farthermost gorges of the Grand Canyon, where the *hay gu* have never gone. Most of the people believe they no longer exist. But you have seen them."

ON THE FRIDAY before the Tribal Council meeting, Gabe played his trump card with Billy. He hadn't even shared this idea with Whitney.

"Billy," he began carefully. "I'll be going back to Seattle in two days. I'd like very much for you to go uptop with me. I'll take you to the hospital and stay with you while the doctors perform the operation. It would . . . please me to know that you'll be . . . well.''

He waited with bated breath for Billy's response. ''You are a good man, *n'home'e,*'' he said at last. ''I am proud. But I will be gone before then.''

''No, Billy. Whitney says you still have time.'' He smiled too broadly and spoke too heartily. ''She's going to come down here this weekend to badger you some more. There's still time to think it over, Billy—''

''I will be gone before you are gone,'' Billy repeated serenely. Then, lulled by the old, familiar lullaby of the rustling cottonwoods, he closed his eyes and went to sleep.

SUDDENLY THERE WAS no more time. The Tribal Council meeting was scheduled for Saturday morning.

Whitney concentrated on the meeting; it kept her from thinking about the fact that on Sunday Gabe would be gone. She hoped for a few emergencies—nothing serious, of course, just something to occupy her time and attention for a few hours.

But on this hot, unusually muggy day, the entire tribe seemed to be afflicted with good health and good luck. Even the tourists in the campgrounds seemed not to be getting into trouble today. No scorpion bites, no run-ins with snakes, no hikers tumbling off ledges, not even any skinned knees or bougainvillea thorns in feet.

She sterilized instruments that were already sterile, double-checked files that were already in perfect order, even picked up Chili's outdated tabloid and tried to drum up an interest in the baby born speaking Latin featured on page one.

Sunday. Sunday Gabe would be gone.

They had made plans, of course, about the future—at least the immediate future. For example, the fact that she lived on the east coast and he on the west bothered him not at all. "No problem," Gabe said positively. "Why do you think God invented airplanes?"

But there was a problem.

The problem was the real world, or more specifically, Seattle. Gabe had a life back there. A successful life. He was going to become a partner in one of the largest, most prestigious law firms in the city. He had women like Mimi Samples at his beck and call.

But there was a deeper problem.

Whitney knew that the life-style Gabe had worked so long to attain—wealth and power, glitz and glamor— wasn't a world she could live in. Nor would she be an asset to him in that world, even if she could.

Let's face it, she told herself bluntly, he needs someone like Mimi Samples on his arm, someone who will set people's secret and deep-seated racial fears to rest, who will prove that, inside, he's just a regular guy, like all the other regular guys.

Someone who will make him seem more American, not less.

It was a superficial life-style he aimed for, in Whitney's opinion; but she understood why Gabe, the perpetual outsider, craved it, and she couldn't find it in her heart to blame him.

But it did create an impossible position for her.

After what seemed like an eternity, the door to the tribal office opened. Gabe and Jesse walked out together. Whitney couldn't tell from either's body language what had transpired. Quickly she locked up the clinic and headed in their direction.

"Hi, guys," she said. Her eyes met Jesse's first, but lingered on Gabe's. "How'd it go?"

Jesse looked even more somber than usual. Whitney tried to guess what that meant. Gabe's expression was harder yet to decipher. Poker-faced and slit-eyed, he looked like a lawyer—or a gunslinger—revealing nothing.

"I'll let Mr. Blade tell you about it, Dr. B," Jesse said. "I've got some loose ends to tie up." He gave Whitney the solemn stretch of his lips that never quite made it to his eyes, shook Gabe's hand, and walked back into his office.

"Well, how'd it go?" Whitney demanded, as she and Gabe headed down the path toward home.

"It didn't," Gabe replied.

"Oh." Whitney didn't know what else to say. "I'm sorry."

Gabe slid his eyes in her direction. "No, you're not," he said sourly. And before she had a chance to defend herself, he added, "and I'm not sure that I am, either."

"Gabe, what happened?"

"Look, babe, I need a little space," he said, instead of directly answering her question. "Want to take a walk with me?"

"Sure," she said instantly. "Where?"

"How about up to the caves where the pictographs are? Maybe we can catch a breeze up there, too. Could be it's just me, but it feels like a steam room bath here."

That's not a walk, Whitney thought; *that's some serious climbing!* But since she knew she'd walk to the ends of the earth with him, what was a little trip up the side of a mountain?

"THEY TURNED IT DOWN. I thought I had 'em. I thought I had 'em right in the palm of my hand." Gabe clenched his right hand, then opened it, looking as though he was surprised to find it empty. "I talked to everyone, promised them everything they wanted. But in the end it was almost unanimous."

Gabe had climbed the punishing trail like a fugitive on the run. He used the stunted piñon trees and tufts of wild grass as supports, grasping them as angrily as if he had wanted to jerk them out of their rock crevices and heave them down to the canyon floor.

Trailing behind at a much more reasonable pace, Whitney could see bloody scratches on his arms and legs from his angry progress through the brush. Because of the unusual mugginess of the weather, she could also see a gray triangle of sweat between his shoulder blades.

She was sweaty, too, and by the time she reached the upper ledge, also out of breath. She found Gabe sitting on the smooth boulder just outside the cave. His head drooped between his hunched shoulders and his hands were braced on his outspread knees. He was panting laboriously. When he raised his head to give Whitney a quick acknowledgment, she saw rivulets of sweat running down his face.

"Nice way to kill yourself in this heat," the doctor in her reprimanded him before the woman asked, "Want to tell me what's going on?"

Still panting, Gabe jerked his head affirmatively a few times, then slid down the smooth boulder to sit on the sand. He drew his legs up, propped his forearms on his knees, and rested his head backward against the smooth rock.

"I talked to Hobie," he said. He took a few more deep gulps of air. "He fired me."

The conversation he'd had with Hobie had repeated itself viciously in his head all the way up the cliff, despite his best efforts to outrun it, and he wasn't quite ready to share it yet.

"I thought you had everything under control, Gabe," Hobie had snarled when Gabe gave him the news. "That's what you told me. I got a fortune tied up there already. I got backers lined up to buy inta this project, and now you tell me there ain't gonna *be* a project? Tell me what went wrong, Gabe. Tell me so's I can understand, 'cause, see, I *trusted* you, Gabe. I thought you knew what you were doing."

"It was the liquor, Hobie. We worked out agreements about everything else, but we couldn't come to any compromise on that one. They just refuse to permit alcohol on the reservation. Period."

"C'mon, man," Hobie snarled again. His voice was getting sloppy; Gabe could tell he was working himself up into a frenzy. "There must'a been *some* money you could'a spread around, *some* votes you could'a bought. Did'ja *try* that, Gabe, my man? *Did'ja?*"

"Not an option here, Hobie," Gabe said uncomfortably. "The tribe's too small, everybody knows everybody else—"

"Did'ja *try,* Gabe?"

Gabe didn't want to have to tell Hobie "No," but he knew the man would eventually learn the truth. "No," he admitted.

"Why not?"

"It, ah . . ." Gabe cleared his throat. "It didn't seem appropriate here."

"Don't *you* tell *me* what's appropriate! I know where you came from, Blade. You're just a half-breed street punk who grew up on the waterfront. What do you know from *appropriate?* A little money handed out under the table is *always* appropriate!

"You mishandled this one bad, friend. I thought you were hungry—that's what I told ol' Trevor Parkhurst and Guy Brandenberg when I picked you for this job. But I was wrong. You're still nothing but a punk, Blade, and you're out of your league. *Way* out of your league! Instead of giving you a partnership, you're gonna be lucky if Trevor and Guy don't hand you a lawsuit. I'll see you when you get back to Seattle, ol' buddy, ol' pal. Count on it!"

"I'll do that," Gabe informed Hobie in his most supercilious voice. "And Hobie, old buddy, old pal? Don't bother sending the limo for me. I'll find my own way home."

CHAPTER NINETEEN

GABE LIFTED HIS HEAD and looked straight ahead at the tumbled limestone walls of the outer canyon.

The moisture in the air blurred its piercing clarity, washing the white limestone with watercolors of soft gray, gentle pinks and cool blues. Even the vivid red pigment of the sandstone walls was muted, not glittering so much as gleaming dully beneath the hazy sun.

But at this moment, all Gabe could see in front of him was failure.

"I *am* sorry, Gabe." Standing up, Whitney brushed sand off her hands and her backside, then walked to where Gabe sat. Straddling the rock behind him, she began to knead his tense neck with her small but surprisingly strong hands. "A while ago you said that you weren't sure you were sorry about the way the vote went. What did you mean?"

He shrugged. "I'm still not sure. But I've come to doubt the wisdom of building here at all. The ambience seems so...fragile. I'm not sure there'd be any left after we finished turning it into a resort."

Then he glanced at Whitney and gave her another ironic shrug. "And I'm not convinced that visitors who have only a weekend to hurry up and enjoy themselves would have time to appreciate it. This place takes a while to grow on you—the way it did on me."

"What about the partnership in your firm?"

"Scratched, of course. Hobie says he might sue. And he's just the type who would. He could even win, because technically I *didn't* follow his business practices to the letter. But damn it—" Gabe struck one fist on the sandy ground "—he hired me because of my instincts, or so he said at the time. I'd understand these people, he said, I'd know how they *think.*"

He scooped up a handful of colored stones and rattled them desultorily in his hand. "Go figure," he mumbled almost under his breath. "But *damn,* I wanted that partnership!" Morosely, he began tossing the stones one by one over the edge of the cliff.

After a silent, moody fifteen minutes, during which Whitney worked her hands up into his hair and began massaging the back of his head, Gabe turned to her, looking vaguely puzzled. "Why is it so hot today? I never noticed this humidity before."

Whitney also felt the weight of the air, pressing down on them. "Summer is the monsoon season," she replied, looking up at the sky. "I think we're going to have a storm."

"But the sky is blue," Gabe protested.

"I know. Our little bit of sky is so narrow we don't see a storm until it's practically on top of us. But you can hear it coming."

As though to confirm her statement, the rumble of distant thunder echoed through the canyon.

A hot wind began as a breeze and then grew stronger, bending the sparse piñon and creosote bushes flat against the rocks on which they grew, and creating dust devils on all the sandy ledges. Then the air became preternaturally still.

"Should we go down?" Gabe wondered aloud.

Suddenly, heavy, black clouds surged into the tiny strip of sky, roiling and boiling in great churning masses.

"Too late now."

A few huge, distorted droplets splattered against the rocky ledge where they sat. With no more warning than that, the dark clouds burst open, releasing a torrential deluge that forced them to run for cover.

"Quick, get in the cave!" Gabe shouted, scrambling to collect their backpacks.

Whitney was literally thrown down on all fours by the force of the cloudburst. Gabe seized her by one elbow and hauled her to her feet, then half pushed, half dragged her into the cave.

GABE TOOK OFF his glasses and swiped at the rain spots with his shirt, then settled them back on the bridge of his nose.

Hunkered down on their heels, he and Whitney watched the rain from the shelter of the cave. It fell from the sky like a solid column of water, beating the unresisting desert scrub flat against the rock on which it grew. The wind howled across the plateau, lowering tornado-like tails into the canyon to scoop up the column of rain and make it curve upwards.

Echoes from the bottom of the canyon welled upward, hollow and heavy, bouncing off each other, creating a bedlam of unearthly, portentous voices of doom.

The whole uncanny spectacle made a mad, prophetic kind of sense to Gabe. It was simply another aspect of the anarchy he had felt in this place from the first time he had ever come here. *There are no laws of nature here,* he thought, with a vague sense of exhilaration and awe. *This is the way the world began, and this is the way it would end.*

"My God, will you look at that!" Whitney exclaimed a moment later.

The east wall had suddenly sprouted a myriad of waterfalls. They gushed over the top and right through the middle of the red rock, then fell hundreds of feet straight down, as if someone had turned on colossal faucets inside the stone.

"We're surrounded by two thousand square miles of flat desert," Whitney told him. "When it rains, all that water drains into the canyons and washes down into the Colorado River. Magnificent, isn't it?"

Gabe agreed. The waterfalls springing from the middle of solid rock were awesome, as was the rest of this topsy-turvy land, with its violent, fragile beauty.

"It shouldn't last long," Whitney predicted. "And the water runs off pretty fast here in the desert. We'll be able to get down before dark."

"That's good, because I forgot my flashlight." He searched his backpack and his pockets, coming up with nothing more useful than a half-burned-out book of matches.

"Billy's," he said, shoving the matchbook back into his pocket. "Last time I saw him he was so hung over he couldn't get the match to the cigarette without burning his nose," he explained sheepishly.

Gabe felt as useless as he'd ever felt in his life. He was out of his element, very much out of his element, and he knew it. What was worse, he knew that Whitney knew it as well. "Did you remember *your* flashlight?"

"Yes—"

"I figured," said Gabe, feeling more useless than ever.

Whitney smiled, still plowing through her backpack. "Don't worry about it, Gabe," she advised. "All we need is one. And I've still got some of that delicious trail mix you got from Gwe. Oh, and my hand-held, of course."

She switched it on. Nothing. "Look, it's soaked!" she muttered disgustedly. "Lot of good *that's* going to do me. I just hope no one needs me for a while."

"Well, *I* need you. Right now." Gabe reached to the other side of the cave entrance where Whitney sat on her heels, and pulled her across, tumbling her into his lap. "I'm not much of a boy scout," he whispered into her ear. "But I've been told that I'm excellent in other areas."

Whitney knew that from personal experience. And after all, how often did you *really* need someone to rub two sticks together to start a fire? Gabe's method was so much more . . . effective! she thought.

"This getting stranded might turn out to be a good thing," he continued. One leg stretched in front of him and the other knee bent upward, he made a chair for Whitney between his widespread thighs. "Gives us a little more time together with no interruptions."

Whitney ran her hand through his damp hair and down the side of his face. "Oh, Gabe," she said softly, "I wish you didn't have to leave." Her hand stopped at the right angle of his jaw and cupped it in her palm. She pressed her lips lightly to his.

"I'm going to miss you too, babe." He seized the hand that was caressing his cheek, opened it, and kissed the center of her palm. Then he proceeded to kiss the soft pads at the base of each finger.

"God, I'd like to make love to you right now!" he groaned into her hand.

Whitney cuddled closer. "Why don't you?" she suggested.

He smiled ruefully. "You know why."

She sat up and reached for her backpack, from which she extricated a familiar little foil packet and held it out between her fingers.

Gabe's confounded eyes traveled from her fingers to her face, and then back to her fingers again. "Where did that come from?"

"From my backpack," she replied innocently.

"You know what I mean. Do you always take condoms along when you travel?"

"I'm a doctor, Gabe," she said with mock-seriousness. "I don't take chances." She tried to keep her face straight, but broke into peals of laughter at the consternation on his face. "No, actually, I had it from the last time we came up here."

"The last time? But we didn't do anything the last time!"

"Exactly," she said logically. "Which is why I have it *this* time!"

"Let me get this straight," Gabe said, taking the proffered packet and then settling Whitney comfortably in his lap. "You *expected* last time that we might get involved?"

"I didn't know," she said in the same no-nonsense tone. "But I thought it was a possibility, yes. After all, I'd had my eye on you for weeks."

"It didn't show. In fact, I felt like you were very disappointed in me for coming on to you the way I did."

"Disappointed?" She grinned impishly. "Yes. But not in you."

Gabe took off his glasses and slipped them into his breast pocket. "Let me make it up to you now," he suggested.

He lowered the knee that had formed the back of Whitney's chair and she turned to face him, straddling his thighs.

She took possession of his mouth, tempting him with playful, teasing kisses. Clasping her hands behind his neck, she raised herself up and slowly, seductively rotated her pelvis against his in a series of undulating bumps and grinds, laughing down at him the whole time.

When she felt his quickening, her smile broadened. When she felt it swell hard and thick beneath her, the smile tightened, became as taut as the rest of her body. Her eyes fluttered to half-mast, her head fell back, and her hips began to thrust toward his with an urgent, instinctive rhythm of their own.

Gabe reached between them to unbutton her damp shirt, then opened it so that the white cotton framed her small, golden breasts. He didn't fondle them, only took them in with hot, greedy eyes. With only the touch of his eyes, Whitney felt them pucker at the tips, felt them quiver with anticipation.

He curved his hand around each breast in turn, plumping them in his palm, rolling the nipples gently and then harder between thumb and forefinger. When at last she felt his lips on her rain-damp skin, she drew a long, shuddering breath. The yearning heaviness deep in her stomach opened to an emptiness that ached to enclose him.

Except for the rain echoing outside, it was like reenacting the last encounter they'd had up here, only doing it right this time.

This time Gabe was no longer trying to play the gentleman.

This time he knew he could do as he pleased, that she had given him that permission, that she wanted it as much as he did.

He lifted her to her knees with one hand at the small of her back. With the other, he unzipped his shorts and freed himself, then pulled hers out of the way.

Gabe noted the expression on her face. It wasn't the sweet, dreamy look of the last encounter—it was as needy, as greedy, as sensual as he knew his own must be. Fixing his eyes on hers, he allowed her neither to close hers nor to look away, so that he could see his effect on her, see her desire climax, see it in her eyes when he made her his.

CHAPTER TWENTY

THE RAIN CONTINUED.

The next time they looked out of the cave, it was to see that the east wall had become a curtain of water. The wall directly in front of them had also sprouted its own collection of waterfalls.

"Even if the rain stops, that's tons of rainwater falling into the canyon, Gabe," Whitney worried uneasily. "Where's all that water going to go?"

Gabe didn't have the vaguest clue, but he could guess. He knew that Whitney was thinking along the same lines as he was. And he didn't want to put it into words any more than she did.

"We often get five or ten feet of runoff when it rains," she continued, trying to inject a note of optimism into her voice. "Like that night you pulled Hobie out of the wash. But the last big flood was in 1928, and the one before that—the one that washed out the entire canyon and killed people—was way back in 1910. Billy told me about it."

"What'd he say?"

"It was a flash flood, he said. A wall of water fifty feet high just came over the east wall and tore through the canyon like a river. It broke weaker sections of the walls. And the waterfalls kept pouring more water on top of it. The village, he said, was under five feet of water for days, and the lowest part of the canyon had twenty feet or more."

"How did the people manage to stay alive while the canyon was under twenty feet of water?" Gabe asked skeptically.

"They climbed up to the rock houses that they use for granaries in the cliffs—the little pueblo-style houses they say the first people built when Coyote led them down here. Actually, they're the ruins of prehistoric Anasazi settlements, but you certainly can see why the Indians believe the houses were built especially for them."

"Yep," Gabe said. "And you can also see how old stories improve with the telling. I'd be willing to bet that if you halved all those numbers Billy gave you, you might be closer to the truth."

He put his arm around Whitney's shoulder and squeezed it comfortingly. "Besides, even if there *is* a flood today, I'm sure the Indians will know how to handle themselves." He chucked her under the chin. "After all, don't they say they've lived in the Grand Canyon forever?"

Whitney didn't even hear his gentle attempt at humor. She slipped out from under his arm and began to pace, feeling suddenly claustrophobic in the confining shelter of the cave. "I have to get down there! If there are problems, they'll be needing me!"

"Well, you weren't there in 1928, and you weren't there in 1910. If there *is* a flood, they'll probably get through it without you this time, too. Meantime—" he subtly steered her away from the cave entrance, where the view was not encouraging "—why don't we try to get some rest?"

"I'm beginning to think we're not going to get home tonight," she confessed uneasily, glancing again at the column of water outside their cave.

"Well then, a nap will make the time pass faster," Gabe returned.

He was worried, too.

He knew that the indentations in the rimrock were water trails cut by old floods, which meant that floods in this canyon must be both frequent and frightening.

Gabe arranged the two backpacks on the ground to use as pillows. Then he took off his glasses, slipped them into his pocket, and he and Whitney curled up on the warm, sandy floor.

"What's the first thing you're going to do when you get home?" Whitney asked after a while. Apparently sleep was eluding her.

Gabe thought for a minute. "Have a cold beer. Turn on the TV. Call someone on the telephone."

"Who will you call?" she asked curiously.

"Oh, I'm not sure yet. Not Hobie Stoner, that's for sure! I guess I'll probably call my secretary, find out what's been going on in the office since I've been out of town. If I still *have* an office!"

"Are you worried about that?"

"Not really. I'm not totally valueless, even without Hobie Stoner. It's just that it'll be my same old office, not the big one on the fifteenth floor with the corner window. But I'll manage."

"And your secretary? What's she like?"

"My secretary?" Gabe chuckled softly. "Well, my firm is pretty impersonal, so I really don't know much about her. But I *do* call her *Mrs*. if that answers your question!"

"It helps some," Whitney admitted. Her voice sounded relaxed, as if she might actually be dozing off. She nestled against Gabe in their favorite spoon position. "Tell me about you when you were growing up," she suggested sleepily. "I think it's time I knew something about the man I'm in love with...."

Love? He looked down at her, startled. "Love" wasn't a word in his vocabulary, unless it was preceded or followed by "making." It was a word he avoided at all costs, because in this day and age, it could land you in court.

"Who do you think I am?" he said roughly. "Billy?" His voice was not accommodating.

"Um-m-m," Whitney murmured, nestling closer.

Whether that meant yes or no, or meant nothing at all, Gabe couldn't tell. But he did know there were things he wanted to share with her. She knew the best of him—at least that was the side he'd tried to show her. But for some reason that contradicted every survival instinct he'd cultivated all his life, he wanted her to know the rest of him, too.

"I don't know where I was born," he said, beginning at the beginning, "but I grew up in Seattle...."

He held nothing back.

And finally he found himself telling her about the McDaniels and Chino the Fence.

When he was finished, he just stopped, feeling drained, but also feeling strangely at peace. He waited for Whitney to say something. Anything. After a while he felt the soft, regular movement of her back against his chest, and realized that she'd slept through it all.

GABE SLEPT, TOO. When he woke the light had faded. Reluctant to disturb the sleeping woman next to him, he stayed put and listened carefully. The thunder and lightning seemed a long way off. He decided that the worst part of the storm must have moved on, although he could still hear the steady drum of the rain.

Then it shivered up his spine again, the chilling sensation that had awakened him. The eerie, uncanny feeling that someone was watching him.

He removed his glasses from his shirt pocket and put them on, then scanned the interior of the cave. The rough walls created irregular shadows, some black, some charcoal, some rippling like gray streamers in the uncertain light that reflected through the rain.

Then he saw them. Two yellow eyes watching him gravely from beneath an outcropping of stone.

It was a coyote. A small, stone-colored coyote, so wet and bedraggled that its ribs stuck out like dark bars in the matted gray of its fur.

Gabe froze. He knew little about wild animals, less than that about coyotes. Were they dangerous? Somehow, looking at the little coyote's eyes, he didn't think so. Just a fellow creature, Gabe guessed, caught like we were in the storm, and looking for shelter.

The coyote continued to observe Gabe, its large, tufted ears pointing forward. Panting in the muggy heat, its long tongue lolled crookedly from its open muzzle.

Gabe had once read something about approaching a strange dog: Don't look directly into its eyes—it might interpret that as a challenge and attack. So, lowering his own eyes, he kept track of the coyote with his peripheral vision.

The coyote watched him straight on, its stern, yellow coyote eyes unblinking.

After a while, given the warmth and stillness in the cave, the tranquilizing drone of the rain, the black-rimmed yellow eyes fixed almost hypnotically on him, Gabe's eyelids grew heavy again.

Stay awake! he ordered himself, *stay alert!* But he felt his lids growing heavier and heavier, and without warning they fell shut.

It could have been seconds, or it could have been minutes, but when he opened them again, the coyote had moved closer. It was still staring at Gabe with its yellow coyote eyes, but now, up close, the animal seemed bigger. Its black guard hairs bristled. Despite the warmth of the cave, Gabe felt cold sweat break out on his forehead.

Yet the coyote didn't seem menacing. Once it saw that he was awake, it got to its feet and trotted to the back of the cave, where it disappeared into the cleft that led to the inner cave. Gabe breathed a sigh of relief.

But in minutes the coyote was back.

It trotted toward the place where Gabe and Whitney lay—she still sleeping, he fresh out of wild-animal lore, fearfully hoping that not looking directly into the little coyote's eyes would prevent an attack.

The coyote sat down again at Gabe's feet; then it stood up, and again disappeared into the cleft between the caves. When the coyote went through this routine a third time, Gabe got curious. This was not typical coyote behavior, he was sure.

Carefully he extricated his arm from beneath Whitney's neck, then stood up and slowly, cautiously approached the animal. He held one hand out in front of him, as he'd seen professionals do in wildlife films— whether to calm the animal or to offer it his arm in hopes it'd be satisfied with that and leave the rest of his body alone, he wasn't sure.

Before he reached the coyote, the animal ducked through the cleft in the wall again. After a moment he poked out his muzzle and looked at Gabe quizzically.

"Call me crazy," Gabe muttered under his breath, feeling even crazier to find that he was talking to himself, "but I think that coyote is trying to tell me something!"

Well, why not? Nothing else in this alien world made any sense: not the violent, surrealistic landscape, not the unearthly palette of colors that bled over the canvases of white limestone, not the deluge of biblical proportions plummeting from a clear blue sky. Why not a scrawny coyote who could talk?

Rolling his eyes heavenward, as though he doubted his own sanity, Gabe followed the coyote through the wall.

WHITNEY WOKE TO FIND Gabe gone. "Gabe?" she quavered uncertainly. "Gabe?" she repeated a little louder, her eyes darting frantically all around the cave. Then she screamed his name, the sound ripping out of her throat in a paroxysm of fear.

The sound skirted the walls, echoing hollowly, then faded into the silence of the vaulted ceiling. Seizing her flashlight, for the daylight was almost gone, she walked to the cave entrance and peered out.

The rain was still falling, and the waterfalls had consolidated into curtains. They covered the walls as far as the eye could see, making the red cliffs look as though they were shielded behind thick, opaque glass.

Where was Gabe?

Dread took her heart in its icy hand and squeezed. With eyes that were afraid to see, she stared, panic-stricken, at the ledge in front of the cave. Surely he hadn't tried to climb down? He didn't know this land, the way it could change in an instant! To go down now would be suicide!

Then, over the dreary tattoo of the rain and the deafening beating of her heart, she heard something—a scrabbling, muffled noise that broke the grip of terror imprisoning her. She whirled around.

"Gabe!"

He was stepping through the cleft in the back wall. In his hand he held a flaming match, which he immediately dropped to the ground with a muttered curse. Whitney ran to him, throwing her arms around his waist in a viselike embrace.

"Whitney, listen!" He grabbed her shoulders urgently. "I think I've found a way out! I went through the hole in the back of the inner cave and it turned out to be a tunnel. It's so symmetrical that I think it might be artificial—that means it has to lead somewhere! You've got the flashlight? Good, let's go!"

"Gabe, wait. You don't know this country. Neither do I, but I *do* know that it's unpredictable. We could get to the other end and find that there's no way down. Or there could be drop-offs—you took a big risk going in there at all!"

"There wasn't any risk," Gabe started to explain. "The little coyote came in while we were sleeping, and he . . . well, you won't believe this, but he . . ."

Suddenly he stopped, his face frozen in a puzzled frown. At the same instant Whitney heard what he did—a sound like the thundering of a freight train. Before Gabe could stop her, she had turned and run to the entrance of the cave.

Her mouth fell open in a horrified, soundless O.

As she looked on, a solid wall of water at least twelve feet high leapt over the east wall. It was churning with

sand and debris, and knocking down full-grown trees in
its path. Giant boulders bounced like beach balls on its
foaming surface. It twirled one crazily, and as Whitney
watched, still speechless, hurled it aside on a mountain-
ous streamer of spume.

The peaceful stream of blue-green water had disappeared. In its place was a muddy, sudsy tidal wave that
swept down its bed and spread wall-to-wall across the
narrow canyon.

It took a few seconds at most. Whitney screamed,
only to find Gabe right behind her, his mouth dropped
open into the same dumbfounded O.

After the passage of the initial wall, the water rose
rapidly, until it looked to be about twenty feet above
creek level.

"Gabe, I've got to get down there!" Whitney cried,
clutching the front of his shirt with trembling, terrified
hands.

Whitney was thinking only of the Indians but Gabe's
concerns went further. That water would take days to
empty from the canyon, and it would be a lot longer
than that before the mud had dried up enough that they
could attempt to climb down.

Surely outside help would come—from somewhere!
Gabe had to believe—but how long would it take them
to start looking for survivors in tiny caves hidden in the
cliffs? How long could human beings survive without
food or water?

It was a question he never even considered asking
Whitney.

She paced the ground wildly, beating clenched fists
together in a frenzied gesture that bordered on hysteria.

"I've got to get down there!" she repeated frantically, returning to the mouth of the cave, where in the

darkness she could no longer see the rising water, but could hear it churning through the narrow gorge like a full-grown river.

"We've got to try," Gabe agreed. "But we'll have to wait until morning. We'll never make it in the dark."

DURING THE LONG, dark, terror-stricken night, between fitful naps, they heard the rain stop. Eventually they heard the waterfalls recede and the newborn river settle into a steady roar.

At the first sign of dawn, they hurried into the inner cave, where the little coyote was waiting.

CHAPTER TWENTY-ONE

THE TUNNEL was as silent as a tomb.

In fact, it *felt* like a tomb, as if the air it contained was as old as time. The air was dry and very thin, as though it lacked some essential ingredient.

With a shudder, Whitney recalled their jokes about mice and old Anasazi, but she hadn't hesitated a moment to get down on all fours behind Gabe and follow him into the tunnel.

He shone the flashlight around the dark passageway only long enough to ascertain that they were surrounded by a narrow tube of stone. The tunnel seemed almost too cylindrical to be natural. Its surface was jagged and rough, in some places almost wide enough to allow them to stand, in others narrowing to barely a crawl space.

After a brief inspection, he switched off the light. Suddenly they were engulfed in total blackness. "We should save the batteries," he said reluctantly. "We may need them at the other end."

Following the coyote on their hands and knees, sometimes on their bellies, they inched their way through the tunnel.

All Gabe could see, as he tried to keep up with the coyote's slow trot, were yellow eyes occasionally glancing back at him, as if to make sure he and Whitney were still following. Other than that, he could see nothing at all, but he could smell the wet-dog odor of the coyote's fur, and he found the gamy smell extremely reassuring.

As they burrowed through the mountain like earthworms through garden soil, small stones and jagged fragments of rock scraped their hands and knees. The jutting, chipped projections that stuck out along the surfaces cut like razors when, unwittingly, they grazed them in the dark.

Gabe moved along at a confident pace, slowing down only after an "ouch" or a muttered profanity that indicated he had again dragged a knee across a knife-sharp rock, or crawled too closely to the serrated wall. Whitney, having no point of reference except the shuffle of Gabe's hands and knees and the sound of his breathing, kept as close behind him as she could.

How far they traveled in the tunnel, whether they were moving outward or farther into the mountain, whether up or down, she had no idea. If there were forks in this wormhole, would they know it? If they made a wrong turn, would they know it? If it turned out to be some sort of maze, would they be able to find their way back?

And, of course, if they made it to the other end, what would they find there?

But Whitney kept swallowing the terror that rose in her throat and threatened to choke her. Stronger than her fear of mice and old Anasazi, and stronger than her fear of the unknown, was her desire to get down to the devastated village—if it still existed—and help where she could.

After what seemed like an eternity, she heard Gabe's voice call back to her, "Look, up ahead!"

And sure enough, directly in front of them, she saw a pinpoint of light. It wasn't much, but it was enough to make her sob with relief and scramble faster on the unforgiving floor.

As they closed in on the point of light, the blurred glow grew brighter and more distinct. When they reached the opening, they found that it was a circular cavity high on the side of a sheer wall of rock. It was just barely large enough to admit the body of a man.

Bracing their palms on the lip of the opening, they scrutinized the sheer, vertical precipice below.

Gabe sat back on his heels. "End of the line," he pronounced bleakly. "We might as well go back and hope someone finds us."

"No, Gabe, wait...." After inspecting the rock face for another few minutes, Whitney looked at Gabe with a puzzled frown.

"Gabe, look at those little projections jutting out from the wall. See the way the rock seems to be chipped away around them? And see how evenly spaced they are?"

"I see that," Gabe replied. "Is that supposed to mean something?"

"Well, it could. They look too regular to be natural, don't you think? They look sort of like the rungs on a ladder, don't they?" Suddenly her breath caught. "Do you know what this must be? This must be an escape route, built by the Anasazi thousands of years ago!"

Excitedly, she leaned farther out the opening to peer down the perpendicular rock face. "They built them to escape enemies who laid siege from below! All the tribes of the southwest have stories about these secret passageways, but they've always been thought to be mythological!"

Gabe held onto her by a handful of her shirt. He pulled her back inside, then leaned out on his hands and knees to study the rock face again. With a sinking heart, he also studied the sheer drop below. Beyond the first few carved projections, he couldn't see any more steps of the stone ladder, but he knew they had to be there.

Moving away from the edge, he looked strangely at the little coyote. This was not a trail a four-legged creature would, or could, ever use. He noticed that the coyote didn't look so small anymore. Its matted fur was dry now, and Gabe realized that the dun-colored pelt was thick and full. Its yellow coyote eyes looked just the slightest bit insolent, as if to say "Mythological, hah!"

"... and if it *is* an Anasazi escape route, there'll be indentations in the rock for handholds," Whitney continued even more excitedly. "I think we've found our way out, Gabe! What do you think?"

"I think we have to give it a try," he agreed reluctantly. Nothing awaited them at the other end of the tunnel but probable starvation and thirst and eventual death, and Gabe didn't intend either of them to become research material for anthropologists of the future. "How about you going back to the cave and letting me bring help up to you?" he suggested hopefully.

"Not on your life! If *you* want to wait, that's fine, I'll bring back help for you. But *I'm* going down!"

Gabe sighed. "I knew you'd say that." He eyed the sheer cliff again. "Damn, I wish we had a rope!"

"I don't see what good that would do us at this point," Whitney said, practical as ever.

"True," Gabe admitted, still eyeing the drop without enthusiasm. "Okay, I'll go first. Stay within shouting distance. If anything happens..."

"Nothing's going to happen!" She threw her arms around him, clinging to his neck as though she would never let him go. Her high, sweet voice vibrated like the strings of a violin. "I love you so much, Gabe—don't let anything happen!"

But then, knowing there was no other choice, she did let him go. Gripping the lip of the hole in the wall, he backed out the opening and tentatively placed one toe on the first step of the stone ladder. "I love you, too," he said, in a voice as solemn as a vow.

Gabe allowed himself one last look before he released his hold on the lip of the opening and put his life into the hands of the ancient Anasazi. He saw Whitney's wet, terrified, beautiful face, and the coyote's tall tufted ears and its tawny muzzle resting on her shoulder. He hoped it wouldn't be the last thing he'd see on this earth.

He began the long descent.

"I WENT TO SEE how fast the creek was rising, and it was coming up so fast that I was cut off. Then the water came over the wall. I climbed up a cottonwood tree, and then I saw uprooted cottonwoods flying end over end like sticks. I thought I was a goner for sure—I thought we all were."

Jesse Sinyella's voice still registered shock. "When I came down at first light, I had to swim. The water was still over my head."

Although injuries were few, Jesse was very glad to see his doctor. He caught her in a most un-Indian-like bear hug.

He was even glad to see Gabe. It meant there wouldn't have to be a time-consuming and expensive search for the big shot from Seattle.

Everything in the path of the flood had been washed over the waterfalls and down to the Colorado River.

At least a dozen houses by the side of the normally placid creek had been torn off their foundations. In those houses closer to the village, mud was standing three feet deep in the rooms.

Trees had been uprooted, bridges demolished, whole sections of red sandstone broken from the walls. The electricity was washed out, as were the water, sewer and irrigation systems. As were the five hundred acres of crops. How many horses had been lost hadn't been determined yet.

Under eighteen inches of water at its shallowest point, as much as twenty feet at its deepest, the tiny village held on.

First light revealed Army National Guard Helicopters already hovering in the sky. They evacuated over sixty hikers from the cliffs and ledges, the talus slopes and the trees. They also brought up two hundred members of the tribe, mostly elders and children, to a fleet of buses waiting to take them the one hundred miles to the Hualapai Reservation at Peach Springs.

Whitney was amazed that there were so few serious casualties. The Indians, she realized, had not been taken by surprise. Everyone in the low-lying areas had fled to the protection of the talus slopes and the ancient pueblos of the Anasazi high in the cliffs.

The only major injury she'd encountered so far was on a hiker who had been badly gashed while trying to swim out of the campgrounds. She had sewn up his wounds by flashlight.

In the clinic, part of the roof had collapsed on the examination table, and the floor was coated with a slick, thick layer of mud. Whitney forgot Gabe. She forgot her harrowing climb down the old Anasazi ladder. Assembling as many boxes of medical supplies as she could locate by flashlight, she had quickly established an emergency dispensary in her waiting room.

Later in the day, when she glanced up from her makeshift examining room, she'd caught sight of Gabe unearthing boxes of supplies from beneath her fallen roof. When she saw him next, it was through the broken window of the community center, where he and Jesse and several other men were shoveling mud out the door so that the building could be used as a shelter.

Then, much later, in the steamy heat of the afternoon, she saw him again. He was walking toward her, carrying an armload of bottled water the choppers had airlifted in.

He was encrusted with mud. There were long, bloody scratches on his arms and legs. His knees were rubbed raw, and his haggard red eyes looked like burning coals in his face.

She knew that she looked exactly the same.

"Hi," she said, summoning up a bone-weary smile.

"Here, have a drink," Gabe said. He twisted the cap off a gallon bottle and held it out to her.

"How're you holding up?" he asked, after she had gulped down a large quantity of water and let a good deal more dribble down her chin, streaking the dirt that caked her face.

"Fine. How about you?"

"Yeah, me, too," he said perfunctorily. He removed his glasses and tiredly massaged the bridge of his nose.

"Something's wrong, Gabe. What is it?"

"Whitney, I can't find Billy."

THE SINGLE TRAIL between the village and the outside world remained impassable. For days, the *chop-chop-chop* of Army helicopters replaced the thud of horses' hooves as the National Guard delivered emergency supplies—generators, water, food, animal feed, tools, medicine, and sandbags.

The Indians came down from the cliffs and began to rebuild. A bulldozer or a tractor would have been a godsend. But since there was no way to get heavy equipment into the canyon, all the cleanup and rebuilding had to be done by hand.

Together, Whitney and Gabe shoveled the mud out of the clinic, repaired the roof, and in short order had it open for business. Then they did the same with the house. They helped distribute the relief supplies as the helicopters flew them in. They kept so busy that, in the daylight hours, they hardly had time to think at all.

But at night, they grieved for Billy.

HIS OLD MULE wandered into the village two days after the flood. When the waters receded, searchers went out on horseback, but no trace of Billy was ever found. Even his wickiup had disappeared, washed away as completely as if it had never existed at all.

SOON AFTER the ham radio was up and operating, Hobie Stoner called.

"Gabe, you old reprobate," his cheery voice boomed across Jesse's mud-caked office. "So you're still down there, huh?"

"Obviously I am, Hobie," Gabe replied coldly. "Or you wouldn't be talking to me here. What do you want?"

"Now don't use that tone with me, Gabe, my man." His own tone was that of a wheedling child. "I heard about the flood on the news, and when I couldn't reach you at home, I thought you might not have gotten out in time."

"What do you want, Hobie?"

"Get right to the point—I always liked that about you, Gabe. All right, I'll take a page out of your book. I want you to forget everything I said before. I must've been outta my head, or drunk, or something. Probably drunk—you know how I can get after a few martinis."

Hobie's rueful little apology was obviously intended to provoke a matching apology from Gabe, allowing both of them to save face and put their last ugly conversation behind them. Gabe said nothing.

"Aw, c'mon now, don't make me beg! I want you back. Look, I already talked to Trevor and Guy, and the partnership's waiting for you. It's a done deal. You saved me a pile of money down there, Gabe. I owe you, and I want to show my gratitude. And then I want you to sue those goddamn civil engineers who did the initial surveys—"

Gabe looked at the mike incredulously. "*I* saved you a pile of money, Hobie? How do you figure?"

"Well hell, Gabe, if we'd signed those contracts—"

"You don't owe me, Hobie. I had nothing to do with keeping you out of the canyon. It was pure luck."

"Maybe you had something to do with it and maybe you didn't. Who knows? I believe in luck, don't you? And right now you're rolling sevens and elevens." He gave an artificial chuckle. "All I know is I came *that* close—" Gabe pictured him measuring an inch in the air "—to losing a bundle, and it feels like you figure in there somewhere. Maybe it *was* luck. Maybe you're my good-luck charm, Gabe! My rabbit's foot!"

Hobie was a gambler. Gabe knew that. For all his business acumen, he wasn't above such things as rabbit's feet and good-luck charms. "Whatever works," Hobie liked to say.

The wheedling, little boy voice came back. "I lost my temper, Gabe. Isn't a man allowed to make a mistake once in a while?"

"Sorry, Hobie, but this half-breed street punk isn't about to be *anybody's* rabbit foot."

"Ker-r-ist, Gabe, I'm sorry about that! Look, come back, we'll talk. Actually, Mimi, well, she decided we had to take the big step or she was going to cut out on me, so we're having a big bash tomorra night, as a matter of fact. Gonna announce our engagement. Why'n'cha plan to be here, Gabe? Mimi'll love it, and you and me can talk. Call me when you get in, I'll send the limo to pick you up, okay?"

Gabe opened his mouth to say no. "I'll give it some thought," he said instead, hating himself for it.

He didn't slam the microphone down as he had the last time. He set it down absentmindedly, as if he was still listening to the words that had just come out of it.

Jesse sat at his desk in his filthy work clothes, entering supply requisitions into his computer. He looked up, pursed-lipped, when Gabe finished talking. "It isn't just the resort project, is it?" he said in his phlegmatic voice. "You're sleeping with her."

Gabe turned. "I don't think that's any of your business, Sinyella." The two men had developed a grudging respect for each other during the difficult days since the flood, but that respect had not extended to friendship.

Calmly, Jesse held up one hand, palm forward. "Hear me out. If you want to stay on the reservation until she leaves, I want you to know that I, as Chairman of the Havasupai, will permit it."

Gabe glared at him angrily. "What makes you think I want to stay here, Sinyella? I've got a *life* out there!"

The Indian surveyed him with contempt, although how Gabe knew that he wasn't sure, since Sinyella's facial expression changed not at all. "You don't deserve her," Jesse said, his impassive voice somehow as contemptuous as his impassive face. "If you leave, someday I will tell her that."

Gabe jerked open the door and slammed it shut behind him.

Why does Sinyella always talk like an extra in a bad Western? he fumed, stomping out into the hot sunlight. He was angry all right, but not at Jesse; not even at Hobie Stoner. He was angry at himself.

"I LOVE YOU, Whitney," Gabe said. They were lying naked in Whitney's bed.

He hadn't made a move toward her, and tonight she felt strangely hesitant to make the first move herself. She felt as though, for some reason, he was trying to distance himself.

He had been irritable all evening, the way he'd been when he first arrived in the canyon with his black wool suit and his overbearing attitude. She'd thought he had put that attitude aside along with the suit, but now it appeared she was mistaken.

"I love you, too," Whitney replied carefully. There was something wrong. She knew it as surely as she had known it the day he came to tell her about Billy.

"I spoke to Hobie today."

"Oh?"

Looking straight up at the ceiling, he said, "I'm going back."

Whitney laughed uneasily. "Well, of course, Gabe. I know that."

"Not just to Seattle. I mean I'm going back to representing Hobie Stoner."

There was a long pause. "Well, if that's what you want, that's what you should do," she said finally. But her voice was flat.

"Look, I know you don't approve!" Gabe swung his legs out of the bed and sat on the edge, his back to Whitney.

The thick scar tissue turned white when he was upset. Whitney had never noticed that before. Of course, she had never seen him angry before. She sat up behind him, leaning her cheek against his back and tracing with one finger the long, jagged scar. "I haven't said I don't approve."

"You don't have to," he returned sourly, as if she had criticized him just by thinking it. "I can tell. But you just don't understand what it means, a partnership in a firm like Parkhurst and Brandenberg! Top of the heap! It's what I've wanted all my life—to *be* somebody! Now I'm there. I've made it, don't you see? I can't let it go without giving it a shot!"

Whitney brushed his shaggy hair aside and kissed the back of his neck. "I understand, Gabe," she said soothingly. But she didn't, not really. He was already somebody. Didn't he know that?

Gabe felt her lips follow her gentle fingers down the length of the ropelike scar. He felt her care and concern. He felt her compassion. He felt her love. He felt like he was sinking into quicksand.

Twisting around so that he and she were face to face, he took her small, heart-shaped face between his two hands. "Nothing's changed between us, has it?" he demanded fiercely. "Everything's just the way it was before, right? I'll fly in to see you when I can. You'll try to

get a replacement for a week and fly out to Seattle? Nothing's changed?''

"Nothing's changed, Gabe. Not if we don't want it
to.''

But that wasn't quite true. Things had already
changed. She could tell that his mind wasn't with her; it
was back in Seattle, ascending another step on the ladder of success. She also noticed that her lack of enthusiasm irritated him.

"I would have thought you'd be happy for me," Gabe
said accusingly, as though he was cross-examining her.
It was a tone of voice she hadn't heard from him before, and she didn't like it one bit.

"I'm happy you've attained your goal in life. Is that
what you want me to say?''

"I want you to say what you mean," Gabe retorted.
"The way you always do.''

But she knew that what he *really* wanted her to say was
what he wanted to hear. Suddenly Whitney felt as
though she was in the presence of a stranger. She became acutely conscious of her nakedness. Reaching behind the bedroom door, she took down her terry-cloth
robe, jammed her arms into the sleeves and knotted the
sash around her waist as if it was a lock and key.

"Well then, Gabe," she said, whirling around so
quickly that her hair flew across her face. She pushed it
back with an angry gesture. "I'll tell you what I mean. I
assume you're good at what you do, or a firm as important as you say Park . . . Park . . .''

"Parkhurst and Brandenberg," he filled in automatically.

"*Whatever!* A firm as important as that wouldn't
have hired you in the first place, if you weren't good. But
to ride to the top on the coattails of a man like Hobie

Stoner, probably as unscrupulous a person as ever took candy away from a baby, even if *technically* he stays on the right side of the law—"

"Stop right there," Gabe bristled. His eyes looked cold and hard. Whitney thought fleetingly that she'd hate to face them across a courtroom. "Hobie is a very wealthy and successful real-estate developer—"

"I'm sure he is. And what do you want to be when *you* grow up, Gabe? A clone of Hobie Stoner?"

"I'm *nothing* like Stoner," Gabe retorted heatedly. "I'm just using him to get where I want to go." The words hung on the air, as fine an example of situational ethics as Gabe had ever heard. He couldn't believe he'd said it; he couldn't believe he'd *thought* it.

"Using people. Sounds like good old Hobie to *me!*"

Whitney's words struck an uncomfortable chord within him. *Using people.* It brought back memories of the McDaniels.

Gabe had always dreamed of going back someday, when he was rich and successful, and returning to them every cent he'd stolen. With interest. But at first he'd been too ashamed to face them. Later, he'd been afraid they'd turn him in. Lately he'd begun to admit to himself that it was a guilt he had become comfortable with. Did that mean he was in danger of becoming a clone of Hobie Stoner? Gabe wondered uneasily.

He couldn't think about it now. The goals he had struggled toward all his life were within his grasp, and there wasn't time now to wonder whether they were the right ones or the wrong ones. There was only time to grab them before they got away.

He looked at Whitney with baffled eyes. "Whitney, what's happening to us? I thought we had something here."

"Maybe we've been moving too fast. A month in Shangri-La, well, it was very romantic, but maybe not too realistic. I think what's happening is just reality setting in." It was her doctor's voice, calm, professional and objective, and it gave no indication at all of what was going on in her heart.

"I love you, Whitney," Gabe said dully. "But this is my big break. I have to take it."

Standing at opposite ends of the bedroom, the bed a barrier between them that both knew they wouldn't cross tonight, it seemed there was nothing left to say.

GABE FLEW OUT the next day. From the broken window of her office, Whitney watched him go.

CHAPTER TWENTY-TWO

THE PEOPLE WERE SAD because those they loved died and went away to the land of the spirits. Everywhere Coyote heard the sounds of mourning.

He said to the People, "Do not be sad. The dead will not remain forever in the land of the spirits. They are like the leaves that turn brown and fall in the autumn. When the grass grows and the flowers bloom and the leaf buds open, they will come back again."

But the People did not want to wait until spring. They wanted him to bring the dead back right away. So Coyote took a basket and journeyed to the land of the spirits. He traveled all day, which in those days was as long as forever is now, and when he arrived at the land of the spirits, it was too dark to see.

So Coyote began to sing, and he called the moon to rise, and it shone down on the spirits so that Coyote could see them. They were dancing, and there was the sound of singing, and of drums. But when Coyote's song drifted to them on the air, it reminded them of the land of the living and made them sad; and in that defenseless moment, Coyote gathered them up and put them in his basket and closed the lid. Then he started back to the land of the living.

After traveling half the night, which was as long as forever is now, Coyote was tired. The basket grew heavier and heavier, for the spirits were turning back into *people. A little while later the basket became too heavy for Coyote to carry, so he put it down.*

"I will let them out," said Coyote. "They are so heavy that they must be people by now, and they will not be able to find their way back to the spirit land."

So he opened the basket. But the spirits were not quite people yet, and when they were set free they took on their spirit forms and flew like the wind back to the land of the spirits.

Coyote was very angry at their ingratitude, so he made the law that after people have died, they will never come back anymore.

If he had not opened the basket and let the spirits out, the dead would have come back to life every spring as the leaves and the grass do, and death, which is the root of all sadness, would not have become a part of the People's lives.

WHITNEY MISSED Billy. She wondered how a person could walk on this earth for nearly one hundred years and then just disappear, leaving nothing behind. Not even a memory, it seemed, because among the Indians, no one ever spoke of him again.

"The Havasupai believe that speaking the name of a person who has died makes their spirit homesick," Jesse told her, "and calls them back to the land of the living, where they can never again belong. They then become unhappy ghosts, forever causing mischief among the people."

Out of respect for tradition, he told her that he, too, chose to honor the old storyteller by not speaking his name.

He smiled his slow, somber smile. "The old traditions aren't dead. They live in our hearts. Some say that they're what keeps us down. But others say they're what keeps us from going under."

ONE DAY in mid-September, Jesse delivered to Whitney a letter Big Jim had brought in the night before.

"Good news?" he asked when he saw her smile.

"It's from my mother. She says she can't decide whether to have a big Christmas party to welcome me home, or a small family gathering so they can keep me to themselves. She wants to know which I'd prefer."

"It's good when both options are happy ones."

"Yes, it'll be nice to be home again. Although I'm going to miss the canyon. And all of you."

"Maybe you'll come back someday," Jesse began carefully.

"For a visit, I hope. But my work is done here. My father is anxious for me to get back so he can plug my fieldwork into his data base. I think the next few years are going to be busy ones."

Pursed-lipped, Jesse considered her words. "Where does Gabriel Blade fit into those years?" he finally asked.

"He doesn't," Whitney replied shortly.

There had been two totally unsatisfactory radio calls and a single letter, apparently dashed off by Gabe between more important appointments. None of the three had been anything more than polite small talk. He had sounded hurried and harassed, which probably meant that he was settling very well into his new partnership at Park...Park...*what*ever.

It was painfully obvious that he was again caught up in his relentless pursuit of the life-styles of the rich and famous. Most revealing of all, there had been no discussion of visits, either his to the canyon, or hers to Seattle.

"I haven't heard a thing from him in a month," Whitney told Jesse, a reminder to herself, as well. "I don't expect to hear from him again."

Jesse set his coffee cup down and leaned on one elbow across the desk. "Dr. B. Whitney. The next few years will be busy for us, too. Many of the things Stoner proposed—a larger school, a small hospital—are ideas we hope to implement ourselves. It'll take time, but I believe it will be done. And I would be proud if you would become a part of this."

"Why, Jesse!" Whitney said with a smile. "Are you offering me a job?"

Jesse hesitated. "In a manner of speaking," he granted, sitting back in his chair. "It could be a good life down here, Whitney."

"Oh, Jesse! I don't know what to say...."

"You could start with yes," he suggested, a ghost of humor in his somber eyes.

"I'm honored. I truly am. But as much as I'd love it, I don't belong here. This isn't my place."

"You do not think you could be happy here?"

"It isn't that...."

Jesse gave her a long, penetrating look. "You still hope that Gabriel Blade will somehow rise above himself and make the right choice," he concluded, as calmly as if he was discussing the next planting of the crops, while the raven in his heart beat despairing wings against the cage of his ribs.

Whitney shrugged helplessly, raising her palms upward, then letting them fall. A small, sheepish smile played around her lips. "Dumb, huh?" she admitted.

"But there doesn't seem to be anything I can do about it."

Silently, Jesse picked up his coffee cup and drained it, while the raven cawed as if its heart was breaking apart.

BENNY'WI HAD GOTTEN a job. He sprinkled water on the helipad before each landing to keep down the red dust.

When the helicopter appeared, still only a sunspot in the empty blue sky, Benny'wi turned off the nozzle of the hose and tossed it toward the fence, then slouched casually on one hip, thumbs hooked in the pockets of his jeans, and watched the aircraft touch down.

The usual indistinguishable assortment of hikers and campers descended, then Benny'wi saw someone he recognized.

"Hey, Gabe," he challenged in his cracked half boy, half man voice.

"Hey, Benny," Gabe called. "Got a job, I see."

"Yeah, man," came Benny'wi's proud, solemn reply.

"Benny, do you know where I can find Dr. B?"

Benny'wi jutted his chin toward the Red Rock Café.

Through the grimy glass, Whitney saw Gabe make his way across the helipad. Even knowing his presence couldn't possibly have anything to do with her, she swallowed convulsively, then moistened her lips and raised one hand to fluff her hair. Why was he here? she wondered nervously. What did he want?

He looked very much the way he had the first time she'd set eyes on him, dark business suit and all. While he walked, he took off his jacket and loosened his tie.

She watched him mount the steps of the café and push open the screen door, letting it slam behind in a series of diminishing thumps. He met her eyes across the room, and walked toward her with the loose runner's gait she liked so well.

Halfway to the booth, he began to smile. By the time he reached her, the smile had become a full-fledged grin.

"Mind if I join you?" he said. Whitney nodded. But rather than seat himself across the table, he slid in beside her, which made her feel a little crowded, a little overwhelmed, a little too aware of her own body and the way it had suddenly begun to tremble. She backed into the corner of the booth.

"I thought you'd learned your lesson about wearing suits down here," she said with a wry twist of her lips.

"I came directly from the office," Gabe replied, still smiling like a man with a secret. "It was my last day," he added.

"Oh?" Whitney said. She was surprised, but determined not to let herself care. "Did Hobie fire you again?"

"Nope. I quit."

She gave him a raised-eyebrow look. "You mean to tell me you've given up the fifteenth-floor office with the corner window—I find that hard to believe."

"Actually, from the day I moved up to the fifteenth floor, I realized it wasn't what I wanted. Or maybe it's what I'd wanted once, but not anymore. It wasn't long afterward that I realized what I *really* wanted was out."

"Well, I'm sure they'll offer you a partnership again, and the next time it won't be because of Hobie Stoner—"

"There won't be a next time, Whitney. I didn't just quit Hobie's account. I quit the firm altogether."

"Gabe! Why?" Whitney eyed him warily. He looked like a man with something more to say. "Okay, so if you're not working for Hobie Stoner, and you're not working for Parkhurst and whatever, then why are you down here again?''

"Well, I figured Sinyella could always use an extra pair of hands with the rebuilding and all. Then I thought I'd do a little traveling—maybe see Boston. Get married, maybe, raise a family, put down some roots? Of course, I can get to Boston by myself—the rest kind of depends on you.''

He was so nonchalant that for a moment Whitney didn't register what he had said. Then, suddenly, her slanted eyes narrowed to indignant slits. "So why didn't you *tell* me you were coming back?'' Her voice took on the rasp of a scolding magpie. "Don't *I* get a say in all these plans?''

Gabe caught her gesticulating hand. "Well, actually, after the jerk I'd been, I was afraid you wouldn't let me come back. You were so impersonal when I called—''

"Impersonal? I was just trying to act neutral so you wouldn't feel pressured!''

Gabe reached out to her. "Well, you did a good job of it. I figured you'd given up on me. So I decided not to even ask—that way you couldn't say no.''

"You should have known me better than that,'' she told him in her down-to-earth, ever-practical way.

"Actually, I feel I hardly know you at all. But I want to spend the rest of my life getting acquainted. Will you have me, Whitney? Because one thing I *do* know is that I don't want to live up there in the real world without you.''

She slid out of her corner and into his embrace.

A shadow fell across the booth. It was Gwe. "What'll you have?'' he growled.

"Nothing. We're leaving now. We're going home.'' Gabe slid out of the booth and stood up, smiling broadly

at the dour old Indian. "You can be the first to con-
gratulate us. Dr. B has just agreed to become my wife."

Gwe looked from one to the other. "It is about time,"
he grunted succinctly. Then he muttered something in
Supai which Whitney couldn't quite understand, but
which could be translated, although in earthier terms, as
"May you have as many children as your garden will
feed." It was a traditional Havasupai marriage wish.

As they turned to go, Gwe made a sound in his throat
that neither Whitney nor Gabe had heard from him before. It was a single, harsh "Ha!" that sounded like a
dog's bark. They deciphered it at the same time, and
looked at each other in amazement.

It was a laugh.

"Hey, Gabe," he called after them, barking cheerfully. "Indian and white and Korean—what you think
your kids gonna be, anyway?"

As he pulled open the screen door, Gabe straightened
his glasses with thumb and forefinger, then gave the man
in the grimy apron a quick wink.

"Ours," he said.

FROM THE TOPS of ladders and roofs, voices called casual greetings to Gabe, welcoming him back as if he were
one of them. Walking through the village toward Whitney's bungalow, Gabe felt part of the seamless cloth of
tribal life.

During the time he'd been uptop, his life had immediately resumed its former marathon pace. He found
himself running, not in pursuit of a goal—because he
had already achieved that—but because it was what he
had always done. He felt the old, panicky feeling of Fate
breathing down his neck, waiting, always waiting, for
him to make a mistake.

But now that he was with Whitney, he was able to let the rhythms of life unfold as they would. Even though he wanted her so badly he felt he would burst, another, even stronger part of him held back, savoring the unfolding.

At the base of the red wall on which they had made their precipitous descent, Gabe stopped and looked up.

"Amazing, isn't it?" he remarked, eyes searching the sheer, shadowed rock face. "Even when you know exactly where that opening is, you can't make it out." He paused reflectively, then shook his head and chuckled. "I sure hope that coyote got down all right."

Whitney also looked up at the wall, peering through the long shadows of the late-afternoon sun. "No, not even the steps," she agreed.

Then she glanced at Gabe. "What coyote?"

"You know, the little coyote that was with us in the cave."

Whitney looked puzzled.

"*You* know. The one that showed us the way out."

Whitney frowned. "Gabe, I don't know what you're talking about."

He stopped walking. "The coyote," he insisted. "You don't remember the coyote? He came in soaking wet during the storm, and he showed me the tunnel? I explored it with the matches I'd picked up at Billy's?"

Whitney shook her head.

"Don't you remember? You were standing at the mouth of the cave when I came back, and I was holding my last match, and it burned my fingers?"

His voice became slower as he finished speaking. It dawned on Gabe that Whitney didn't have the vaguest clue what he was talking about.

"I remember you coming out of the cave," she agreed with an involuntary shudder. "How could I ever forget that? I was afraid you might have fallen over the cliff! And I remember the match burning your fingers. But Gabe, what about this coyote? I don't—"

"He was with me, Whitney! He was *right there,* next to me!"

She shook her head positively. "I remember every second of that awful night, Gabe. But I don't remember anything about a coyote."

Gabe stalked away a few steps, frustratedly rubbing the back of his neck with one hand, then abruptly turned on his heel and returned to where Whitney stood. He looked at her strangely.

"He came in while we were sleeping." He repeated the sequence, as if trying to figure out exactly where the story went wrong. "He was half-drowned. I figured he was just looking for some shelter, the way we were. I hoped if we didn't bother him, he wouldn't bother us. But he kept staring at me with those yellow eyes. And then he started acting, you know, like he was trying to tell me something."

Whitney stared at him, bewildered. Even to his own ears the whole thing sounded impossible, but Gabe continued doggedly. "I followed him, and he led me into that rat hole in back of the cave. That's when I realized it was a tunnel. And then, when we crawled through it the next morning, he was right in front of us all the way."

He gazed at her with tense, baffled eyes. "You didn't see his eyes in the tunnel? Whitney, he was no hallucination—didn't you *smell* him?"

"But Gabe, you couldn't have seen *anything* in that tunnel. There was no light!"

It was Gabe's turn to look bewildered. "Of course," he said dully. "There was no light...."

He sat down abruptly on a convenient boulder. Whitney plopped down beside him. "But I saw his eyes. I *saw* them, Whitney! He kept looking back at us, like he was making sure we were still behind him."

He seized her by the shoulders, digging his fingers into her flesh until they hurt. His eyes burned into hers, trying to rekindle a memory that he suddenly suspected wasn't there. "Whitney, the picture I carried in my mind all the way down that damned wall was your face, and that coyote with his nose on your shoulder, watching me go down."

Whitney's voice was no more than a whisper. "I didn't see any coyote...."

They stared at each other in confusion, in disbelief, and finally in dawning incredulity. "It's not possible," she breathed at last.

Suddenly she hurled herself at Gabe and buried her face in his shirtfront. His arms surrounded her, crushing her against him in fierce denial.

"No, no, of course not," he assured her, unaware that his own voice was as shaky as hers. "It's not possible. Things like that just don't happen!"

"But Billy knew everything that went on in the canyon." Her words were halting, as if they were being spoken against her will. "He said the wind told him, and the leaves, and the rocks...he wanted you to have a spirit animal, Gabe. What if he knew we were in trouble...? What if he sent *his* spirit animal to you, to guide you through the tunnel...? What if...?"

He crushed her closer. "No, Whitney! You're a scientist—you know things like that just don't happen!"

But Gabe remembered how small, how frail the coyote had seemed when he'd first noticed its yellow eyes across the cave. By the time they'd reached the other end of the tunnel, however, the coyote had changed. Its ragged coat had become fuller, its dun color had become a sort of tawny gold, and its black-rimmed eyes a deeper shade of yellow. The black tips of the guard hairs at its neck shone like quills of patent leather.

It seemed not only a bigger animal, but a stronger, healthier, *younger* one.

If the coyote was indeed Billy's spirit animal—and Gabe was not for a moment suggesting it was—but *if* it was, it somehow pleased him to imagine that the same metamorphosis had taken place in the old man.

"I know things like that don't happen," Whitney repeated like a mantra. Tears streamed, unheeded, down her face. "I know they don't. *I know* . . ."

But, Gabe thought, in this strange, beautiful, topsy-turvy world, where all the other laws of nature didn't seem to apply, who knew for sure? Maybe things like that *could* happen.

Maybe they could.

Maybe they did.

EPILOGUE

IN WINTER, Havasu Canyon was very different. It was cold and damp, and in the mornings, steam rose from the creek. The sun cleared Wii'baaq'a at ten-thirty or eleven o'clock and was gone by 2:00 p.m.

Winter was a time of droopy horsemen riding up the Moqui Trail to the plateau, or packing their supplies down from it. Winter was a time of long evenings, of cold, still nights. The cliffs, layered with snow, looked unfamiliar and ominous under the hard, cold sun and the brittle moon. Ravens as big as turkeys perched on the fences, and in the scraggly branches of the naked trees.

Haze and smoke rose only about fifty feet off the ground and spread like wet cotton over the dank, damp canyon floor.

Sometimes winter storms washed out the trail. Other times snowfalls on the plateau cut off the canyon from the outside world for weeks at a time.

On very cold nights, the moisture in the rocks froze, and the sound of sudden rockfalls rumbled with terrifying echoes through the labyrinth of stone walls.

Old Billy used to say that the People of the Blue-Green Water would endure for as long as their gods, high on Wii'baaq'a, watched over them. Sometimes Jesse Sinyella wondered if that was the way the gods would leave their people? If the man rock and woman rock would

just freeze up some winter night and topple ignomini-
ously from their slender, top-heavy pedestals?

Everything sleeps in the winter, Jesse thought, as he
trudged across the village square one dark, cold afternoon in early January. The greenness is gone, the animals are gone, and most of the children are gone, sent
away to live at the Indian Boarding School in Phoenix.
The people seem to sleep too, waiting for spring, when
the leaves and the animals and the children would return, and life would begin again.

Except for a few stray dogs huddled under the porch
of the trading post, Jesse's stark figure was the only sign
of life in the barren square. His cowboy hat pulled low
over his eyes, he drew his neck, turtlelike, deeper into his
shepherd's coat, and raised the collar up to his ears.

From inside the trading post came the sound of voices,
indistinct and reed-thin on the cold air.

Jasper turned when Jesse entered, gave him an ac-
knowledging grunt, then returned his attention to where
it had been in the first place. Around the wood stove in
the corner, a woman had gathered some of the children
too young for school. She was entertaining them by telling them stories. It reminded him of when he was a kid,
sitting at this very same stove, listening to old Billy tell
about the days of Coyote.

Jesse could only see the back of the woman's head and
her long, black hair, but he knew who she was.

THERE WAS NO protection from the icy cold in the empty,
treeless square, so when Jesse left the trading post, he
trudged down-canyon as quickly as his hard, husky legs
would carry him. A little farther along, he cut across a
copse of dark firs, and entered a ramshackle frame
house half-hidden by the trees.

"Mother, I'm home," he called in Supai.

A woman emerged from a room at the back. "My son," she greeted him also in Supai. "You are early."

Without a word, his mother ladled a bowl of soup from a pot simmering on the back burner of her stove, and set it before him.

She also poured two mugs of coffee, one for herself and one for Jesse, then sat down across from him to watch him eat.

Jesse made short work of the soup. "Thanks," he grunted when he had finished.

He had learned that uptop. Indian men never thanked women for food, any more than women thanked them for bringing home the occasional poached deer. However, Jesse's mother liked these manners he had learned.

Jesse leaned back in his chair, wrapping his chapped hands around the warm coffee mug. His mother waited. She could tell he had something to say. She knew he would say it in his own time.

"Mother," he said finally, shifting his eyes everywhere except into hers. "There is a woman I would like you to talk to."

This was one of the things he had learned uptop that she *didn't* like. This reserve, this awkwardness, especially with women. He had been a quiet child, a watchful boy who kept his own counsel. But until he went away to school, he had never been shy. She mourned whatever experiences among the *hay gu* had brought about this change in him.

"What woman?"

"Her name is Tsquiva. She is Jasper's daughter."

"I know Tsquiva. She has only this winter returned. You went to school with her—you did not notice her then."

Jesse gave his mother his slow, solemn smile. "She has been gone a long time. I have changed. *She* has changed. And it is time I took a wife."

Jesse's mother pursed her lips, Indian-style, and thought. "Jasper's daughter has a child," she finally said. "That is why she came home."

"Good," Jesse replied stoutly. "We need more kids down here."

"I will speak with her," she said.

AFTER JESSE HAD GONE back to the tribal office, his mother took off her apron. She dressed carefully, putting on a pair of stockings and her best black shoes, then her warm woolen coat. Lastly, she pinned on top of her head her black straw hat with the black flower on the brim.

Taking one last look in the mirror over her dresser, she knew she made a good impression. The woman in the mirror was heavyset, with long graying hair and a round, solemn face. Her posture was erect, and she looked dignified, as befitted the mother of a chief. The mother of a chief who had finally chosen a wife.

Although her face didn't change, her heart sang.

ONCE SHE ARRIVED at the trading post, chilled to the bone, she stalked haughtily past Jasper, as if she had more important things to attend to, and stationed herself behind the canned goods. From there she had an unobstructed view of the young woman Tsquiva, who sat beside the wood stove in the middle of a group of small children.

The woman was called Tsquiva, which meant "tattooed one," because of the freckles scattered over her nose. This was unusual in an Indian, even one as fair-skinned as the sun-deprived Havasupai.

She was tall for a woman, Jesse's mother could tell, even though the younger woman was seated. Her profile showed her face to be round and firm and smooth-skinned, and her voice was low and womanly. She had the strong, broad body of most Havasupai women, although somewhat slimmer than most, probably due to the years she had lived uptop with the *hay gu,* who preferred their women that way.

A baby not yet old enough to creep was wrapped in a shawl on Tsquiva's lap. Jesse's mother moved closer, still hidden behind the canned goods, to hear what the young woman was saying to the children in the familiar, flowing tongue of the Supai.

. . . Coyote walked alone upon the earth. The land smelled rich and fertile, but the People had not yet come to cultivate it. . . .

Relive the romance...
Harlequin and Silhouette
are proud to present

by Request™

A program of collections of three complete novels by the most requested authors with the most requested themes. Be sure to look for one volume each month with three complete novels by top name authors.

In January:	**WESTERN LOVING**	Susan Fox
		JoAnn Ross
		Barbara Kaye

Loving a cowboy is easy—taming him isn't!

In February:	**LOVER, COME BACK!**	Diana Palmer
		Lisa Jackson
		Patricia Gardner Evans

It was over so long ago—yet now they're calling, "Lover, Come Back!"

In March:	**TEMPERATURE RISING**	JoAnn Ross
		Tess Gerritsen
		Jacqueline Diamond

Falling in love—just what the doctor ordered!

Available at your favorite retail outlet.

REQ-G3

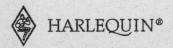
HARLEQUIN®

Silhouette

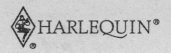

Harlequin proudly presents four stories about *convenient* but not *conventional* reasons for marriage:

- ♦ To save your godchildren from a "wicked stepmother"

- ♦ To help out your eccentric aunt—and her sexy business partner

- ♦ To bring an old man happiness by making him a grandfather

- ♦ To escape from a ghostly existence and become a real woman

Marriage By Design—four brand-new stories by four of Harlequin's most popular authors:

CATHY GILLEN THACKER
JASMINE CRESSWELL
GLENDA SANDERS
MARGARET CHITTENDEN

Don't miss this exciting collection of stories about marriages of convenience. Available in April, wherever Harlequin books are sold.

MBD94

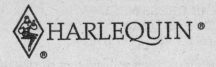

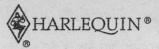

HARLEQUIN®

COMING SOON TO
A STORE NEAR YOU...

THE MAIN
ATTRACTION

By *New York Times* Bestselling Author

This March, look for THE MAIN ATTRACTION by popular
author Jayne Ann Krentz.

Ten years ago, Filomena Cromwell had left her small town
in shame. Now she is back determined to get her sweet,
sweet revenge....

Soon she has her ex-fiancé, who cheated on her with
another woman, chasing her all over town. And he isn't
the only one. Filomena lets Trent Ravinder catch her.

Can she control the fireworks she's set into motion?

HARLEQUIN®

Don't miss these Harlequin favorites by some of our most distinguished authors!
And now, you can receive a discount by ordering two or more titles!